I0761175

Talking through the Door

Arab American Writing

Other titles in Arab American Writing

Bread Alone
Kim Jensen

Loom: A Novel
Thérèse Soukar Chehade

Love Is Like Water and Other Stories
Samia Serageldin

The Man Who Guarded the Bomb: Stories
Gregory Orfalea

Modern Arab American Fiction: A Reader's Guide
Steven Salaita

My Name on His Tongue: Poems
Laila Halaby

The New Belly Dancer of the Galaxy: A Novel
Frances Khirallah Noble

Remember Me to Lebanon: Stories of Lebanese Women in America
Evelyn Shakir

Through and Through: Toledo Stories, 2d ed.
Joseph Geha

An Anthology of Contemporary Middle Eastern American Writing

EDITED BY

Susan Atefat-Peckham

Foreword by Lisa Suhair Majaj

Syracuse University Press

Syracuse, New York 13244-5290

First Edition 2014

14 15 16 17 18 19 6 5 4 3 2 1

∞ The paper used in this publication meets the minimum requirements of the American National Standard for Information Sciences—Permanence of Paper for Printed Library Materials, ANSI Z39.48-1992.

For a listing of books published and distributed by Syracuse University Press, visit www.SyracuseUniversityPress.syr.edu.

ISBN: 978-0-8156-3347-1 (cloth) 978-0-8156-5260-1 (e-book)

Library of Congress Cataloging-in-Publication Data

Talking through the door : an anthology of contemporary Middle Eastern American writing / edited by Susan Atefat-Peckham ; foreword by Lisa Suhair Majaj. — First edition.

pages cm. — (Arab American writing)

Collected works of fiction, nonfiction, and poetry by chiefly Arab Americans and Iranian Americans.

ISBN 978-0-8156-3347-1 (cloth : alk. paper) — ISBN 978-0-8156-5260-1 (ebook)

1. American literature—Arab American authors. 2. American literature—Iranian American authors. 3. American literature—20th century. I. Peckham, Susan Atefat, 1970-2004, editor of compilation. II. Majaj, Lisa Suhair.

PS508.A67T38 2014

810.8'08927—dc23 2014015246

Manufactured in the United States of America

For My Dear Son Darius

We talked through the door. I claimed
a great love and that I had given up
what the world gives to be in that love.

—Rumi, translated by Coleman Barks

CONTENTS

FOREWORD, *Lisa Suhair Majaj* · xiii

ACKNOWLEDGMENTS · xix

INTRODUCTION

Voices from the Threshold: A Few Thoughts on Middle Eastern American Writing · 1

ELMAZ ABINADER

Mothers and Daughters (nonfiction) · 21

Preparing for Occupation (poetry) · 43

Flying to Arabia (poetry) · 45

DIANA ABU-JABER

Tainted Love (fiction) · 49

SUSAN ATEFAT-PECKHAM

Marvari—*The Pearl Tree* (poetry) · 55

Fariba's Daughters (poetry) · 56

Dates (poetry) · 57

Them? (nonfiction) · 58

JOSEPH AWAD

from *"A Novena for My Mother"* (poetry) · 63

Memories of Tiger Rag (poetry) · 65

For My Irish Grandfather (poetry) · 66

Windows (poetry) · 69

Aunt Anna (poetry) · 70
For My Lebanese Grandfather (poetry) · 71
Christmas at Sithee's (poetry) · 72

BARBARA BEDWAY
Death and Lebanon (fiction) · 73
Why We Are in the DAR (fiction) · 84
Turning Lebanese: A Family Story (nonfiction) · 89
In Her Own Hand (nonfiction) · 91

JOSEPH GEHA
Where I'm From—Originally (nonfiction) · 95
Stepping Out (fiction) · 103

SAMUEL HAZO
Understory (poetry) · 119
The First Sam Hazo at the Last (poetry) · 120
Ahead of Time (poetry) · 122

JOE KADI
Writing as Resistance, Writing as Love (nonfiction) · 125
Coiled Tongues (poetry) · 128
Moving from Cultural Appropriation Toward Ethical Cultural Connections (nonfiction) · 130

PAULINE KALDAS
Cumin and Coriander (fiction) · 145
The Top (fiction) · 151
Shifting Spaces: 1990–1993 (nonfiction) · 159

JACK MARSHALL
Deal (poetry) · 167
G–D (poetry) · 170
Arabian Nights (poetry) · 173

CONTENTS

KHALED MATTAWA

Selections from the Ibn Hazm Epistolary · 175

D. H. MELHEM

Preface for Walt Whitman (poetry) · 181
28. [bright world in morning light . . .] (poetry) · 181
53. Hudson Continuum (poetry) · 182
then/now, part one (poetry) · 182
[Bookladen on Friday . . .] (poetry) · 183
[Charon drives his ambulance . . .] (poetry) · 186
[mother . . .] (poetry) · 189

EUGENE P. NASSAR

Summer 1958 (nonfiction prose poetry) · 191
Summer 1964 (nonfiction prose poetry) · 204

NAOMI SHIHAB NYE

Yellow Glove (prose poetry) · 213
Arabic (poetry) · 214
Jerusalem (poetry) · 215
Holy Land (poetry) · 217
The Only Word a Tree Knows (poetry) · 218
Renovation (nonfiction) · 219
Amir & Anna (poetry) · 223
Your Weight, at Birth (poetry) · 224
Supple Cord (poetry) · 225
The Only Democracy in the Middle East (poetry) · 226
Because of Poems (poetry) · 226

NAHID RACHLIN

The Calling (fiction) · 227

ROGER SEDARAT

My Mother's 20 Persian Gold Bracelets (poetry) · 237

San Antonio, 1979 (poetry) · *238*
Khomeini's Beard (poetry) · *239*
Outing Iranians (poetry) · *239*

CONTRIBUTORS' BIOGRAPHIES · *241*

FOREWORD

AT THE END OF THE 1990S, when the late Susan Atefat-Peckham began working on this collection, Middle Eastern American literature was gaining increasing visibility on the American cultural landscape. Although early in the twentieth century authors of Arab and Muslim background were publishing work in both English and Arabic, by midcentury authors writing specifically from, and of, Middle Eastern ethnic backgrounds seemed to have fallen into relative silence. It was not until around the 1980s, when a new generation of authors of Middle Eastern descent—usually, although not always, American born—began publishing in journals and anthologies, as well as in their own books, that a growing body of Middle Eastern American literature began to come into view.

Three anthologies paved the way for this emergence, or reemergence, of Middle Eastern American writing, and for its increasing visibility on the American literary scene: *Grape Leaves: A Century of Arab American Poetry*, edited by Gregory Orfalea and Sharif Elmusa (1988); *Food for Our Grandmothers: Writings by Arab American and Arab Canadian Feminists*, edited by Joanna (now Joe) Kadi (1994); and *Post Gibran: Anthology of Arab American Writing*, edited by Munir Akash and Khaled Mattawa (1999). These collections, each groundbreaking in its own way, made visible the existence of a body of Middle Eastern American writing by authors of Christian, Muslim, and Jewish background, established a sense of this literature's historical and cultural roots, and helped to create ground space for future growth. *Grape Leaves* linked early *Mahjar* (immigrant) and contemporary Arab American writing, asserting the century-long presence of this body of literature as well as insisting on both the specificity of its Middle Eastern thematics and on its Americanness. *Food for Our Grandmothers* brought women's voices front and center, challenging the stereotypes that continue to beleaguer Middle Eastern women, while at the same time exploring feminist concerns and complexities. *Post Gibran* traced this literature's cultural and multicultural roots in the Middle East back to the narrative of Gilgamesh, while at the same time emphasizing its contemporary explorations on American terrain. Although all three anthologies focused on Arab identity as a unifying framework—a focus emerging from the simple fact that most authors of Middle Eastern background in the United States at that time were Arab—complexities of identification and inclusion were nonetheless evident. In *Food*, for instance, Kadi included two Armenian American and one Iranian American contributor, noting that although these contributors were not Arab, as Middle Easterners they shared many things in common with Arab contributors. Kadi's meditation on the complexities of which terminology to use—Arab? Middle Eastern? West Asian/North African?—remains compelling today precisely because there are still no easy answers: words bear the inescapable traces of historical, cultural, and political legacies, and every definition, every boundary line, both includes and excludes. Is this body of literature American? Ethnic? Arab American? Middle Eastern? (The fact that virtually every grouping of literature by authors of Middle Eastern origin has included Christian, Muslim, and Jewish writers suggests that religion is far from a defining category here, but there is nonetheless an ongoing discussion, too, about the relationship of Arab/Middle Eastern American literature to Muslim American literature.)

Had Atefat-Peckham's collection been published in the early years of the past decade, as planned, it would have played an important role in furthering this discussion of what it means to write from the space where "Middle Eastern" and "American" meet. Atefat-Peckham's tragic, untimely death in a car accident in 2004 meant the deferral of this publication and its contribution to Middle Eastern literature's expanding visibility, and of discussion of its identity, location, and implications. Yet her collection is no less important today. The writers whom she chose to include here have for the most part become well-established writers, recognized for their contributions not just as Middle Eastern ethnic writers, but as American—and, in some cases, international—writers who are not constrained to an ethnic "niche." Meanwhile, by bringing together Iranian American and Arab American authors of various national and religious backgrounds, the collection widened the scope of this body of literature. If, at an earlier time, there were so few Iranian American authors that the category "Arab American" could be invoked as more or less all-encompassing, the commonalities of experience and literary expression among Arabs, Iranians, and other Middle Easterners in the United States (e.g., Chaldeans, Copts, Armenians) compel us to expand our categories and consider the ways in which Middle Eastern identity more generally conceived has shaped the experience of writing from that meeting point of "East" and "West."

The question of what it means to write as a Middle Eastern American was even more pressing because this collection was initially brought together in the years soon after the terrible events of September 11, 2001, when being "Middle Eastern" was too often identified as the antithesis of being "American," and when the lines between Arab, Iranian, Pakistani, Sikh, and various other "foreign" identities, Middle Eastern or not, were frequently blurred in the general rush of grief, anger, and fear. Atefat-Peckham's focus on a Middle Eastern American literature that could communicate from an ethnic sensibility without relinquishing its full claim to full American identity was crucial at this juncture, as was her sense of the role literature could play in achieving such communication. As she commented in the context of discussing her own poetry book, *That Kind of Sleep*, in an interview originally published in *Poets and Writers* on October 12, 2001, "I found that really what I was trying to do was build a bridge between the two cultures. . . .

Literature, the visual arts, and music are a way for us to connect to one another. Art is empathy."[1]

Meanwhile, her simultaneous focus on the diversity of the Middle Eastern American community and its literature connected to a growing awareness of the need to interrogate and speak beyond concepts of singular identity. Although literary texts participate in creating "imagined communities," to use Benedict Arnold's well-known term, such imagined communities are never homogenous; nor are they static. In recent years, Middle Eastern American writers have sought to grapple in increasingly complex ways with the relationship between identity and literary articulation. In the introduction to his anthology *Inclined to Speak: An Anthology of Contemporary Arab American Poetry*, published in 2008, Hayan Charara acknowledged that whether the writers included in his collection "like it or not . . . identity is, for their readers, typically both an entry and exit point to their poems."[2] Yet he also stressed that Arab American poems "do their part to trouble and reshape any notions of a literature or a people called Arab American." The same might be said of Middle Eastern American literature more generally. While readers often approach such texts seeking stable answers to questions of identity, authors increasingly seek to disrupt overly easy answers—and seek, in many ways, to change the questions altogether.

Indeed, what the Arab American critic Steven Salaita terms the "searching diversities"[3] of Arab and Middle Eastern Americans not only complicate any overly rigid consolidation into any singular identification, including ethnic identification, but also have complex effects on cultural expression. Contemporary Middle Eastern

1. Jodie Ahem, "Interview with Poet Susan Atefat-Peckham," *Poets and Writers*, online only, posted February 12, 2004, http://www.pw.org/content/interview_poet_susan_atefatpeckham.

2. Hayan Charara, *Inclined to Speak: An Anthology of Contemporary Arab American Poetry* (Fayetteville: University of Arkansas Press, 2008), xiii.

3. Steven Salaita, *Arab American Literary Fictions, Cultures, and Politics* (NY: Palgrave Macmillan, 2007), 5.

American writing increasingly explores the ways in which writers might resist the kinds of orientalist overdetermination that, as Atefat-Peckham shows us, have situated the Middle Eastern American writer within an almost impossibly overdetermined history. However, this resistance is increasingly articulated not simply by asserting opposing identities or correcting misperceptions, but also by attempting to change the way we think about identities in the first place. The emphasis on claiming both American identity and ethnic heritage that defined earlier generations of Middle Eastern Americans has shifted toward a greater focus on exploring and articulating transnational connections and diasporan sensibilities, with a simultaneous critique of the very notion of American identity itself. Indeed, much contemporary Middle Eastern American literature suggests that the idea of a stable cultural identity, even a hyphenated one, has been splintered—perhaps productively so—by what Charara calls this literature's "varied and complicated engagements with language, style, form, meaning, tradition, class, gender, ethnicity, race, nationality, history, ideology, and of course the self."[4]

Middle Eastern American literature has always explored that process of "talking through the door," finding those openings between cultural spaces through which voices can slip. But the nature of that communication has never been singular or predictable; nor has the nature of the door—that opening, that linkage—remained exactly the same at all times. This collection goes far in showing us the kinds of communication that are possible between cultural spaces, and the kinds of doors that we might seek to open. Yet as the "great love" mentioned in the Rumi epigram to this volume also seems to subtly suggest, perhaps one of the most important legacies Atefat-Peckham's anthology offers us is an understanding of the importance not just of finding ways to communicate between cultures and communities and peoples, but also of "talking through the door" between the different facets of one's own self.

4. Charara, *Inclined to Speak*, xvi.

I never met Susan Atefat-Peckham personally, but like so many others I was devastated by news of her death. I remember reading e-mails about the tragedy from writers around the world, and feeling the world to be a small, fragile place. With her passing, Middle Eastern American literature lost a sensitive, intuitive, empathetic voice. Yet through this volume her voice is somewhat returned to us, albeit only in part, both through her own literary texts included here and through the warmth and vision that she brought to her understanding of Middle Eastern American literature. Although she did not see this book come to fruition, her words resonate beyond her passing, and offer sustenance.

Lisa Suhair Majaj
October 2013
Nicosia, Cyprus

ACKNOWLEDGMENTS

I HAVE WORKED sporadically on this project since 1998 and owe grateful acknowledgment to many family members, friends, colleagues, and publishers.

My gratitude to all of the writers included, and to the many more in our vibrant literary community, for their patience and kindness, especially to Elmaz Abinader, Naomi Shihab Nye, and Gregory Orfalea, for their help in contacting others.

Thank you to Nora Staal and Christina Van Regenmorter for their faithful assistance typing the manuscript.

At the University of Nebraska–Lincoln, I thank Stephen C. Behrendt, Ted Kooser, Hilda Raz, Doris Smith, and my many fellow graduate students who inspired me to believe I was capable of assuming this mammoth task.

At Hope College, my gratitude to Myra Kohsel, Peter Schakel, Kathleen Verduin, and especially to Jesus A. Montano, and to the Hope College administration for their financial support of my work on issues concerning the Middle East and Middle Eastern Americans. May honest judgment always guide you.

My heartfelt thanks to my new academic home, Georgia College and State University, Arts and Letters, and the MFA program in creative writing. Especially I thank David Evans, Marty Lammon, and Beth Rushing for their encouragement of my work in civil and human rights, and for their sensitive support regarding teaching and race issues.

My love and gratitude to Joel Peckham, who stands with me on raising our children with an awareness of their rich heritage, both Iranian and American.

I feel indebted to the loving examples I have found in my blessed parents, grandparents, two sons, and countless aunts, uncles, and cousins, and to the Middle Eastern blood that ties us together.

I would also like to gratefully acknowledge the following authors who have generously contributed their previously published and unpublished work to this project, and to the publishers who originally printed, sometimes in different forms, the following titles by the following authors:

Barks, Coleman

["We talked through the door"] excerpt from "Talking through the Door," Jalal al-Din Rumi, *The Essential Rumi*, trans. Coleman Barks with John Moyne, A.J. Arberry, Reynold Nicholson (New York: Harper Collins, 1995), 78. Copyright © 1995 Coleman Barks. Reprinted with permission.

Abinader, Elmaz

"Mothers and Daughters," *Children of the Roojme: A Family's Journey from Lebanon*, Copyright © 1997 by the Board of Regents of the University of Wisconsin System. Reprinted courtesy of The University of Wisconsin Press.

"Preparing for Occupation," *In the Country of My Dreams* (Sufi Warrior Publishing Co., Inc., 1999): 36–37.

"Flying to Arabia," *In the Country of My Dreams* (Sufi Warrior Publishing Co., Inc., 1999): 13–14.

Abu-Jaber, Diana

"Tainted Love," from *Crescent* by Diana Abu-Jaber. Copyright © 2003 by Diana Abu-Jaber. Used by permission of W. W. Norton & Company, Inc.

Atefat-Peckham, Susan

"*Marvari*—The Pearl Tree," "Fariba's Daughters," and "Dates" are reprinted by permission from *That Kind of Sleep* (Coffee House Press, 2001). Copyright © 2001 by Susan Atefat-Peckham.

"Them?" *North American Review* (November–December 2001): 5–6.

Awad, Joseph

"A Novena for My Mother," reprinted from *Shenandoah Long Ago* (Poet's Press, 1990), 1–6. By permission of the author. Copyright © 1990 Joseph Awad.

"Memories of *Tiger Rag*," reprinted from *Shenandoah Long Ago* (Poet's Press, 1990), 12–13. By permission of the author. Copyright © 1990 Joseph Awad.

"For My Irish Grandfather," reprinted from *Shenandoah Long Ago* (Poet's Press, 1990), 21–24. By permission of the author. Copyright © 1990 Joseph Awad.

"Windows," reprinted from *Shenandoah Long Ago* (Poet's Press, 1990), 29. By permission of the author. Copyright © 1990 Joseph Awad.

"Aunt Anna," reprinted from *Shenandoah Long Ago* (Poet's Press, 1990), 34. By permission of the author. Copyright © 1990 Joseph Awad.

"For My Lebanese Grandfather," reprinted from *Shenandoah Long Ago* (Poet's Press, 1990), 20. By permission of the author. Copyright © 1990 Joseph Awad.

"Christmas At Sithee's," reprinted from *Shenandoah Long Ago* (Poet's Press, 1990), 10. By permission of the author. Copyright © 1990 Joseph Awad.

Bedway, Barbara

"Death and Lebanon," *The Iowa Review* 12, no. 1 (1981): 50–58.

"Why We Are in the DAR," *The Iowa Review* 28, no. 1 (1998): 72–77.

"Turning Lebanese: A Family Story," *The New York Times*, May 22, 1982, 1.

"In Her Own Hand," *Ohio Magazine*, November 1985, 23–24. Reprinted with permission, *Ohio Magazine*.

Geha, Joseph

"Where I'm From—Originally," in *Townships*, ed. Michael Martone (University of Iowa Press, 1992), 57–66. By permission of the author.

"Stepping Out," *The Nebraska Review* 22, no. 1 (1994): 36–48. By permission of the author.

Hazo, Samuel

"Understory," "The First Sam Hazo at the Last," and "Ahead of Time," from *As They Sail*. Copyright © 1999 by Samuel Hazo. Reprinted with the permission of The Permissions Company, Inc., on behalf of the University of Arkansas Press, www.uapress.com.

Kadi, Joanna

"Writing as Resistance, Writing as Love," *Thinking Class: Sketches from a Cultural Worker* (South End Press, 1996), 9–11.

"Coiled Tongues," *Thinking Class: Sketches from a Cultural Worker* (South End Press, 1996), 89–91.

"Moving From Cultural Appropriation Toward Ethical Cultural Connections," *Thinking Class: Sketches from a Cultural Worker* (South End Press, 1996), 115–27.

Kaldas, Pauline

"Cumin and Coriander" and "The Top" from *The Time between Places: Stories That Weave In and Out of Egypt and America*. Copyright © 2010 by The University of Arkansas Press. Reprinted with the permission of The Permissions Company, Inc., on behalf of the University of Arkansas Press, www.uapress.com.

"Shifting Spaces," *Letters from Cairo* (Syracuse University Press, 2006), 105–11.

Marshall, Jack

"Arabian Nights" and "Deal" are reprinted by permission from *Arabian Nights* (Coffee House Press, 1987). Copyright © 1987 by Jack Marshall.

"G–D" is reprinted by permission from *Sesame* (Coffee House Press, 1993). Copyright © 1993 by Jack Marshall.

Mattawa, Khaled

"From Cordoba" [God made souls in the shapes of spheres . . .]. By permission of the author.

"From Cordoba" [You look at grains of iron . . .]. By permission of the author.

"From Cordoba" [The soul too in this world of clay . . .]. By permission of the author.

"From Granada" [All fictions lose their story lines . . .]. By permission of the author.

"From Jativa" [If the lover cannot dissuade the beloved . . .]. By permission of the author.

"From Cordoba" [Nothing in the world matches two lovers . . .]. By permission of the author.

"From Almeria" [Fidelity is to keep her secrets . . .]. By permission of the author.

"From Almeria" [The world oppressing you and the love that spurns you . . .]. By permission of the author.

"From Valencia" [There is a breaking off when the beloved . . .]. By permission of the author.

"From Cordoba" [After many weeks of resisting the impulse . . .]. By permission of the author.

"From Fez" [There are times when the lover says NEVER . . .]. By permission of the author.

Melhem, D. H.

"Preface for Walt Whitman," *Country: An Organic Poem* (Cross-Cultural Communications, 1998), 14. Reprinted by permission of D. H. Melhem.

28. [bright world in morning light . . .], *Country: An Organic Poem* (Cross-Cultural Communications, 1998), 51. Reprinted by permission of D. H. Melhem.

53. "Hudson Continuum," *Country: An Organic Poem* (Cross-Cultural Communications, 1998), 78. Reprinted by permission of D. H. Melhem.

"then/now, part one," *Rest in Love* (Confrontation Press of Long Island University, 1975), 17. Reprinted by permission of D. H. Melhem.

[Bookladen on Friday . . .], *Rest in Love* (Confrontation Press of Long Island University, 1975), 23–25. Reprinted by permission of D. H. Melhem.

[Charon drives his ambulance . . .], *Rest in Love* (Confrontation Press of Long Island University, 1975), 41–46. Reprinted by permission of D. H. Melhem.

[mother . . .], *Rest in Love* (Confrontation Press of Long Island University, 1975), 75. Reprinted by permission of D. H. Melhem.

Nassar, Eugene P.

"Summer 1958," *Wind of the Land* (Syracuse University Press, 2002), 43–55. By permission of the author.

"Summer 1964," *Wind of the Land* (Syracuse University Press, 2002), 69–78. By permission of the author.

Nye, Naomi Shihab

"The Yellow Glove," *Words under the Words: Selected Poems*, A Far Corner Book (The Eighth Mountain Press, 1994), 116. By permission of the author, Naomi Shihab Nye, 2013.

"Arabic," *19 Varieties of Gazelle: Poems of the Middle East* (Harper Teen, 2005), 90. By permission of the author, Naomi Shihab Nye, 2013.

"Jerusalem," *19 Varieties of Gazelle: Poems of the Middle East* (Harper Teen, 2005), 92. By permission of the author, Naomi Shihab Nye, 2013.

"Hold Land," *19 Varieties of Gazelle: Poems of the Middle East* (Harper Teen, 2005), 94. By permission of the author, Naomi Shihab Nye, 2013.

"The Only Word a Tree Knows," *Words under the Words: Selected Poems*, A Far Corner Book (The Eighth Mountain Press, 1994), 74. By permission of the author, Naomi Shihab Nye, 2013.

"Renovation," *You and Yours*, American Poets Continuum (BOA Editions, 2005). By permission of the author, Naomi Shihab Nye, 2013.

"Amir & Anna," *Transfer: Poems* (BOA Editions, 2011). By permission of the author, Naomi Shihab Nye, 2013.

"Your Weight at Birth," *You and Yours*, American Poets Continuum (BOA Editions, 2005). By permission of the author, Naomi Shihab Nye, 2013.

"Supple Cord," *A MAZE ME: Poems for Girls* (Greenwillow, 2005). By permission of the author, Naomi Shihab Nye, 2013.

"The Only Democracy in the Middle East," *Transfer: Poems* (BOA Editions, 2011). By permission of the author, Naomi Shihab Nye, 2013.

"Because of Poems," *A MAZE ME: Poems for Girls* (Greenwillow, 2005). By permission of the author, Naomi Shihab Nye, 2013.

Rachlin, Nahid

"The Calling," *Veils* (City Lights Books, 1992), 95–108. Copyright © 1992 by Nahid Rachlin. Reprinted by permission of City Lights Books.

Sedarat, Roger

"My Mother's 20 Persian Gold Bracelets," *From Tehran to Texas* (Červená Barva Press, 2008).

"San Antonio, 1979," *From Tehran to Texas* (Červená Barva Press, 2008).

"Khomeini's Beard," *From Tehran to Texas* (Červená Barva Press, 2008).

"Outing Iranians," *From Tehran to Texas* (Červená Barva Press, 2008).

As Susan's father and on her behalf, I am grateful to Deanna H. McCay, acquisitions editor at Syracuse University Press, who has extended her efforts above and beyond the call of duty for the publication of this anthology. Without her help and support this project would not have been possible. She has been truly a great facilitator.

Bahram Atefat, 2013.

THE PUBLISHER would like to acknowledge Lisa Suhair Majaj's contributions to the publication of this volume. Lisa's expertise guided us as we prepared the collection, particularly the editor's introduction. We are grateful for her input.

Talking through the Door

INTRODUCTION

Voices from the Threshold: A Few Thoughts on Middle Eastern American Writing

IT WAS NOT THE FIRST TIME THAT, as an Iranian American student in the late 1990s at a large Midwestern state university, I encountered confusion regarding the classification of my heritage. The University of Nebraska's renowned museum of natural history was exhibiting Persian tiles from the Abbasid period in its Center for Asian Culture. To the right of the display, a map confirmed in bold color what the museum considered Asia: all of modern-day Iran, stretching north to Turkey, south to India, and east to Japan.

Until then I had not known I could be considered Asian, although I had been miscalled Hispanic, Latina, Jewish, Arab, Indian, Russian, Italian, Greek, and Native American, among other ethnic labels. Now living in the state of Georgia, I have been mistaken for African American ("Is it true that your wife is black?" a student of my husband's recently asked him). Wherever I am, whichever the largest dark-haired minority group happens to be, I am thought to be a member of it. But "Asian" was a first. When I approached the museum's curator, he pointed out that the map portrayed modern-day Iran as a part of "prehistoric Asia." And because they did not have a Middle East exhibit, "where else could we display the tiles?" he asked.

While completing a fellowship application several months later, I was unsure which box to mark for race ("other" was not an offered option). According to the graduate school, I was "white," a race defined as "not of Hispanic origin: a person having origins in any of the original peoples of Europe, North Africa, or the Middle East." I marked "white" and also facetiously marked "Asian," punctuating each with small question marks. The chancellor called me in response to say that I could not apply for the fellowship, for I was not Asian.[1]

Our country harbors an insidious history of renaming people for convenience's sake, and in this light, I use the designation "Middle Eastern American" with trepidation. Unlike academic fellowship applications and admissions committees that consider Middle Eastern Americans to be "white," literary academia has at times placed Middle Eastern American writing under the rubric of Asian American literature. But this has not solved the problem of classification.

Scholars have begun to use the category "Asian American" to encompass increasingly divergent traditions. What began with the inclusion of Chinese, Japanese, and Filipino/a American texts in anthologies of Asian American literature expanded later to include the texts of American Koreans, South Pacific Islanders, and writers whose lives and cultural contexts had been influenced by Asia.[2]

1. Asian is defined as "Asian or Pacific Islander—A person having origins in any of the original people of the Far East, Southeast Asia, the Indian Subcontinent, or the Pacific Islands. This area includes, for example, China, Japan, Korea, the Philippines, Australia and Samoa." This and the definition of the racial category "white" were taken from "Ethnic Origins" (provided by University of Nebraska-Lincoln's Student Information System—SIS). The University of Nebraska State Museum of Natural History (Morrill Hall) and the Graduate School, which are both a part of the university system, define the Middle Eastern peoples according to different terms. Whereas Morrill Hall cited cultural and historical grounds for identifying Iranians as "prehistoric Asians," the university cited the Iranian language, Farsi (which is rooted in the Indo-European tradition), as well as the geographical location (just below the Caucasus Mountains), as grounds for calling Iranians "white."

2. Amy Ling, "Teaching Asian American Literature," *Heath Anthology Newsletter* (Georgetown University, 1996), http://www9.georgetown.edu/faculty/bassr/tamlit/essays/asian_am.html (accessed March 5, 2014).

Asian American literature diversified even further when it began to include writers of Indian and Middle Eastern background, whose numbers surged in the latter half of the twentieth century. The literature of Middle Eastern Americans—like that of Indian Americans—possesses distinctly different historical, religious, linguistic, and cultural traditions from other groups included in the "Asian American" category.

I also hesitate to use the term "Middle Eastern American writer" because I do not wish to imply or support the notion that ethnicity is the only, or even the strongest, driving force behind the work writers produce. One writer in this anthology asked me, "Why do we have to be Middle Eastern American? Why can't we just be American?" Yet I wonder whether we *are* as simply American as anyone should be. I believe we are, as writers of literary merit.

But we are no less American when we celebrate our ethnic community. Our ethnicity textures our experiences. Our conversations as people of Middle Eastern descent inevitably raise issues of common experience, which in the post–9/11 climate unfortunately includes infringements on our civil and human liberties.

Nonetheless, I am concerned that an anthology such as this one not be used by the academy to marginalize the literature it includes. A. R. JanMohamed and D. Lloyd affirm that the creation of "special units" in the humanities (such as ethnic studies, women's studies, and gay/lesbian studies) has resulted in the relegation of those areas to the margins of the academy.[3] All writers included in this collection, and the many excellent Middle Eastern American writers for whom space did not permit inclusion, write about various facets of what it means to be, simply, an American—whether or not this includes discussion of ethnicity. For many of these writers, ethnicity sometimes provides a looking glass into contemporary America, but it is not the only window.

3. Abdul R. JanMohamed and David Lloyd, eds., *The Nature and Context of Minority Discourse* (New York: Oxford University Press, 1990).

Many of us share concerns over literary isolation. But there are other considerations; Joe (formally Joanna) Kadi, for instance, often discusses the importance of solidarity. This anthology does serve, ultimately, an important purpose that outweighs the risks of literary isolation. It celebrates and discusses the heritage we share and the writing we produce, offers some measure of peace, and opens intelligent dialogue about how the Middle East exists in America today.

When I first conceived this project years ago I was interested in presenting Middle Eastern American writers as a nonmonolithic group. The writers included here are descendants of multiple cultural heritages and reflect in some way the perspectives of various ethnic and cultural backgrounds: Egyptian, Iranian, Iraqi, Jordanian, Lebanese, Libyan, Palestinian, Syrian. They are from diverse socioeconomic classes and reflect multiple spiritual sensibilities: Jewish, Muslim, Christian, atheist, and so on. The Middle East is not a simple construct and never has been. Middle Eastern Americans are as diverse in ethnicity, religion, class, and sexual preference as any American subculture. Whether our sensibilities are Arab or Persian, Christian or Jewish or Muslim, we wish to separate our voices as little as possible and allow them all to coexist here as, simply, American voices.

When conceptualizing this project in early 1998, I keyed "Middle Eastern American writer" into an Internet search engine to see what Arab, Turkish, and Persian names I would find. The computer surprised me instead with Czech, Dutch, and British names of white American writers from Michigan, Missouri, and Ohio. Our times have changed dramatically in the years since I began collecting the works in this anthology. The project received enthusiastic writer support and publisher interest a good while before the current media furor over the Middle East. My motives in publishing this anthology remain the same as when I began collecting the works: that these writers be celebrated for their merits as writers. Now, in particular, the intrinsic value of cross-cultural understanding among Americans of diverse ethnicities, and between Americans and people of Middle Eastern cultures, will be evident to any perceptive reader.

An informed cross-cultural understanding of contemporary Middle Eastern American writing relies on familiarity with Western literary and cultural portrayals of the East that shaped cultural interactions for centuries. Western interest in Middle Eastern themes first noticeably surfaced in medieval Europe and continued with a resurgence of the "oriental" in eighteenth- and nineteenth-century France and England, finally reaching its peak in the European Decadent movement of the 1890s as well as in the early twentieth century. Take, for example, fragments of the unfinished "exotic" Eastern romance that begins one of Chaucer's *Canterbury Tales* (ca. 1387), "The Squire's Tale" (as influenced by Sir John Mandeville's famous travel narrative regarding Genghis Khan); or Daniel Defoe's empowerment of the East-West, man-woman female voice in *Roxana* (1724);[4] not to mention more subtle influences such as the smaller, albeit vivid, aesthetic details in Oscar Wilde's *The Picture of Dorian Gray* (1891). The Decadent's "oriental" interest in Middle Eastern icons such as Salome also appeared in the period's music and visual art, inspiring a number of musical compositions, most notably the violent discord of Richard Strauss's opera *Salome* (1905).[5] Similarly, the portrayal of femininity changed dramatically in later Pre-Raphaelite paintings, ultimately leading to the image of the femme fatale. Sultry, black-eyed, wavy-haired models were in, whereas pristine, bun-tied, tight-mouthed models were out.

4. This empowerment was far from complimentary. Roxana, taking on the stereotyped Eastern female role, ruins herself with sexual laxity and overzealous boldness. Although the text can be seen as empowering the female, it is a pathetic account of both the views Englanders held toward the peoples of the Middle East and the class and gender subjugation of the Western female; the Western woman must either become "oriental," that is, a "sex fiend," to gain power or must masculinize herself into what Defoe calls a "man-woman."

5. The opera *Salome*, a story of sinister feminine obsession, premiered in 1905 and was widely condemned as blasphemous and salacious. Within two years the piece was performed at more than fifty opera houses.

Eastern influences on European art from medieval to modern times shaped European and ultimately American perceptions of the Middle East and the Middle Easterner. Marwan M. Obeidat's *American Literature and Orientalism* (1998) suggests that the influx of Near Eastern material into Europe served to satiate the public's taste for the didactic, cathartic, and "exotic"; an unflattering image of Muslims was created, often weakly researched, which led quickly to legend and stereotype.[6] Obeidat sites several other studies that relate to his, including Frederic I. Carpenter's *Emerson and Asia* (1930), Arthur Christy's *The Orient in American Transcendentalism* (1932), Dorothee M. Finkelstein's *Melville's Orienda* (1961), David H. Finnie's *Pioneers East* (1967), and Franklin Walker's *Irreverent Pilgrims: Melville, Browne, and Mark Twain in the Holy Land* (1974). The most intriguing portions of Obeidat's study involve discussions of the historical and cultural relations between the Christian West and the Muslim East in the European literary tradition, as well as the concept of "romantic orientalism" and the impact of the Barbary conflicts on early American nationalism. Obeidat emphasizes Sufi influences on Emerson and the exploitation of Eastern exoticism in novels such as Twain's *The Innocents Abroad* (1869) and Melville's *Clarel* (1876).

I am interested in connecting issues of the past with contemporary times. The Christian West viewed the Muslim East with "suspicion and hostility" (Obeidat, 9). The end result was a distorted perception of the peoples and the religion, which to some extent has held well into the twenty-first-century United States. Even now, contemporary political rhetoric is revealing; what has been presented as an "inevitable war" with Iraq as a result of a war on terrorism, for instance, is referred to by some as a "crusade." Early distortions in the eleventh century resulted from a lack of personal contact with the region. Western Christians, often on military fronts, relayed secondhand or thirdhand accounts colored by religious zeal, condemning

6. Marwan M. Obeidat, *American Literature and Orientalism* (Berlin: Schwarz, 1998), 3. Hereafter cited parenthetically in the text (Obeidat, page number).

Muhammad as little better than the devil, and they commonly believed that Muslim rule laid the groundwork for the appearance of the Antichrist (Obeidat, 10). Three Christian and one Arab scholar first translated the Koran, albeit inaccurately, during the Crusades (1095–1291). By the time George Sale's version appeared in 1734, many scholars in the West believed the Koran to be not only lascivious and frivolous but also dull, monotonous, and forged from the Bible. Muhammad, often referred to by deformed names such as "Mahound," was credited with creating only a corrupt form of Christianity—pagan, anti-God, Satan protecting, heretical, evil, and based on idolatry. From the 1200s onward, many church scholars approached the Koran as the subject of refutation and polemical hostility. Among early anti-Islamic polemicists were John of Damascus and Nicetas of Byzantium, who regarded Muhammad as a liar and a Christian heretic (Obeidat, 11). According to Obeidat, throughout the Crusades, works such as William of Tripoli's *Treatise on the Condition of the Saracens* and Ricoldus de Monte Crucis's *Confutatio Alcorani seu legis Saracenorum*, as well as the many works of Ramon Llull, confirmed that the Muslim Prophet was "a lustful, voluptuous, veritable devil." Arguments surfaced claiming that what was most vile about Islam spiritually was also most culturally typical of the Middle East (Obeidat, 12).

Needless to say, many of those participating in this vicious stereotyping also did not recognize the nonmonolithic makeup of the Middle East, nor did they distinguish their erroneous conclusions about Islam from the varied Middle Eastern ethnic and spiritual communities. Meredith Jones summarizes the stereotype of Muslims that appeared in *Chansons de Geste*: "[Muslims] are giants, whole tribes have horns on their heads, others are black as devils. They rush into battle making weird noises comparable to the barking of dogs . . . they eat their prisoners."[7] Dante's *Inferno* depicts a cloven

7. Meredith Jones, "The Conventional Saracen of the Song of Geste," *Speculum* 17 (1942): 203.

Muhammad, chest torn apart, face ripped open—a grotesque and beastly portrayal, even by medieval standards. In 1100, in *La Chanson de Roland*, dogs are depicted feasting on "Mahumet" (Obeidat, 14). The Saracen conversion at the poem's end underlines a cultural as well as religious victory; its resolution is not so different from what can be achieved through assimilation and acculturation. A similar treatment appears in the Spanish *Poem of the Cid* (1140).

In Britain, one of the earliest portrayals of Muhammad appears in John Lydgate's lines (ca. 1400) in which the Prophet lies drunk and dying as swine eat him: "Off Machomet the false prophet and how he beying dronke was deuoured among swyn . . . Like a glotoun deied in dronknesse, / Bi excesse of mykil drynkyng wyn, / Fill in a podel, deuoured among swyn."[8] Muhammad didn't experience better publicity in the Elizabethan period, during which a common legend about Islam was promulgated: the failed miracle in which the hill did not come to Muhammad, so Muhammad went to the hill (similar to our own contemporary American idiom: "If the mountain can't come to Muhammad, then Muhammad will go to the mountain"). This story of the hill often went hand in hand with the legendary hostility and treachery of the Turks (the Ottoman Empire was now pushing at the perimeter of Europe). The Renaissance stereotype of the "despicable Turk" stood in for the medieval "vile Saracen" in plays such as Marlowe's *Tamburlaine* (1587–90), the hero of which is a Muslim who is part pagan, well read in the classics, unkind to Muslims, and somehow responsive and sympathetic to Christians (Obeidat, 17). The narrative ends with his conversion to Christianity.

Renaissance writers used texts of the Muslim East to satisfy the cathartic desires of a people who feared the outcome of bloody military battles, but who also lusted for the exotic, the mysterious, and the fantastic. A. Galland's translation of the *Arabian Nights*

8. John Lydgate, *Fall of Princes*, quoted in Marwan M. Obeidat and Ibrahim Mumayiz, "Anglo-American Literary Sources on the Muslim Orient: The Roots and the Reiterations," *Journal of American Studies of Turkey* 13 (2001): 47–72.

(1704–17) offered a magical and romantic portrait of the Orient. Despite increasing interest in the picturesque oriental other, polemical attacks continued well into the seventeenth and eighteenth centuries with texts such as *First State of Muhametism, or an Account of the Author and Doctrine of That Imposture* (1678) and the *True Nature of Imposture Fully Displayed in the Life of Mahomet* (1697). The titles are revealing.

The British romantics updated fantastical portrayals of the "oriental" until they soon outnumbered polemical attacks. Robert Southey (*Thalaba*, 1801) and Thomas Moore (*Lalla Rookh*, 1817) glamorized the Orient with plentiful stereotypes. Typical of the period were Middle Eastern lusty men, sultry women, passionate romances, sensuous paradises, and fantastic settings, as portrayed by Byron, Shelley, Coleridge, and others. In the first two cantos of *Childe Harold's Pilgrimage* (1812–18), Byron sympathized with the Christian Greeks (for whose cause he later gave his life) and castigated the "barbaric" Turks. He wrote with firsthand familiarity and experience that other Western European writers did not possess, and he attempted to understand and use the Eastern literary aesthetic in his writing by incorporating the Muslim calendar in *The Gaiour* (1813), for example, as well as by using traditional Eastern images and metaphors—pomegranates appear in the setting; the heroine's eyes are depicted as a gazelle's eyes; and for his heroine, he chose the name Leila, an often-used lover character of Eastern poetry (Obeidat, 23). Obeidat reminds us that Edward Said, in his groundbreaking study *Orientalism* (1978), collected the various beliefs and clichés described above through centuries of European philosophies, religious systems, and literatures. After the romantic period, "the West's superiority over the East became 'more definite,' at least on the material level"; nonetheless, any judgment since the Crusades, argues Said, has been cast within the context of "Orientalism" (Obeidat, 24). "Orientalism," then, is ultimately a cultural doctrine willed over the Orient because the Orient becomes inferior to the West; this doctrine forced a "difference between the familiar (Europe, the West, 'us') and the strange (the Orient, the East, 'them')." So the orientalist makes the "Orient" speak, using a generality of labels like "the Muslim" or "the Arab" versus "the Westerner" (Obeidat, 24).

Early American contact with "oriental" material appears minimal, but a few points of contact besides secondhand British texts existed; American travelers included John L. Stephens, George W. Curtis, Bayard Taylor, Mark Twain, and Herman Melville, as well as small missionary groups, naval expeditions, and soldiers fighting in the Barbary Wars. Although American Transcendentalists often found parallels between Indian mysticism and their own spiritualism, they inherited much negative stereotyping from their British contemporaries regarding the "oriental." Obeidat catalogues the "oriental" tales carried by American journals such as *The Columbian Magazine*, *The American Magazine*, and *The Literary Magazine, and American Register*—tales filled with intrigue, such as "Bathmendi" (1787), "Salyma and Ossmin" (1788), and "Omar and Fatima" (1807). Even a notable author such as Benjamin Franklin wrote a few "oriental" tales of his own: "A Narrative of the Late Massacres" (1764), "An Arabian Tale" (1779), and "On the Slave Trade" (1790). Ultimately the Barbary Wars (1801–5, 1815–16) initiated true American-Eastern contact. Early American attitudes toward the "Barbary pirates" held until the 1970s, when the Middle East once more came to the public's attention through political issues such as the Arab-Israeli conflict, the Iranian hostage crisis, and extremist terrorism in Europe in the 1980s.

Until contemporary times, mainstream attitudes in the United States held the "reductionist view of North African privateering and a horrific image of 'the Barbary,' exaggerated and enlarged" (Obeidat, 25). Royall Tyler's *The Algerine Captive* (1797) presents a picturesque account of American life and subsequently a nationalistic approach toward the "oriental." The text references "our great government," but this travel narrative concerns itself also with the fabulous "other." It describes Algerian Muslims as a "ferocious" race and portrays Arabs eating prisoners. Although the text criticizes America's own Christianity, it also dismisses the entire Islamic argument as invalid and inconsequential. In the end, the narrative proves patriotic and political, suggesting the superiority of the American government and its people (Obeidat, 27). Muslims appear as drunk, emotional and excitable, polygamous, and slave-abusing cretins in Richard Penn Smith's *The Bombardment of Algiers* (1829). Joseph Stevens Jones's *The Usurper; or, Americans in Tripoli* (1835) does not paint a more dignified picture: "Now how shall the darling passion of my soul be glutted. Plunder! Aye, plunder alone can raise our sinking realm. Peace has no charms for me . . . ," yells the motivated dey of Algiers.[9] In the play, he takes American hostages, who spend a good while expostulating on their patriotic devotion to their country and the superiority of the American government. They are the martyred, seeking refuge from the "cruel, barbaric, and savage" Arabs. In the end, America triumphs as the American flag rises. Later representations of the "Orient" are no less stereotypical, and Obeidat (34) cites the examples of Edith Wharton's *In Morocco* (1920), Hemingway's *The Green Hills of Africa* (1935), Kenneth Roberts's *Lydia Bailey* (1947), Norman Mailer's *Barbary Shore* (1951), and Violet Winspear's *The Sheik's Captive* (1979).

The popularity and ubiquity of television since the mid–twentieth century has furthered the spread of misinformation. Just as *Tamburlaine* presented the Middle Eastern villain as Renaissance entertainment, television in the 1990s replaced the Russian male with the Middle Eastern male as the popular villain in dramas such as *JAG*, *X-Files*, and other action and adventure shows. Hollywood films such as *Naked Gun II* feature a comic scene of Middle Eastern terrorists, and there are countless others. A "noble savage" rendition of a Saracen in Hollywood's version of *Robin Hood* was thought to be a positive portrayal by some, though not by this writer. Popular fiction writers, such as Tom Clancy, have also often used the Middle Eastern villain, catering to the public's appetite for this common enemy

9. Joseph S. Jones, *The Usurper; or, Americans in Tripoli*, 1835, in *America's Lost Plays*, ed. Barrett H. Clark (Bloomington: Indiana University Press, 1965), 14: 153–54.

even before September 11. As a vigilant friend read passages of one novel to me in the late 1990s, I attempted to unveil the distortions. Ironically, on the morning of 9/11, Tom Clancy's voice was one of the first I heard aired on television attempting to avert the racism that many feared would surface as a result of the attacks. Even Disney's animated feature *Aladdin* bursts at the seams with stereotypes, from the goofy, bulb-nosed "oriental" storyteller who opens the piece to the relentless portrayal of evil characters as dark skinned. The evil vizier bears the closest ethnic resemblance to a Middle Easterner, whereas Aladdin, the good hero, sports the California surfer-dude look. Only Jasmine vaguely resembles a Middle Eastern woman, but her physical appearance is wrought with gender stereotypes I will not address here.

Contemporary portrayals of the Middle Eastern villain in popular media reached its height during conflicts between the United States and the Middle East, beginning with the wars in Iran and Iraq and the Israeli-Arab conflict and culminating in the period of grief and anger after September 11. The resulting negative ramifications have affected Americans of Middle Eastern descent as well as those who physically resemble them. We have heard tragic stories of victims of terrorism worldwide and witnessed the grief of victims' families. Our personal sense of security has been severely fractured. We have read about or witnessed hate crimes—a Jewish man savagely beaten in Boston in the early 1990s (just after the outbreak of the Gulf War) by a group of young white men who thought that he was Arab American, or a Native American gunned down in Arizona when mistaken for a Middle Eastern American, ten years later, post–9/11. And there are many more stories like these. Physical violence, emotional abuse, and racial discrimination are plentiful. The "Orient," while providing some people with an enemy they love to hate, and providing others with a source from which they draw their patriotism, has paid a high price. The images projected by literature or the media, in journalism, film, or television, have slowly, over the centuries, become, for some, a reality. Post–September 11, efforts have been made to prevent racial profiling and to promote cross-cultural understanding, but much remains to be done. A reality that began in medieval Europe still affects many immigrant Middle Eastern Americans, in particular, many first- and second-generation Middle Eastern Americans who, having been born and raised here, are an integral part of contemporary American culture.

Barbara C. Aswad confirms that the first travelers from the Middle East appeared on this continent long before Columbus arrived in 1492: "Among the belongings of Columbus was a book by the Arab geographer al-Idrisi which mentions that eight Arabs sailed from Lisbon and landed in South America, long before. . . . We are also told that Istephan, a Moroccan Arab, served as a guide to the Spanish explorers and conquerors in what is now Arizona and New Mexico in the 1500s (Mehdi 1978). The major populations arrived approximately a century ago primarily from the Syrian-Lebanon region. Most were Christian."[10] A large portion of these early immigrants, peasant farmers, left their homelands to avoid Ottoman conscription and taxation, and to realize the great wealth, prosperity, and freedom of the American Dream. The fast-changing economics of the Middle East, cash cropping, competition for goods resulting from the opening of the Suez Canal, and, finally, diseased Middle Eastern vineyards forced many to leave the Middle East. The author Michael W. Suleiman, as quoted in Aswad, describes pre–World War I immigrants as "a quiescent community, keeping their politics to themselves, and not feeling part of American society. Rather, they followed the politics of the homeland, some supporting the Ottomans, others supporting revolt against the Ottomans and others remaining neutral. Many feared repercussions upon return."[11] Elmaz Abinader

10. Barbara C. Aswad, "Arab Americans: Those Who Followed Columbus (1992 Presidential Address)," *Middle East Studies Association Bulletin* 27, no. 1 (1993): 8, http://www.jstor.org/stable/23061491. Aswad cites Beverlee Turner Mehdi, *The Arabs in America, 1942–1977* (Dobbs Ferry, NY: Oceana Publications, 1978).

11. Ibid. Aswad cites Michael W. Suleiman, "Arab Americans and the Political Process," *The Development of Arab-American Identity*, ed. Ernest McCarus (Ann Arbor: University of Michigan Press, 1994), 37–60.

explores this period of economic crisis through family narratives; the characters in her memoir *Children of the Roojme: A Family's Journey from Lebanon* experience these unfolding crises and the destitution and desperation of Ottoman occupation.

It wasn't long after the proliferation of hostility, stereotyping, and cynicism in "oriental tales" published by eighteenth- and nineteenth-century American journals, discussed above, that Arabic newspapers and English-language works written by Middle Eastern Americans were published in the United States.[12]

If asked to identify a Middle Eastern writer, most Americans today would likely cite Gibran Khalil Gibran (1883–1931). Many consider him among the founders of Middle Eastern American writing as well as among the most widely known American poets read by the American public, while at the same time the most ignored or blatantly scorned by academics. He was a member of the New York Pen League, the first Arab American literary society formed by a group of writers from Lebanon and Syria who often wrote in Arabic and published their work in collaboration with translators. Gibran and other writers of the Pen League were part of the first wave of immigrants who arrived in the United States at the turn of the century.[13] Gibran, like our current-day Samuel Hazo, Jack Marshall, Khaled Mattawa, D. H. Melhem, Joseph Awad, Naomi Shihab Nye, and others, combined interests in family, longing for home, spirituality, injustice, violence, international politics, gardens, and dance in his writing. Although his love poetry in *The Prophet* brought him his greatest fame, Gibran's social and political texts are arguably his best literary achievements and are often concerned with speaking to the masses and assimilating into his newfound culture ("My Countrymen," "Khalil the Heretic").

12. Ibid. Aswad cites examples such as *Kawkab Amerika* (founded in 1892), Khalil Gibran's *The Prophet* (published in 1923), and the English-language magazine *The Syrian World* (published in the late 1920s) to illustrate this trend.

13. Gregory Orfalea and Sharif Elmusa, eds., *Grape Leaves: A Century of Arab American Poetry* (Salt Lake City: University of Utah Press, 1988), xv.

According to Aswad, "American nationalism in World War I pushed assimilation; restrictive immigration quotas of 1924 favored European migration and curtailed immigration from the Third World countries overall. Some American chauvinists feared that immigrants from some cultures would not assimilate to Anglo American traditions. . . . Those citizens who possessed second languages were not praised but made to feel ashamed. Their literature and history was deliberately and systematically ignored (Novak 1975). The melting pot ethos was in and was strengthened in the Arab community by the new second generation (Aswad 1974, 1992; Naff 1985; Pulcini 1993; Suleiman 1994)."[14] In this anthology, Barbara Bedway writes of aging family members desperately wishing to learn English; in Eugene Nassar's work, the younger generation is slowly lost to cultural assimilation.

While the Depression sent many immigrants home without jobs in the 1930s, those who stayed joined national and community groups. In the southern United States, where shopkeeping was stigmatized, Arabs and other minorities (who at the time were regarded as superior to African Americans) joined the mercantile business.[15]

14. Aswad, "Arab Americans," 8–9. Aswad cites the following: Michael Novak, foreword to *The Syrian-Lebanese in America: A Study in Religion and Assimilation*, ed. Phillip Kayal and Joseph Kayal (Boston: Twayne Publishers, 1975); Barbara Aswad, ed., *Arabic-Speaking Communities in American Cities* (Staten Island: Center for Migration Studies Press, 1974); Barbara Aswad, "The Lebanese Muslim Community in Dearborn," in *The Lebanese in the World: A Century of Emigration*, ed. Albert Hourani and Nadim Shehadi (London: Centre for Lebanese Studies and I.B. Tauris, 1992), 167–88; Alixa Naff, *Becoming American: The Early Arab Immigrants' Experience* (Carbondale: Southern Illinois University Press, 1985); Theodore Pulcini, "Trends in Research on Arab-Americans," *Journal of American Ethnic History* 12, no. 4 (1993): 27–60; and Suleiman, "Arab Americans and the Political Process," *The Development of Arab-American Identity*, ed. Ernest McCarus (Ann Arbor: University of Michigan Press, 1994), 37–60.

15. Aswad writes also of the comparison between the treatments of Arabs and African Americans: "[The Arab American's] hard work was stressed by most academics. . . . However, it is also important to be aware that European and other immigrants were able to 'make it' to the middle class, while American blacks did

Arab American immigrants of the northeastern United States, where many jobs were classified by ethnicity, were offered jobs in textile mills. These immigrants were peddlers, small shop owners, factory workers, and farmers. Women, essential contributors to the working family, also engaged in these occupations.[16]

The end of World War II brought with it a change in Middle Eastern immigration. New immigrants included refugees from the Palestinian-Israeli conflict, students attending American colleges who married Americans (and never left the United States), as well as other upper-class exiled elites who left their homelands for political, religious, or social reasons. Changes in immigration laws favored "educated" émigrés from the Third World—professionals who were already heavily influenced by the West. Besides those from Lebanon, Syria, and Palestine, Arab immigrants from Yemen, Egypt, Iraq, and Jordan, and Middle Eastern immigrants of ethnicities other than Arab, such as Turks, Iranians, and Kurds, also emigrated during this period. The Immigration and Nationality Act of 1965 (which ended favoritism toward European immigrants) was particularly influential in this regard. After the Israeli-Arab War of 1967, popular interest in the Middle East peaked: "The interest was not only due to the fact of US ethnic revivalism or . . . political turmoil in the Middle East and the fact that the US had replaced England and France as

---

not because of the politics of racial inequality in the US. The various national labor laws between 1930 and 1960 benefitted immigrant populations by enlarging job opportunities, controlling access to those jobs and providing supplementary income to the unemployed. These same benefits seldom helped the black worker until the Civil Rights movements of the 1960s (Smith 1987: 151–54)." Aswad, "Arab Americans," 9–10. Aswad cites J. Owens Smith, *The Politics of Racial Inequality* (New York: Greenwood Press, 1987).

16. Excepting Philip K. Hitti, sociological histories of these immigrants and their communities did not begin until after World War II, although the scribes of these communities wrote prolifically about upholding ethnic traditions and boasted proudly about their lives and ancestry. Philip K. Hitti, *The Syrians in America* (New York: George H. Doran, 1924).

the dominant neo-colonial power in the area. The issues of protection of some Arabs for their oil and the increasing alliances with Israel caused frustrations in the American communities."[17] It was during this time that emotional and physical harassment of Middle Eastern Americans became more public and frequent, recurring with even more frequency during the Gulf War in 1991, and again in 2001 after September 11. This increase in immigration as well as the inflammatory political tensions inherent in America's relationship with the Middle East coincided with a surge in the production and publication of Middle Eastern American literature in the latter half of this century.[18]

"If a literature's life and energy are determined by the activity surrounding it," then Middle Eastern American literature "is experiencing a renaissance," writes Elmaz Abinader.[19] Middle Eastern Americans have been writing and successfully selling books since the 1920s with Al-Mahjar ("immigrant poets"; otherwise known as the New York Pen League). Abinader cites Ameen Rihani, Gibran Khalil Gibran, Mikhail Naimy, and Elia Abu Madi as the major figures of

17. Aswad, "Arab Americans," 11.

18. Since the early 1980s, studies defending the public image of the Middle Eastern American have increased, the major proponents being third-generation Middle Eastern Americans. They explored their roots for the first time. Numerous books emerged on the subject, such as Sameer Y. Abraham and Nabeel Abraham, eds., *The Arab World and Arab Americans: Understanding a Neglected Minority* (Detroit: Wayne State University, 1981); Edmund Ghareeb, *Split Vision: The Portrayal of Arabs in the American Media* (Washington, DC: American-Arab Affairs Council, 1983); Jack G. Shaheen, *The TV Arab* (Bowling Green: Bowling Green State University Popular Press, 1984); and Michael Suleiman, *The Arabs in the Mind of America* (Brattleboro, VT: Amana Books, 1988). Among the best sociological books written about Middle Eastern American ancestry is Gregory Orfalea, *Before the Flames: A Quest for the History of Arab Americans* (Austin: University of Texas Press, 1988).

19. Elmaz Abinader, "Children of Al-Mahjar: Arab American Literature Spans a Century," *U.S. Society & Values: Electronic Journals of the U.S. Department of State* 5, no. 1 (2000): 11.

the period. From the 1950s onward, while Middle Eastern American writers such as Hazo, Melhem, and Etel Adnan were rarely identified by ethnicity, they were prolific. And scholarly attention to Middle Eastern American writers is gaining ground with the critical work of Evelyn Shakir, Lisa Suhair Majaj, Loretta Hall and Bridget K. Hall, Gregory Orfalea, Sharif Elmusa, Barbara Aswad, and Nathalie Handal, among others.

Scholarly progress depends on facilitating access to the works through anthologies and clarifying issues of classification. Amy Ling, in her essay "Teaching Asian American Literature," affirms the difficulties involved in definitions: "At what point does an immigrant become an American? Should American citizenship be the sole criterion? Can't a lengthy residency [qualify]? Where do mixed-race people fit . . . ? [What about those racial authors who choose] not to write [about their] ethnicity? Is Asian American literature defined by the ethnicity of the author or by its subject matter?"[20]

The answers to these questions will depend on the individual. Middle Eastern American writers, while possessing a distinct cultural and religious history, share many themes in common with Asian American writers: political marginality, the importance of tradition in alien environments, ethnic denial, isolation (Connie Young Yu, "The World of Our Grandmothers"), the power of the extended family and the community (Li-Young Lee, "I Ask My Mother to Sing"), the integration and assimilation of children into the dominant culture (Monica Sone, *Nisei Daughter*), the loss of the mother tongue (Sui Sin Far, "In the Land of the Free"), the difference between what America represents and what it really is (Carlos Bulosan, "Silence"), and the widening gulf between parents and children (Maxine Hong Kingston, *The Woman Warrior*), among others. Many of these themes are shared by immigrant writers in general, regardless of racial background. The ultimate goal of all writing is to humanize. It is easy to hate an invisible and silenced enemy, but as Ling suggests,

20. Ling, "Teaching Asian American Literature."

if readers who generally have no contact with people of a particular ethnic background are able to see, through the work, that they are "just people after all," then "they have made a giant leap towards greater understanding."[21]

Mutual understanding might be this anthology's most important purpose. I ask readers to acknowledge and respect "our" differences (meaning the differences among the writers in the anthology as well as the differences between readers and these writers), and then to consider that we are simply the family who lives next door. We share much in common. The people of the Middle East and the people of the United States, while speaking different languages and following different political systems, and while nursing wounds born from long conflicts, must come to understand that they are global neighbors if there is to be any lasting and peaceful coexistence. Without empathy, this task is impossible.

The goal of art is empathy. In Middle Eastern culture, the best and most successful writing or art is considered to exist in service to one's community. As the editors of *Grape Leaves: A Century of Arab American Poetry* suggest, writing for the Middle Easterner is not isolated in the academy, "as too often is the case in the United States—but rather is a public treasure used on important occasions as a connector of people."[22] This anthology includes sixteen accomplished writers whose works take up a multitude of themes: from the familial cross-cultural misunderstandings and conflicts of Iranian American writers in Nahid Rachlin's and Roger Sedarat's work to the mysticism of Khaled Mattawa's poems, from the superstitions that govern characters in Diana Abu-Jaber's prose to the devastating homesickness in Pauline Kaldas's characters. And while the goal of this volume is to collect the work produced by a number of Middle Eastern American writers and to provide empathy to readers who seek a new understanding, it also aims to recognize these writers'

21. Ibid.

22. Orfalea and Elmusa, *Grape Leaves*, xiv.

vital contributions to contemporary American literature—to underline connections rather than to isolate differences. The themes surfacing in this anthology consistently demonstrate an ardent effort at reconciliation, connection, and finding one's place among others.

We live in times of crisis and change. We struggle for a foothold in a country that is at once repulsed and intrigued by the many voices of its immigrants. And we struggle for a place in time that calls on us to speak the many languages of this world, a time that calls for an opening of many doors to intelligent discussion.

Dr. Susan Atefat-Peckham, Editor (2003)

ELMAZ ABINADER

Mothers and Daughters

1918

Mayme tucks her dress beneath her thin legs and sits down. The other passengers on the ship around her scrape tin spoons across metal plates. She slowly rubs the left side of her face and closes her eyes. Now she can think. People have stopped moving around; she has stopped moving around. Although she needs food, she does not want to eat. She prefers to sit, to let her back curve in a posture she would correct on her daughters—to drop her head slightly, to not look at anything very hard; to place her hands together, not in prayer. The deck rocks beneath her long flat feet. Her daughters, Zina and Camille, sit quietly on the bed above hers. Soon the lower deck will be dark. Boats stir a sickness inside Mayme, and the view from the rail petrifies her with its infinity. The passengers cannot watch her down here; the girls will not see. *Lie down girls, sleep. Sleep for days. Hold your shiny rosaries of olive seeds and close your eyes.*

Mayme cherishes solitude and quiet. She did not have it in Abdelli, not even in the old days before the war. When they moved into the big house, she imagined she would sit on the veranda sipping tea and watching the water, but she did not. If she could have escaped through an open window for a little while, just a little while, and disappeared while Shebl's friends drank black coffee and smoked Turkish pipes; if she could have shrunk and crept along the roads like a mole, she would have loved her home. In the early years of their marriage, she liked company, and set food for everyone at a moment's notice. After all, she was the sheik's wife, and from her hands came plates of stuffed grape leaves, stacks of homemade bread. She placed a diamond of baklava on each plate. They called her Sheika and thanked her. She bowed, smiled, and backed into the kitchen, never speaking or mingling with them as they sat on their chairs watching her come and go.

Now without light or examination, she pauses, stops, stares as she could not in the busy "palaces" in Abdelli, in the basements and ruins she was sent to live in, or in the shanty in Batroun, where she could not look beyond the flicker of the fire. Now Mayme is taking her daughters away, and that's all that matters. No one will notice if she rests for just a little while, or if she remembers, allows herself to think back and remember the faces, hands, and voices of the dead. And when the deck has gone quiet, Mayme will think of her nieces, the children of Shebl's brother Yousef. His wife—she forgot her name, although they spoke often—had run away, leaving the two daughters on their own. They were not only the same ages as Mayme's own daughters, they had the same names, except in that family, Camille was the elder and Zina the younger.

No one could have known the girls would die. Not the women who had named them the same, nor the fathers who lived in America; not the mother who had left them, nor the mother who stayed, and maybe not even their uncle, Rachid, the new sheik. Could anything have been done? When they try to explain, people will say: The girls were born into a hard time—it was World War I, the Turks occupied Lebanon, and those who weren't dying of starvation were ill from the Spanish flu. Everyone counted these events in his history.

Mayme knew to keep her daughters close to her, to veil them in her skirts, to create chores for them so they would not stray and find a body or touch food that was contaminated. Mayme made them sing. *Love singing, girls. Listen to my scratchy voice as I beat the bread. Repeat and sing.*

After the wife's disappearance, the nieces had no mother to whisper to them, to take them away from the sickness, or to take them to another world. *Who actually found them?* she asked Zihr el Ban. Zihr was visiting Mayme in Batroun and brought the news of her nieces' deaths. As the village teacher, she knew all the children. Zihr explained, "After the girls' mother left, they refused to leave the house. The older, Camille, found food, washed herself and her sister, and went to church each day. Suddenly they disappeared. Some thought their mother had come for them, but she had not. The flu took them quickly." Mayme tried to picture the two girls in their house, alone, dying.

A few years after Shebl left Mayme, her two girls were not allowed to visit their cousins. Shebl had left many debts and no money. Rachid had to liquidate his brother's property to satisfy the creditors. He sold the furniture, sold off the crops, and eventually rented out the house. He allowed Mayme and her two daughters to live in the basement, but they could not return upstairs to the large rooms. Also they could not cross their land or enter their groves. Rachid needed the crops to feed his large family, so he guarded the land carefully, allowing no one to trespass. Yousef's house was on the other side, so it was impossible to visit the other Zina and Camille. After a while, Mayme did not think of them, filling her time only with thoughts of her own escape.

TWO GIRLS, Camille and Zina, had died in a room beneath their father's house. Did they then lie there slumped against the wall until an angel gathered them in his arms? Two other girls, Zina and Camille, lay together in the dark on their way to America. These thoughts were hidden in the darkness, or in the depths of Mayme's lungs, until she breathed out all the air, clean. Start over.

THE BASEMENT of their harra had once been a small store. Crates, drawers, and bins on the dirt floor served as their furniture. Mayme sang loudly to puff away the clouds of dust that filled the air. Perhaps her girls did not see the brown particles shaking from the walls, rising from the floor, floating into her mouth. Mayme tasted the dust, saw it, and tried to rub it from her daughters' skin until they cried.

Rushing through the room, she took little breaths as she worked, trying to beat the dust from coming in every crack. She sang, prayed, waved her hands through the air, watching it fly. The girls' steadiness sometimes bothered her. She tried to move them: get water, sweep, dance, walk around . . .

TWO YEARS BEFORE, when Mayme's mother died, Mayme could barely see because of the dust. She splashed her eyes with water before she cleaned her mother's body. It had become soft, like a rolled carpet, and in her arms, her mother's body hung to the ground. She moved quickly—get the priest in and out, the doctor, the neighbors, or they would all choke.

While she was preparing food for the visitors, her youngest daughter, Camille, only two, came out of the pantry where she slept and stared at the wooden box sitting in the middle of the parlor. Her *sittie*'s old mattress, dressed in a tight white sheet, was pushed against the wall. The blankets had been folded and placed at the foot. The day before, Sittie had laced strips of rags through Camille's hair, and Mayme could see it needed to be fixed. Camille looked through the door toward the bleached morning. Putting her tiny hands on her hips, she examined Sittie's bed again. It was smooth and unwrinkled. She turned toward her mother and her sister. Mayme chopped onions with slow careful slashes and watched her daughter. She hadn't thought of what to do with the little girl. Her mother had died in the night, and the funeral bells were not rung, so Camille had slept through the commotion. Zina poured chick-peas into a bowl. The large box in the middle of the floor had its lid propped open. Camille slipped her feet into her felt slippers. Mayme raised her eyes and saw her little girl approaching the coffin. "No, miss." Her voice became shrill and immediate. "Don't go near."

"Where's Sittie?"

"I'll comb your hair out later." Taking some bread and yogurt to where Camille had stopped, Mayme instructed, "Go and eat your breakfast outside, and when you're done, go down to see your cousins."

Camille held the bowl for a moment, and her mother waved her out twice. She walked away from the box and out the door; then she sat on a stone with her food. The first neighbor who came to pray greeted Camille. The little girl scooped her yogurt with pieces of bread and mumbled, "*Mahraba.*" She did not look at the others who clutched rosaries and wore black scarves pulled down over their eyes. Throughout the prayer, Mayme lingered in the doorway—a shadow on the threshold.

Mayme prayed for her daughters and for herself. Her mother was gone, and her husband has been in America since before Camille's birth. This was the only life the girls knew—the life of this basement, this loneliness and foreboding. They have taken on the traits of gypsies. Camille often wandered through the village alone looking for animals of any kind: oxen pulling wagons, asses carrying loads, or a bird sitting on a stone wall. She said they waited for her too. That one partridge on the pomegranate tree blinked sideways into the sun and watched for Camille's golden hair. A work mule in its journey across the tobacco fields shook his head to see Camille march up to him and talk in a high voice. Sometimes she was chased away by a farmer, but some old women listened and smiled.

As she walked, Camille limped, because her left leg had been injured. She stayed on the road to avoid climbing down through the thickets. Her foot skimmed the pebbles, and she raised and dropped it again. It didn't hurt anymore, but she was slow to get going. The scar was nearly gone, and Mayme prayed there would be no permanent damage from her daughter's foolishness.

About six months before, despite her mother's warning, Camille had dawdled in an open doorway during a thunderstorm. "Don't wander out into that rain, little miss." Camille put one foot in, one foot out. In, out, in, out. Mayme steadied her eyes on her own fingers twirling threads around needles. She hoped the girl would tire soon and sit down. The scream that came from Camille was not part of the game. Mayme rose, shook the strings from her fingers, and ran to the door. Camille crumpled forward, and the back of her knee burned red. She had been struck by a hailstone the size of a tomato.

Carrying the child to Sittie's bed, Mayme laid her on her stomach. The spot blazed from the heat, and the knee swelled. What could she do? Zina ran into the storm to get her great-uncle, and Mayme watched as Camille's leg turned blue.

Uncle Nassif looked at the little girl's leg, which had doubled in size. She had started to run a fever. He shrugged. "You had better take her to Batroun." Zina and Nassif helped wrap Camille on Mayme's back and tie her with a shawl. Pulling on a scarf and shoving her shoes in her satchel, Mayme started on the long journey with Camille sleepily bouncing up and down.

The treatment for blood poisoning was cleaning out the wound with a spindle and thread. The doctor watched as Mayme imitated his actions. Camille's face and dress were soaked with tears. She moaned, and Mayme's own eyes filled with water as she worked the needle and then replaced the bandage. For two months, each morning and each night, she let the blood while Camille's sobs choked in her chest. Mayme talked to the leg and told it Camille might be a dancer, if she would not cry.

When the mourners started a second rosary, Mayme gave instructions to Zina to serve the food, and she went to find Camille. Her daughter had stopped at the top of the hills, from where she could see her cousins. The bright morning sun cast short shadows on the dusty ground. Uncle Yousef's girls were returning from the well. Camille held her sister's hand and carried a jar with the other. Mayme's Camille descended and stopped the girls and asked with her head lifted, "Whose Camille are you?"

"*Bint Yousef*," the older one replied. The younger echoed, "*Bint Yousef, unna Zina*."

"Whose Camille are you?" Yousef's Camille asked.

"*Bint Shebl*," Camille automatically replied to their ceremonial greeting. She followed them, and her curls, still in rags, flopped against her shoulders.

On the way home, Camille asked Mayme where her cousins' mother was. Gone where? Mothers don't leave, except for a day when they go to the souq as Mayme does to get food.

Once a week Mayme held a bracelet or a ring up to the light, polished it with an old cotton shirt, placed it in the belt at her waist, and headed north. Taking the roughest mountain roads, she walked quickly, speaking to no one. Many women she knew traveled to Tripoli too, but Mayme had to go alone. She did not want them to know about her jewelry; besides, she moved faster than most. From the road a traveler might sense a rabbit scampering through the field below. Her mother had taught her this route and how it wove in and out of the mountains, coming near the road only twice. She kept her hands on her waist, impressed with the shape of her treasure.

When she reached Tripoli, she went to a man she knew, a Syrian, interested in nice things. She did not stop to examine anything in the bazaar. The odor of fresh lamb sifted by her. Her eyes did not notice the bolt of brocade fabric open on a table or children's shoes lined on the street. No one's eyes met hers except when she raised her jewelry up to the man. *My bracelet.* She related the story of how it had been brought from Brazil or France and there wasn't another like it in all of Syria or Lebanon. She fingered the design and told him to feel it too. Mayme begged the merchant to take another look. He nodded his head as he did to all the village women and handed her small bags of flour, a skin of oil, a handful of salt, lentils, and rice.

Behind the church Mayme wrapped the food in her bag and placed it under skirts, between her legs, and she left the city through the fields of a friend who owned a house there. She would be lucky if the Turkish soldiers didn't search her; she would be blessed if they didn't rape her. They stood at the archway of the city, throwing flour into the wind, spilling salt onto the ground, taking the last shawl, the pair of shoes, a locket from a neck, pulling the hair of the women down into long black waves. A village woman had been raped by soldiers. Some remembered her in their prayers.

Climbing down the cliff, Mayme let her body drop into the brush. She crawled on her stomach in the ditch, scraping her elbows on the stones. Dust filled her nostrils and sweat soaked her body. When she heard horses on the road above her, she lowered further until the dirt filtered into her dress and the rocks ripped her sleeves. Her face turned hot and red and the bags skimmed the ground. Their weight pulled on her stomach, her arms, and her breasts; her face scraped shrubs and her knees absorbed tiny rocks. Mayme prayed on her stomach and wiped sweat and tears. She crawled along the road. She would feed her daughters. In spite.

On the day Mayme and Shebl moved into their new house in 1903, Mayme tilted her head in the parlor and twirled under the mural that her husband had commissioned a well-known artist to paint. The figure on horseback revolved, the Virgin Mother turned, the angels descended. It was beautiful, and visitors paused under it when they entered. And many came, to sit in a circle in the salon, drinking coffee and tea. This is when Mayme heard the voices around her—the persistent declarations—but she imagined they were only the wind fanning leaves, the door cracking open, or her voice singing as she worked at the stove. The women of the village talked among themselves. Grabbing their right calves, they shook them. "If Mayme could get pregnant, so could this leg." Mayme's legs were thin, long, and muscular; her body stayed lean. And the women commented again. Her husband might have many children, but no one was ever sure. *Poor Shebl*, they thought, *eighteen years with a barren wife, and he so handsome, and the oldest of the brothers. What else could he do?* Mayme did not care about his other women, though they came to her house.

As a couple they did not fit. Shebl's tall robust frame overshadowed Mayme's entire body. She would look up and see him gazing out to the fields. He was bright, with gray eyes and blond, nearly white hair. A lighthouse. Even when he sat, he dwarfed the furniture. But the face, when it bothered to look, to examine, to pause, melted into softness. Is this what made him a Don João? That face, with the thick line of a pink mouth, talking quietly to others as if every word were an intimacy? Mayme was not a tree. A twig perhaps, small, tight, and drawn into herself. None of her features protruded. Her dark eyes were recessed, her nose sloped. She pulled her hair back. She did not mind what they said because her house was so beautiful.

NOW YEARS LATER, just the sound of trotting horses made her cringe. Mayme stopped. She was afraid of becoming too exhausted, and she would not be able to run if it was necessary. She sat in a pile of weeds. She could make herself very small, by pulling up her thin legs and wrapping her arms around them. Below her a young couple leaned on one another. They did not seem to be hiding. The girl talked rapidly to her lover. Without speaking he raised his hand and outlined her nose with his finger. Shebl was not Mayme's lover.

When she married at thirteen, Mayme did not know what to expect from a husband. Would he beat her? At twenty-one, she begged him to take her to Brazil with him; at twenty-eight, she hoped that he would sleep with her in their new bed. Perhaps Mayme did not pray enough, eat correctly, or work hard. She asked priests, gypsies, old wives. "Rub the olive oil, pray to Saint Anne, relax." In Brazil she bought incense and fried bananas, and bathed in freshwater ponds.

Three years later, dressed in a hat from Paris, a still childless Mayme returned to Abdelli. Her husband combed his hair back off his browned face and wore a white suit and white hat and carried a cane. Wicker baskets, chests of statues, vases, and jewels were carried up to the mount, and the couple received guests for weeks. Neighbors came to see Mayme's new dresses and statues, and to listen to them speak Portuguese. The men followed Rachid, Shebl, and Yousef to the table to survey the plans for the new houses. They admired the large rooms, the kitchens upstairs and down—the way a sheik should live. Mayme brought her sister-in-law Elmaz to sit with them. She gave her a new shawl, served her, and remarked on the beauty of her daughter's hair. Elmaz was pregnant with her third child.

When Mayme put away her hat, she did not know she would not wear it again. Fires were lit and the ground for their houses was cleared. The three brothers started to build on the outskirts of the village. Men carried stones from the quarry for the plaza behind Rachid's house, and Yousef imported tiles from France for his floors. The Italian marble for Shebl's stairs weighed down the ox cart on its way up the hill. He had traveled to Persia to buy rugs, and he returned with two hundred little bells to tinkle when the wind blew. He and his brothers supervised the work on the houses. Walking back and forth along the road with the carts, they ordered a larger window, perhaps a balcony in back as well. Every day a hundred workers waited for the meals that Mayme made. Running from the house where pots boiled in the kitchen to the fields, she raked, picked, and pulled. She steamed onion skins to make paint for the outside of the house. Taken from its French knot, her hair fell in a long braid on her back.

After the homes were completed, Shebl opened a business in the bottom floor: a bank, a general store, and on one side, the chapel, which the district bishop dedicated to Saint Elias. He constructed a public oven outdoors and hired a man to bake and sell, then he departed. He did not watch over his house, store, or land. While Mayme tended to the customers and his twelve-year-old brother, Elias, kept the books, Shebl traveled. Mayme baked bread, milled flour, picked figs, tobacco, and olives, and pounded coffee. Thin, barren, looking ten years older than her husband, Mayme stopped mid-action to watch: she thought she saw him standing with his cane at the end of the road. As she carried the laundry out to lay on rocks, she may have heard his boot thump overhead. When he did return home, he handed Mayme the merchandise to shelve, he ate her meals and slept in their bed. He did not wait for long—Mayme became pregnant.

AFTER SHE FELT the weight in her womb, a heartthrob in her own, the business slowed down. The Turks took away Lebanese autonomy, and money was scarce. No one could buy their goods. Shebl lent money, then borrowed more. He lent, spent, and promised. Taking the baker's place, Mayme propped her belly against the public oven, and she beat dough against the stone all morning. Her husband, now sheik of the village, and his brother Rachid worked together as they had in Brazil: dining with friends in Tripoli, Beirut, Batroun. Mayme's thin frame stooped under her new weight. Would she ever walk without pain? She rubbed her legs. Some did not believe she was pregnant—not even Elmaz, who had her fourth child before Mayme had her first. And the women offered quite casually to feel her stomach, to listen to the rhythms and gushes inside of her. Mayme did not draw back.

The day her labor pains started, her mother was in church praying. Victoria, Elmaz's oldest, heard Mayme scream, and she brought the midwife and several neighbors. In the cold of November, Mayme lay on the floor as her womb contracted. The baby wrestled inside of her. The women's faces hovered above her, and she breathed as hard as she could. She shivered and saw their faces swing. When she released the pain, they withdrew to look below. Inside the dampness of her clothes, in the fog of her own cold breath, she heard the midwife say, "It's a girl."

Mayme thanked God and screamed, "I have a daughter," lifting her arms to heaven, to her friends. But the women moved away from her. The midwife did not stay. Each neighbor retreated, backed out the door. *What a shame*, they said, not sorry, half expecting it. *Barren eighteen years and only a girl.* Her husband would leave her now, they guessed. Then the room was empty.

With the baby still tied to her, Mayme crawled to the bed and screamed for help. She leaned her body against the leg of the bed and buried her sweating face into the cool linen. She tried to reach the daughter between her legs and wept as she bent over. Her mother ran in and saw her daughter and her granddaughter drenched in blood and water. Kneeling, she lifted the child and cut the cord. She bathed them together—placing her hand on the face of her daughter and her daughter's daughter.

She laid the girl, Zina Marie, on her mother's chest. She was a small olive-skinned girl with a ruffle of brown hair. Mayme hugged her all the day and night, held her head, and felt the moon in the palm of her hand. Untying her own long brown hair, she let it rest on the fingers of the baby.

When Shebl returned a few days later, Mayme stood at the door. He had heard that a child had been born in his house and he hurried through the groves and orchard, up the stony paths to the bottom of the stairs. His wife waited in the doorway, and in her arms a child lay, tiny and dark. He examined her, lowering his flashing gray eyes until they became agate. His shoulders fell into a slight curve until Mayme thought she looked at him eye to eye. He put out his arms, and Mayme laid the infant in them. The baby barely reached his elbow. He kissed his wife and daughter over and over, then stretched beside them on the bed. That night he arranged a twenty-one-gun salute. The smoke misted up to the stars, and Shebl, too, thanked God. He prayed until the sun rose.

The road was quiet once more. Rising from the dust outside Fripo Mayme wiped her face and ran home. Mayme didn't like the girls to be alone at night—Camille especially. She wandered away too often. Mayme might find her behind the church crawling in the bushes or walking on the edge of the mountain singing to herself. Something could happen. Last month Zina had been bitten by a scorpion. Anything could happen.

Pausing at the bottom of the stairs leading to the main rooms of the house, Mayme allowed her hand to graze the railing, but she turned and entered the basement, where she really lived. A small fire glowed orange on the faces. The two girls sat on the dusty floor, and beside them the Michaels boys rested. Tanous and Boulos had the Spanish flu.

When their father died from it, and their mother had fled to Batroun, Mayme had taken them in, sick as they were. The four of them shared one room—small, square, and damp. Crates served as chairs and tables. The girls slept on fabric bins; Mayme used her mother's mattress.

Months before when the men carried out the sofa, the chairs, and the Persian rugs, the girls sat where their beds had been and cried. Mayme spun around trying to stop them, grabbing at their sleeves, pulling on her possessions, shouting. Above her head in the mural, the horse, white and sleek, posed without flinching; the light around the Blessed Virgin did not die. Mayme stopped a man with a chest. Opening each drawer, she ran her hands around the empty wood. Where were their clothes and the sheets? The mattresses and linens lay in a heap where the master bed had rested. When the men were gone, Mayme sank onto the pile. Zina began to fold what articles were left. Rising, Mayme ran to the priest's house. He listened and wrote a letter for Mayme: *My dear husband . . . your brother said we must leave the house . . . your brother let a man take the furniture . . . we must leave tomorrow . . . money is needed.* Closing the door behind them, the mother and two daughters carried their clothes and two mattresses below.

BEFORE SHE COULD UNTIE HER PACKAGES and shake the dirt from her clothes, Mayme saw something scampering along the wall. She raised her fingers to her lips to signal the girls to stay still. Holding a hot poker over her head, she crept to the corner. Camille screamed and jumped as a rat ran toward her feet. Mayme swung her weapon and smashed the rodent again and again, then dropped it. The smell of burning fur penetrated the dusty air. Both girls began to cry: Zina leaned against her mother, and Mayme wiped some dust from Camille's face. She was covered with dirt. Mayme rocked them, enraged. The brightness of her daughters' rosy cheeks had become coated with brown. She imagined the Bedouins lived like this, walking through the desert, turning their eyes away from the sand blowing on them. They covered their faces and wore long black robes. As she sat, the gravel she had picked up on her journey filled her underclothes and settled around her waistband, around her ankles, between her toes. Yes, it enraged her that her own body crumbled away into tiny bits of gravel. That her children spit on their hands to wash them and created palms of mud. And now tears on Camille's cheeks ran roads down her face. "Take my handkerchief, little miss." Mayme removed her scarf, and dirt cascaded from her hair onto her lap.

Mayme rose and pulled the groceries from inside her clothes. Sometimes she wanted to speak of America where her husband lived and how they all would have food and clothes. But the checks did not come often. She spoke of none of it—not the future, nor the past.

Mayme handed Zina a small bag of flour. "Steal yourself to the house of Yousef and give this to your cousins. Stay with them awhile and let me know how they are." Zina pinned her hair up and wrapped her mother's shawl around her shoulders. As she walked in the shadows, only bugs chanted in the still night. She crept among the fig trees in her father's grove. In the valley, her cousin Boutros sat inside a tent. A small fire glowed. She did not speak to him; instead she climbed onto the road and hurried toward the last house.

Camille lay in her bed; the Michaels brothers also slept. Mayme covered her eyes and pressed her sweaty face. Since Shebl had left, Mayme spent only half each night sleeping. She thought of the strong cedar-and-velvet furniture they had placed atop the red ornate rugs in the master bedroom. Gone. Fortunately, she had tucked away her jewelry—a few bracelets and a brooch for her daughters. She put her hand inside her shirt and reached under her arms into her *hoobee*, a secret place they could not guess or get to. Inside the deep cave of her underarm hung the wrapped and tied pieces of jewelry. She never took them out except to show her daughters where they were. They too hid treasures: a piece of cake, some cheese, an apple in their *hoobat*, and when they thought no one spied them, they rustled through their blouses to reach the treats, warm and crumbly.

Before Mayme slept she prayed very quietly for her husband to come and recover her possessions. Shebl would send money, she told Rachid, but he did not believe her. She wept before Rachid and pounded her tight fists on his table. "Nothing is yours anymore, Mayme," he said quite clearly.

She wondered if she had heard a snicker from the kitchen. Elmaz had replaced her as the sheik's wife. She dressed her six children and paraded them to church—two girls and four boys, holding hands and walking in shiny shoes. Elmaz claimed she wore the first hat in the village. Mayme's eyes narrowed. *You are nothing, Elmaz; I may have nothing, but you are a peasant.* Rachid looked away from Mayme, talked to his son, tended his ox, drank his coffee. She cried, "At least let me have the goat for some milk for the girls, some yogurt for soup—something." He turned his back but left the goat with her.

Mayme could have blamed Elmaz—they argued between themselves about food, clothing, ownership, who could tat, and whether

Mayme could continue managing the silkworms that she had bought. Elmaz won nearly every battle, because she had Rachid nearby. No one took anything from Elmaz, because she had attended a convent school and was one of the few women in the village who could read. People addressed her as Sheika; they admired her clothes, her children, and even if they plotted against the house of Nader during the war, they were intimidated by Elmaz's certain manner. She always stood on solid ground, boomed across rooms, pointed fingers at anyone who bothered her children. But Mayme did not blame her, because with all her children to look after, Elmaz too was often alone.

Mayme curled on a blanket on the floor and waited for Zina to return. Zina worked hard and was obedient. Every task Mayme performed, Zina did too. Unlike Camille, Zina, now six, had known her father and hoped for his return. Her brown eyes followed the needles closely, her hands separated the grape leaves carefully; her back rippled as she lifted the mattress to flip it over. She never spoke of her father. She prayed for him and cried only once.

One afternoon Mayme heard Zina whimpering at the door. Mayme lifted the handle and saw her daughter standing with a basket, as empty as when she left. Her mother had instructed her to pick some figs, just one basketful, since they were not ripened. They had only flour and beans for dinner. Zina had surveyed the grove and tried to see which of the fruit would be near ready. When she walked forward, her cousin Victoria stepped into her path. "Where are you going, Zina?"

"To my father's fields," she said, looking up and brushing the loose strands from her face.

Victoria moved closer. "You cannot have any figs." She pointed her finger at Zina. "You can have nothing of your fruit, until your father sends money." She breathed into Zina's face and wagged her finger. Zina drew a short breath and watched the finger and then looked at Victoria.

Victoria's mouth folded into a line as Elmaz's did when she didn't like the people in the room. Zina glanced at her finger again, turned, and ran home to her mother.

Zina had wanted her cousins to like her so much. When they walked to church in front of her, she stared ahead as Victoria held Selma in her arms. Although only two years older than Zina, Victoria wore dresses cinched at the waist like a lady and stood erect always. Zina followed behind, talked to her sometimes, but now it was Victoria who made Zina's lips quiver and her fists draw tight. Mayme knew Zina would see more of what Rachid's family did to hers, but she could not tell Zina that her father was a bad businessman, that he had left them with debts. And all was taken away: no house, no furniture, no clothes, food, sheikdom, and no love. *I will never forget*, Mayme's oldest daughter muttered. You must not forget, her mother didn't say. How could she explain? Aren't cousins supposed to love each other? Telling her war is wicked wasn't enough or accurate. *Because I live, crawled in, and ate dirt. Because I couldn't breathe for years and years. Because my monthly bleeding stopped when my husband went away. Do not forget.*

Her wiry body shook and her voice crackled. "What do you want from me, Rachid? Shebl has sent me nothing." Zina heard Rachid's voice again, rising against her mother. They stood in the parlor, but Zina could not understand the words anymore, because her ears flopped back like a rabbit's (so she thought), but she saw. Rachid slapped her mother's thin face and he slapped her again. She sank to the tiles, her bones cracking against the hardened clay. Mayme curled forward, black and weeping—the rugs piled for dusting, the blankets folded for the season, heaps of tossed-aside fabric. Her daughters surrounded her—Camille's small hand patting her shoulder and Zina looking up to see Rachid walking away clasping his hands behind his back.

Zina watched the wiggling fingers, the curve of the arms, the shoulders like shelves. His long feet spread outward as he clicked down the corridor and went through the door. Mayme dropped her head and wept, "Naum, Shebl, where is everyone?" She called to her dead brother, Naum, and her absent husband. She began to cough, and her body echoed with emptiness. Grunts forced themselves from her throat; she covered her mouth and stood. The power of her lungs threw her body around the room. Both daughters watched the convulsions. Mayme dropped her head again. She understood why Yousef's wife had run away. Zina and Camille approached her. "Naum!" their mother screamed.

Perhaps like the little cousins, the other Camille and Zina, these three females were alone. Truly alone. Perhaps what lay outside their door had nothing to do with them. This could be a stranger's village. What signs did she have that she belonged here? The village women had walked into her house as if they didn't know her and taken her clothes. "My husband said I could have this; Shebl owes him money." Then the furniture disappeared. Camille would not be able to remember how beautiful the house was. She would never read her father's books, or see her mother dressed in a gown with gold bracelets ringing her thin arms. Mayme had no family; everyone was dead or gone. She didn't even have her brother, although he visited her in the dream.

Over and over she and Naum entered a cave with pails and small shovels to bring the dust to whitewash the house. How many times did she have to go there? Ahead Naum's candle sprayed stars on the walls; long rays curled over her head. Their voices echoed in the tunnel. Naum's arms flashed in the light as he scraped the walls. When Mayme walked toward him, she began to feel dizzy and stopped. His voice swirled around her as the cave began to move. The ground growled and the ceiling flaked down onto her hair. She stood stiffly. "Naum!" Her voice faded behind the rumble of the cave, the collapse of the ceiling. She dropped her implements and fell to her knees and crawled backward to the opening. Mayme could not remove her eyes from the descending cave. Dust billowed into clouds, rocks rained onto a heap. She imagined the flattened body of her brother below, breathing inside the earth. Perhaps he could burrow like a mole and arise beside her. Wrapping her arms around her head, Mayme covered her ears, shut her eyes. "Naum," she shouted, louder and louder, into the storm until her voice rang flat. When she opened her eyes, Mayme saw a wall of rocks. Staring at the mountain of rubble, she screamed his name again.

Once she had explained to Yousef's wife why the men had to go away. "Think of the things you can give your girls with the money they bring back. Brazil was good for Shebl and Rachid. If it wasn't for their manager, who stole everything, they would be there now. America will be the same. A land of dollars, not of pennies, you know." Both women were suckling babies—Yousef's wife had her Zina, and Mayme held Camille. Later Zihr told Mayme, as she poured lentils into a pot to soak, that the mother had left. As Zihr spoke, Mayme watched the cloud of brown water settle onto the beans. "Where did she go?" No one knew. "So how do they know she won't be back?" Zihr responded, "She won't be."

Mayme stirred the beans. Yousef's wife did not come back—Zihr had been right. The Michaels boys left too. Their mother had died in Batroun; so they went to Tripoli to look for work. Mayme waited but knew she herself must leave soon. The "little miss" had tried the day before to get banana peels from a dog, but he had growled her away. Mayme found her daughter staring at the animal, who was tearing the rinds apart and making fierce noises. She wanted to go somewhere where food grew on boughs that bent down so her daughter could reach it and eat as much as she wanted. In Brazil in the jungles, fruit fell to the ground and rotted and an animal would come along, sniff it, and pass by. She wanted to be in a place where there was only singing, so instead of the bellowing of the empty stomach, the roar of anger, Zina might hear music. Angels.

Mayme decided to get the figs herself. Grabbing the basket from Zina's hand, she started for the fields. Mayme had always been pleased with her agility. She could climb anything, carry more than many men, although her bones were brittle. Approaching the groves from the west, she pulled herself up a tree on the edge of her land. Kneeling on a thick limb, she cradled the basket in her lap. As she stretched toward the outside fruit, Mayme slipped and fell to the rocky ground. As she hit the stones, she knew she had broken her back. Lying on the ground, she felt a rod bury itself inside of her. Mayme could not move and began to yell until a nephew found her and carried her home.

When the doctor arrived, Mayme lay on the basement floor stiff from pain. "We have to set the bones, Mayme. Can you sit up?" the doctor asked. She could not move her head to answer him. He dragged her body along the floor and raised her upright against a post. Pulling her shoulders back, he tied her to the pillar. Mayme screamed. He warned her, "Do not move for any reason or your back will be damaged forever. You must stay this way for a month." Mayme winced and tried to move, but the pain shot so hard and far she became dizzy. There was not much to do. Tied to the post, she watched as eight-year-old Zina cooked the meals, washed the clothes, and ran all the errands. Eventually Mayme could sew buttons and comb her daughters' hair. She wanted to twist her body away and walk, do the floor, tuck Camille into bed, but she could not even wiggle. She cut the vegetables for canning, crocheted a tablecloth, and leaned her head back to pray.

The month passed slowly. Her uncle brought food for them, a neighbor helped with the clothes and fed the silkworms, but Mayme was captive. She could talk, yell, wave her arms a little, and nod off to sleep. She prayed the rosary almost five times every day. And she tried to take deep breaths, but her breast pulled tightly. Since she could not go outside, the dust would bury her.

One late afternoon, Zina took a basket and went to buy some flour. As the night became cold and dark, Mayme pulled a little at her restraints but could not get up. She asked Camille to go to the neighbors to get an ember to light the fire. Turning from where she lay, Camille said, "I don't think so." *Camille*, Mayme shouted over and over. The little girl rose and walked around the house. "No, no, no."

Mayme pulled at her ropes in anger. Her voice bounced, squeaked, and growled. She poked her chin out, kicked her legs. Her clothes wrinkled into a ball beneath her. Camille moved as far away from her mother as she could. Mayme wrestled with the ropes again. She looked around her for something to throw. Picking up a knife by the blade, she flung it, handle first, at her daughter. The knife flipped in flight and stabbed Camille in her left leg, then dropped to the ground flashing its blade. The girl fell, and Mayme screamed. Her blood rose up and her voice echoed in their little room. She fought the ties but could only scream more loudly until her voice surrounded her, shook the dust from the air, stabbed the walls. Camille's godfather ran in. The girl's leg bled into a pool on the floor. He grabbed the broom handle and reached for a cobweb from the ceiling. He placed the web atop the wound. The bleeding stopped within a minute. Camille lay sleepily on the floor soon after, and Mayme wept quietly at her post. Later Zina made a strong fire, but Mayme shivered all night.

Perhaps her mind was gone. Mayme did not understand how she had crippled her daughter. From her position, she watched Camille's wound heal to a broad purple scar. The girl could barely rest her leg on the floor before she had to lift it again. For the next two months, the mother carried her youngest daughter everywhere, although Camille asked to be allowed to walk. When she became too heavy for Mayme's still tender back, she let the girl go. Camille limped without complaint.

For six months, Mayme received nothing from Shebl. Zina stood once again watching Rachid's fingers. This time she could not stay idle. She pulled and shouted while his fingers clenched behind his jacket, danced in his hands. In front of him in the archway of the house, a tax collector beat her mother. Mayme had screamed, as the man grabbed her by the shoulders, "Zina, get your uncle!" Zina ran toward her uncle's house, where Rachid stood, outside, like a spectator, squinting his eyes from the sun. Mayme was being kicked. Rachid's fingers danced. "Come, can't you see what is happening?" She grabbed his arm and he shook her off. She fell into the dust, then ran from his unmoving figure. Her mother writhed on the ground. When Zina helped her mother to her feet, she looked across the road. Their audience had departed.

WHEN THE SPANISH FLU invaded the village, Mayme nursed her husband's mother and father as they both lay dying on their beds. All of the men were gone. Rachid's trips to the north sometimes lasted weeks. Elmaz was pregnant and did not let her children come to the sick house. Neither did Mayme. She left her girls alone when she went to wash down her in-laws and feed them. And as she had every morning for the last year, she harvested the silkworms that lived on shelves in their pantry. The silkworms crackled like rain on a tin roof. She stopped for a moment while the chorus rustled. A loud moan came from above. Mayme climbed the stairs to the room of her in-laws. Their large bodies had withered quickly in this last week, their faces had turned to slate. As she entered the room, her husband's mother shrieked and tried to chase Mayme away.

When Mayme returned home that day, Camille stood outside their basement talking to a woman in modern western clothes. The stranger wore a felt hat tilted to one side and had a golden cross pinned to her lapel. Mayme rushed toward them as the woman handed a pear to her daughter. "Who are you?" Mayme grabbed the fruit.

This American lady was from the *Ship of Hope*; they had come to care for the stricken, she told Mayme. The Spanish flu was a worldwide epidemic.

"But we are not sick here—" She started to point to the house of her husband's parents.

The woman interrupted her. "Your daughter tells me your husband is in America."

Mayme nodded.

The stranger continued, "I need a woman to come to Batroun to work for me. Do you sew and crochet? Could you and your daughters go to Batroun?"

Mayme invited the woman into her basement home. Zina prepared anise tea and Camille sat on the floor. Mayme wanted to know about the job, but she asked many questions about America and Pennsylvania, where her husband lived. The lady of *Hope* had only traveled through the state once and remembered some steel mills and very green hills. The lady talked on about her mission and Mayme's opportunity. Mayme watched the woman's hands, pale and smooth, as they lay in her lap. Her eyebrows were very thin, but she wore no color on her white cheeks. Mayme could work by pieces. The nurses and doctors needed some sewing and darning; the sheets and towels needed patching. Could she do this? Could she find a place to live? They would give her some food and a little money. Mayme did not know how much would be enough. Anything would do. Could she come soon?

She would take the job even though she could imagine the warnings: stay away from this woman, she is a Protestant. But Mayme had known Protestants and missionaries in Brazil, and she was not worried. Instead of thinking of this, she tried to recall the names of people in Batroun who could house her and her daughters. Some owed her husband money. What were their names?

Before she left, the stranger shook Mayme's hand. She would see her at the clinic, and she told her the address. Somewhere to go. When the woman was gone, Mayme surveyed their basement room. Her daughters sat quietly. Dust settled everywhere. Impossible to clean. Yes, she would take the job, but she would not leave until she could do no more for Shebl's parents. They died a week after the stranger's visit. They died together.

Mayme placed a basket of pots and pans on Zina's head. Clothes and shoes had been rolled up in the mattress; Mayme would carry these, and Camille, who now was four, cradled only some sheets and towels. Each girl was pinned with an important piece of jewelry on her undershirt—Zina a ruby ring, Camille a broach. They were leaving without much notice. Mayme did not stop to see Elmaz's new baby. The other villagers tended to the sick in their homes. Mayme tried to imagine the village fading behind her, dissolving into a cloud, and finally into dust. Yet she was sure that they would walk with everything they had and with all their strength and find it there again when they stopped, when they rounded a bend, when they shut their eyes, or left them opened.

None of the three wore a hat, although the day was hatefully hot. The rocky road sizzled like embers beneath their bare feet. Mayme sang to the girls as they walked. She recited the only Portuguese word she remembered from Brazil: *sarava*. They repeated it obediently. They recited the rosary and they sang.

Other families traveled the road. Some had carts piled with furniture and children. They stopped and talked to the three females, shared water and stories. They met a group of five on their way to America. "We are going to live in Brooklyn, U.S.A.," a girl of eight announced. Mayme asked them if they would send a letter to her husband. "See us in Batroun." They snapped a whip and rolled away. "Do not forget!" Mayme shouted after them.

As the family left the hillside and reached the main road, they also left the rocky surface to walk on limestone. It seared their feet; they could hardly bare to allow each foot to touch. Mayme began to walk faster, but Camille could not keep up. She cried as her flesh burned on the road. She stood in the shade and would not move. Mayme stopped and looked at her in frustration. The girl was only four years old. Mayme tied the mattresses onto Zina's back and put Camille on her own shoulders. Beside them motorcars formed clouds as they passed. Walking with their heads down, they hurried along the road. Below them the sea rolled in and out, the white houses on the hillsides pearled the hills, but they bent with their loads and rushed toward Batroun.

Preparing for Occupation

This is my place. My territory, Landing
strip of my anxieties. Heaven
upside down. It's my place, and I won't change it
for any other. I fell, and I'm not sorry.

—From *Jucio Final*, by Blas de Otero,
translated by Hardie St. Martin

Buy only short books, ones that read quickly with plots
you can keep track of when the pounding starts on the door.
Drive no nails into the wall, no pictures, no pencil sharpener
or mirror. Your face doesn't matter any way. You are no one.

Teach your children at home. Or leave them idle to wander
the streets to find a funeral parade; a crowd to join.

Use only votive candles so they can burn out before morning.
Stash your cigarettes in your pocket. Leave nothing
in the cupboards to remind them but a child's toy.

Adopt no pets. Hook up no phones. Print no cards, address
labels or stationery. Test your batteries daily.
All your clothes must be light, in similar colors and never need
ironing. Your only family heirlooms are habit, memory, name
and
song. Believe that placing your daughter upon your shoulders
will be home enough for her as she feels
for something familiar.

Avoid meeting the neighbors unless you've known them
since birth. Be careful of the bird flirting with you in the yard;
one of you may soon fly away.
One of you has migratory patterns.

You've been here thousands of years. But aren't your people
nomadic anyway? Can't you pitch your tent in a grove
on the outskirts? Move in with relatives? Cross into another
country, clogging the border with shanty towns, waiting
to return? I've seen you together; you prefer to be together.

Because this house bears the prints of your children
upon the wall, because the kitchen is furrowed
from your journeys made to the table from the stove,
the stove to the table, because the floor is pocked
from the weight of your davenport, doesn't mean
you can't move on.
The walls have echoed your voices, your sighs floated
up to the ceiling and gathered like clouds in a refugee sky.
Remember the time your son opened the door so quickly
the bulghur flew off the table and around the room?
Grains are in the corners still.

You will miss nothing: the window that refuses to open,
the sputtering light of the refrigerator, the leaking pipe
in the girls' room; the cat that crosses the fence in the morning.
He is not your family although you recognize him.
This is not your town, although you walked its streets
on your wedding day. Local water mixes with your blood.
This is not your country despite its dust covering
your shoes, the songs you have memorized; the poets
you claim as your own. Don't look down.
Look up. When the geese are passing in their vee formation,
join them, tuck your treasures under your wings.
From the refugee sky, you can count the bodies below you,
examine the shipwreck of your home while others pick
through the remains.

Flying to Arabia

It's their hair they love the most,
these women, sitting on the plane
from Frankfurt to Jeddah—the way
it falls against their beaded backs,
or is it the bracelets ringing
their elegant arms, or those fine
Italian shoes, polished and pointed?
And yet when the descent
into the city begins, they drop
their magazines and rise
one at a time to teeter down
the narrow aisle, their high
heeled feet barely touching
the carpet.

These women let the doors flap
behind them and face the mirror

for one last look at a speck
in their iris, at the lines
grooving their mouths
at their eyelashes lowering.
They pluck one stray hair
with their slender fingers.

These women shake wrinkles
from their abayas the black
fullness flutters like an errant curtain.
Their eyes close darkly
as they slide their arms into the large shoulders,
shrug them on.
They pull black veils from Milanese leather bags.
And they come foot after foot,
like a magician's scarf. Their hands are quicker
than their eyes. So quick
their fingernails nearly rip them. But do not, what

Can I say of these women, they do not
receive their veils like a bride
or a corpse but let their bodies
go slack; their arms fall to their sides.

These women land in Jeddah covered
invisible—inside the folds
their hearts beat unheard. They clutch
children, carry huge packages, attach
themselves to anything that can be seen.
What can I say of these

Women captured in their clothing,
bobbing toward each other
like bottles in the ocean.
I stare at the tented faces,

burn through their invisibility. They alone
recognize their radiance, their hips
in quiet hula, whisper to each other, point
to the sky through the window and glide away
huddled in conspiracy.

DIANA ABU-JABER

Tainted Love

DURING THE AFTERNOON STILLNESS when the heat concentrates in the air and the palm trees turn to glass, Sirine is sitting with Um-Nadia in the back kitchen when the phone rings. Um-Nadia picks it up and Sirine can tell by the way she says, "Yes? Oh ho. Oh no, you bad man—yes, yes, you bad thing—no, no, *you* are, you bad, extra naughty . . ." that she's talking to Odah the Turkish butcher who's had a crush on Um-Nadia for at least as long as Sirine's known him. Um-Nadia always tells Odah that she is saving herself for the mysterious Mr. X. Now she cups her palm over the receiver and tells Sirine, "He says he's put aside some special legs of lamb and for you to come and pick the best." Sirine unties her apron; she considers wrapping the scarf around her neck, but the window thermometer reads 89 degrees. Everyone has been saying what a warm autumn it is.

Sirine walks along the lip of Westwood Blvd. The big street looks cooked and yellow as a lizard skin in the late afternoon; there are Iranian restaurants, markets, and bakeries up and down the block, quiet now but mobbed at the dinner hour. This is a scene that she's looked at almost every day for over eight years. There's the swoop of traffic over the hill, the gray curbs, cement-busted sidewalks, and the busy jumble of Persian businesses—Shiraz Beauty Salon and Victory Market, Shusha Bakery, and Shaharazad Drugstore, with their shop signs written in English and Arabic scripts, and long, velvety-looking sedans and scrappy little compacts parked nose to nose along the streets.

Sirine doesn't quite come to a corner; she waits for a break in the cars and then runs across the middle of the street. She walks past an open fruit stand where they give her free kumquats, past a fallen power line, power company workers, and some police who ask her what tonight's special is, past the Persian Marxist Revolution Bookshop, where the clerks wave to her, down to the Topkapi Butcher Shop at the bottom of the street. It's a compact place, sleek and enameled as a tooth. No one can speak much above a whisper in there or voices will clatter and echo all over the place. Odah's shop is always crowded with Turks, Arabs, and Persians, as well as Italians, Poles, Bosnians, and Russians; almost all of the customers are identically dressed women in black babushkas and heavy black shoes. Sirine's uncle calls it the old lady store.

Usually Odah has one of his countless sons or nephews just run the shipment of meat up to Nadia's Café. But Sirine doesn't mind coming in to look over the wares and to watch Odah and his handsome sons hustling from the case to the scales, handling the big joints, the meat with its bright fresh bloom of marbling and blood.

She is somewhere deep in the ragged line that starts at the door and leads up to the counter, watching a tiny woman who apparently speaks no English gesture to one of Odah's sons—trying to demonstrate the cut of meat she wants—when someone stumbles into the line. The old ladies gasp and their purses swing on their arms. Sirine turns and recognizes the back of the man's shoulders. He seems to be half-crouching trying to hide himself behind the line of customers. "Aziz?"

He turns, peering around anxiously, a film of sweat beading over his temples. "Who?" He pauses and finally recognizes Sirine. A big smile breaks across his face and he says, "It's Cleopatra!" He scoops up her hand and kisses it.

There are loud grumbles and several of the elderly women shove Aziz out of line. Behind them, one white-haired woman with electric blue eyes shakes a knuckly finger at him and says, "No budging!"

"Who are you hiding from?" Sirine steps out of line. She looks out the big front window and spots the edge of a woman's black veil whipping up the street. "Hey. Isn't that that student?"

Aziz's eyes go round and innocent. "Is who what student? I have no students, only assassins." He drags a handkerchief out of his pocket and mops his face, then pulls his bright blue silk shirt away from his chest. Then he scans the room once more and says, "No really, I'm just experiencing a little technical difficulty. A complication, as they say. Having a little more fun than one Aziz can handle." He smiles his gigantic smile and takes Sirine's hand again. "It's good as can be to see you again, my dear. Look at how lovely you are without an apron on."

Sirine ducks her face a little. "Oh, now."

"Where are you spending your free time? Is that Han monopolizing your life? You know, he doesn't write poetry."

She sinks her hands into her pockets, tries to think of something that she's done with herself. "Well. I've been working on things," she says defensively.

He raises his black eyebrows. "You sound like my students, they're forever working on things. Why don't you come to my office and I'll teach you how to write poetry? I can tutor you." He leans over her, brings his face close, and she can smell something like licorice on his breath.

"Well . . ." She wraps her arms around herself, grabs her elbows. "English was my worst subject."

"We'll write everything in classical Arabic," Aziz says.

"I don't know if Han would appreciate you giving me private lessons."

"Han?" He sounds as if he's never heard the name before. "Why?"

"Sirine of my dreams!" A voice bursts in echoes over the white tiles of the shop. All the old ladies stop their arguing and turn. Odah emerges from his side office. "Sirine of the trees!" Odah is about five-foot-three, built with thick wide shoulders, no neck, and a big head covered with wooly black hair. His big soft nose looks slightly squashed against his face and his eyes are huge and dolorous. The happier Odah is, the sadder he looks. "Sirine, come in back here! I want you to see!" He grabs her hand and they hurry behind the counter, Aziz following. They go down a hallway and through a door into the refrigerated room behind the store. Their breaths turn to steam. Long, uncarved sides of beef hang from the ceiling. Odah leads her to a small silver cooler, the size of a footlocker; they lean over it and their breaths make pale spirals. Aziz says, "Open sesame!"

Odah looks at him. "Who are you supposed to be?"

"That's just Aziz," Sirine says.

He sticks out his hand. "I'm Aziz the poet," Aziz says.

"Oh, a poet." Odah doesn't seem to notice Aziz's hand. "Never mind about that." He squats over the cooler and it opens with a gasp. He tilts it, showing off a row of bright pink lamb legs. "You get first choice. The very best spring lamb."

"But it's October," Aziz says.

"In New Zealand it's spring!" Odah's voice ricochets off the shining gray walls. He puts his hand delicately to his chest, then recovers and bends back over the meat. "And this," he says, tenderly cradling a few cuts propped in butcher paper, "is for my rose, Um-Nadia. You tell her, yes? Special from Odah."

After Sirine has selected the lamb and gone back to the front of the shop, Odah presents her with Um-Nadia's package of cuts, wrapped in gold foil with a single pink ribbon. He taps it then taps his chest, saying, "Remember, from me."

"Now there is a true romantic," Aziz says, watching as Odah disappears back into his office. "He must be married."

"No, he's divorced. A bunch of times."

"Ah, no wonder. A chronic romantic. But romance is one of the fundaments of life, a crucial element, like bread and water, wouldn't you say?" He looks at her closely, his smile easy and soft, and Sirine notices for a moment how smooth his tan skin is and the brightness of his dark brown eyes. Then she realizes he is holding her hand again. She releases herself and plunges her hand back into her pockets. She feels her blush starting all the way at the center of her sternum. "I guess. I never thought about it that way before," she says.

"Perhaps you're not meeting your minimum daily requirements," he says. "You look a bit pale to me. A bit anemic. Dr. Aziz thinks you might be needing more poetry, more music, more kisses, more laughter, and also more dancing in your life. And he is prepared to write the prescription."

She's trying to think of a response when the white-haired woman who'd stood behind Sirine in line—now on her way out—taps Sirine's shoulder with a white-papered packet of meat, raises one finger, and shakes it at them vigorously, saying in broken English, "Monkey business!"

Suddenly there's a wild clattering, a juddering noise that fills the tight little space like roaring water in a drum, and a vivid blue blur spins around them: a bird has somehow flown into the shop and it batters itself against the plate-glass window trying to escape. The old ladies scream in twenty different languages, dropping their packages and straw baskets and wheeled carriers, and run out of the shop, as do Odah and his sons. Aziz drags Sirine out as well, laughing. "Oh no, oh dear!" he cries, laughing and shaking his head. "They think it's the Evil Eye."

"It *is* the Evil Eye, you idiot poet!" Odah rumbles at him as they shove through the door. "Do you realize what this means for me! All new charms!"

Sirine's heart is speeded up and she's out of breath. She presses one hand down against her chest, as if she could slow herself down, and she peers into the window. The poor bird is still spinning its wings against the window, a crazy, round blueness. Odah turns to her, bows, and then takes the pink-ribboned package from her. "I am terribly sorry," he says, his wide eyes shining. "But it is impossible now. I can not allow Um-Nadia to have this under the current circumstances."

"Why not? We left the shop—it's okay."

Odah shakes his head ominously. "Something—or someone—" he eyes Aziz, "has allowed the Evil Eye to enter my shop. Everything is tainted. Believe me, if I find out who is responsible—"

"Time to go check on my poetry class," Aziz says, and begins walking backward away from Sirine and Odah. "I left them writing something. It's been lovely, you two." He turns and strides up the hill toward campus.

Sighing heavily, Odah puts the meat on top of the mailbox like it's a special delivery package. "Fine," he says, and crosses his arms.

✢

While Sirine and all the customers are still gathered on the sidewalk, two young officers pull up in a cruiser. Odah tells them that the Evil Eye is inside his store. One of the officers puts his hand on his gun and the other says, "I think we should call the fire department." Then everyone stands there awhile watching the bird pinwheeling through the shop, and Odah sighs heavily several times, occasionally crying out, "Oh, the bad omen!" Finally, Sami—the smart son—thinks to prop open the door. And just as suddenly as it came in, the bird flies out the door, then rises calm as a sigh into the trees. And watching it go, Sirine feels some dark tension slip out of her body as well. She walks back from the butcher shop feeling oddly peaceful. When she turns the corner, she thinks she sees a flash of blue in one of the bushes and she moves closer, wondering if it might be the escaped bird. But then she hears Mireille call her name from up the street. And she backs up, thinking perhaps it's best to leave the Evil Eye alone.

SUSAN ATEFAT-PECKHAM

Marvari
The Pearl Tree
—for Joel

He asks if I remember them—I remember
few, I say. Leaning deep into leaves,
my uncle pinched and turned white berries
from the pearl tree in hands as old and twisted
as the branches. He rushed to where I waited,
uncurled his palm and tossed them, rolling
into linen spread on my lap. He squeezed
my fingers into his and pushed the silver point
through each fruit, tugging on the thread
until my palms were wet with juice.

I feel the grip and weight of a white necklace
soft and warm in the curve of my neck. I return
to the garden, alive again with yellow flowers
and the fresh scent of cucumbers. I am tall
enough now, but he holds my fingers back
and thrusts his own arthritic hand in leaves,
his mind fixed on a memory. One wet finger
unfolds and reveals a palmful of pearls.
He asks if I remember him.

Fariba's Daughters

Iranian law states that once a girl turns nine, she
is of age and must wear the chador in public places.

Fariba pulls her scarf off when we are alone,
holds her head taut like a winter oak, dark
and bare. She likes her books under
the mattress, under the wooded tucking
of blankets, between mattress and box spring.
She asks me if it's good to read, and reaches
under white to pull the book from its hiding.

I hear her voice, clear and strong, talking
of school, asking how freedom feels,
asking if I had sex before marriage like girls
in the West, or if I was a good Iranian virgin.
I tell her what freedom is. It is noon
and the prayers outside are loud. I ask her
why she never teaches her daughters
a different way. Her stare is hard. Almost
as hard as the roll of her eyes when someone
wants more doukgh, more bakhlava.
She is worn from wanting.

This is my favorite—Jean Paul Sartre, they say
his wife was smart, she says. But I can see her
daughter Attar turning with the scarf, winding it
around her head and loving to see herself as her
mother in the dresser mirror. I ask Fariba
why she wears it. For my daughters, her fingers
catch in her hair, for my daughters.

I remember when Father said I wasn't to wear
a chador to the bazaar. I was not old enough

to choose my way, that I would be safe.
So Grandmother pulled me under her chador,
wove me into her folds, just me and her under
cloth so postars would leave us alone. *Bepau*,
she said, Watch it. And I thought it was fun
and safe and soft standing against Grandmother's
lap, seeing from an opening near her hands.
Perhaps there is some joy in being captive,
some comfort in knowing we obey.

Nebraska winter drops in tufts. Does Sartre
still hide in wood? What does Fariba read
today? Attar turning, almost nine. What color
will her first scarf be? Woolen snow drifts
and weaves its way. Daughters are warm
wrapped in their Grandmother's chadors.

Dates

Three days and they wrapped
his washed body in muslin,
no lumbering sounds of coffins
carried, only the white ripple
of cloth. I sat back where all
women sat, staring from behind
a wooden net, carved and set
aside. The others swayed
as if crows under the mirrored
dome of the mosque webbed
in their chadors, breathing cloth
in and out of their wailing,
in and out. Their black heads
bobbed against the carved light
of the wooden boundary, the roar

and echo of men beating themselves
downstairs, pounding their chests
tightly, fists on flesh, to the rhythm
of a prayer for the dead.

A woman stood and held a tray,
the edges of her chador clenched
in her teeth and wrapped so tightly
around her face that it cut angles
into her cheeks. She offered us
a silver tray of fruit as chanting
grew, beating grew, that fleshy
rhythm. And the woman
with dates walked the aisles
offering the shriveled skin
and its sweet stench on a silver tray,
making her way from one woman
to the next. Somewhere under
Iranian earth, seamless cloth lay
on its side, a turned face frozen
under a concrete canopy, legs bent
toward Mecca. She lowered the tray.
I reached for a date, and my mouth
watered to taste its sugar.

Them?

MY TEN-MONTH-OLD SON Darius slept upstairs, and while I folded the laundry, September 11 happened. I find myself now explaining to my four-year-old son Cyrus that "mean guys knocked down buildings with lots of people inside" and that "they kind of look like us—isn't that too bad?" I never tell him about the airplanes—he loves airplanes too much. We travel often, and if he sees white powder anywhere, he knows not to touch, "because there might be bugs in it." And after another long, convoluted explanation, I say, "Well, fighter jets drop bombs, and sometimes people die because bombs don't understand. But sometimes fighter jets drop food too. Do you understand?"

He says, "Well, Mamma. I tryin' to understand you."

He watched me sob when the World Trade Center collapsed, draped his little arm all the way around my shoulders. A native New Yorker, I grew up with the skyline; the twin towers opened to the public the same year as my birth in NYC. A large black-and-white photograph of the skyline taken from the Staten Island Ferry hangs in my bedroom hallway. I stare at the "new" skyline. I only see air.

I am Middle Eastern American. Angry when Americans assault Middle Eastern and Muslim Americans or those who resemble them. I'm tired of our country ripping itself apart over racial tensions. Some Americans say, "Bomb them to the stone age." I've read the sign, "Kill them all; let Allah sort them out." But other Americans are tired of violence. After an angry person shot a sparsely attended Iranian restaurant, people filled the place the following day—some who had never eaten Iranian food, Americans who wanted simply to be there, leave generous tips, and show their compassion.

Compassion connects us. My work fills linguistic, cultural, and religious distances, juxtaposing Eastern and Western cultures. My book *That Kind of Sleep* was released in early September, and now, in large cities and small towns, I am reading poems about loving Iran. I wonder what I should expect. Rotten tomatoes? A punch in the face? Pity? Recently, I felt the agitation of a man in the audience as he asked me again and again if I approved of military action. American air strikes on Afghanistan had begun that morning, and I read at a Barnes & Noble that afternoon. He wanted an answer.

We are global citizens.

And I need to read those poems to anyone—to underline our shared humanity. I've felt my heritage in my blood in the small childhood moments of New Jersey when, wearing an authentic Iranian costume, I whirled like a crazed dervish on our Persian rugs. But growing up during the hostage crisis of the late seventies in the

United States and Europe, I learned that being Iranian American on the playground was unsafe. If someone figured I was Greek, Italian or Spanish, all the better. For the first time, now, I feel the urgency of claiming my heritage and writing more, of speaking to the issues that concern Middle Eastern Americans. I have two sons. They are of Middle Eastern descent, because of me. I am responsible, at least as the mother of my sons, to attempt change in my small part of this world. Watching those planes fly into those buildings, I knew I would have to overcome shyness, shame, and fear. And speak everywhere. The young listen. One child asked, "What have we done? Why are they doing this?" Another said, "Isn't Islam supposed to be a peaceful religion?"

I reminded them that often the people of a country are in contention with their government. Even today, in cities across Iran, Iranian youth protest against the government. My parents were visiting Tehran on September 11. I called, frantic, and asked them about the general feelings of the people there. They said youth held candlelight vigils in the town square for American victims; Iranians observed moments of silence for the dead. Who would have ever thought? This was not reported here. Iran was quick to condemn the September 11 attacks. In fact, recently Iran, home to 2.3 million Afghan refugees, extended a humanitarian hand, allowing international relief workers to truck US food through the country for Afghan refugees, and agreeing to help with search and rescue of US military personnel who might become stranded in Iran.

God to Muslims, like to Christians and Jews, embraces peace, equality, love, and justice. September 11 is not the product of fundamentalist Muslims—it is the product of madmen and fanatics. This is not to say that there is no rational reason for anti-American sentiment in the Middle East. Many in the Middle East disagree with our government's policies, and the vast majority of them would not fly airplanes into our buildings, or threaten us with chemical or nuclear weapons.

When I was a freshman in college, just after the blaze of extremist terrorism in Europe, I heard someone say, "We should send nuclear bombs to the Middle East and flatten it like glass." What about my grandparents, my aunts, uncles, cousins, and friends who live good, generous lives in Iran, who cared tenderly for me as a baby, who speak beautiful words—all of them incinerated in one plume, all of them, glass? Our words have far reaching consequences on those we will never meet and know. Think of that, the next time you hear a racial slur and say nothing.

At the end of a long conversation Cyrus asks me, "Why are those guys mean?" I say, "Because they think we're mean." He says, "Why?" I say, "Because." He says, "Because why?" Exasperated, I say, "Because some things are because." Today, when his "huge" Lego tower crashes to the ground he says it crashes "like the buildin' in the other New York." Only in this building, he says, "no one is died because no one was in there, Mamma." I see Darius sitting next to him, clueless, but clenching two small airplanes that Cyrus has put in his hands. Cyrus explains that Darius "rescued everybody with his airplanes." So, he knew about the airplanes.

Our stories can save us.

My cousin Ali, a freshman at the University of Isfahan in Iran, e-mailed me about how he had made the mistake of leaving his large bag of fresh fruit in the community refrigerator. When he returned it was gone, eaten of course, by the upperclassmen. They wrapped their arms around him later and told him the story of the "Woolen Bear" who burrows into the dorms and steals any food in the refrigerator. I hadn't heard from Ali in ten years, but now he writes me to ask for advice about being a college freshman because I am a college professor. He asks if it's different in the United States. Then the e-mail takes a serious turn at the end. Writing in early September, he asks, "Why do Americans hate us so much? Please explain it? Why? Perhaps you understand them, as you live among them."

Them? I love my cousin, but I don't get around to answering his e-mail until after the 11th. When I sit down to reply, I look beyond the laptop screen, out the window in front of my desk. A dog barks at the leaves, the Michigan wind picks up, and I feel a chill rise as I settle my fingers on the keyboard.

JOSEPH AWAD

from "A Novena for My Mother"

4.
Flashing on my window through the night,
Her waving spectre followed when we went
To live with Sithee. Cramped and recondite,
That third floor room was never meant
For dad and me. There was a curtained door
To a roof and a clothesline's creaking din.
On stormy nights the wind would howl and roar
And pound on the door like someone wanting in.
Cold with fear, I'd slip from early bed,
Camp on the stairs to hear the radio's drawl
Or worried parlor voices (what they said
Of mother chilled) or Sithee, in her shawl,
Rocking my sister, shushing her bleating cries,
Crooning, in Arabic, soulsweet lullabies.

5.
Crooning, in Arabic, soulsweet lullabies,
(Her long black hair, unbound, mysterious)
Hugging us, baking us *hubbus*, cakes and pies,
My grandmother opened house and heart to us.
Father's bachelor brothers became my brothers.
Aunt Anna, whose love would fasten us together,
Quit her job to be our "second mother."

New Year's eve brought snow and bitter weather
And the party at Aunt Mary's where we sleighed
On frozen coal hills while the grownups sang
And laughed and polkaed. How the accordions played!
And when the curfew blew and the church bells rang
In the falling snow, I wept. But at my ear
My father whispered, "She'll be home next year."

6.
My father whispered, "She'll be home next year."
That summer, I went with cousins and Uncle Frank
Picking huckleberries. Blazing days were here.
Sithee and Charlie showed me how to yank
The tenderest grape leaves from their ghostly groves.
With Aunt Kitty I rode a Trailways in the gloaming
To her Jersey in-laws' farm, where swimmers dove
From a swinging tire. I'd feed the chicks and roam
The butterfly fields. Flash, racing me, would bark.
Hot nights I twisted while the thundering trains
Shook the walls and moaned in the far dark,
The starlost night of "isolation's" pain.
Back home, the streets, the morning light seemed strange.
Once more I watched the season's colors change.

7.
Once more I watched the season's colors change.
On Chestnut Street the trees were towered gold.
My father, faltering, told me he'd arrange
For me to visit mother "before the cold."
I had made that trip before, then stood outside,
Forbidden to enter, looking up at mother
Through her window. After that endless ride
We could only wave and smile, each to the other.
This time we went inside. We found her room
Where paned October sunlight crossed a hall.

I entered with small steps. Her eyes consumed.
We dare not touch. By a crucifix on the wall,
She lay there lost in cerements of white.
Softly, fondly she asked, "Why don't you write?"

Memories of *Tiger Rag*

The house would jump with light and sound.
Melancholy would fly away
When uncle Al and uncle Joe
And their swinging twelve-man band
Rehearsed in *Sithee's* living room.
When they rose as one to sway and play
The roaring score of *Tiger Rag*,
My secret soul would strut and shag.

"Al Awad," was their billing,
"And his Royal Vagabonds." Long
Afternoon, at the upright,
Al tinkered, plinked, exploring chords,
Bending an ear to heed a key,
Orchestrating a popular song,
Arranging it in his easy style,
Replaying it with a dreamy smile.

Uncle Joe was a cabinet maker.
He hammered and sawed by day.
By night he rattled and rolled the drums,
Bashing the cymbals with panache.
He crafted the band's music stands,
Emblazoned on each a double "A"
And a treble clef with a sparkling crust
Sprinkled with Hollywood glitter dust.

When a tympany thundered in our house,
All the kids in the neighborhood
Milled like moths at our front window,
Agog, with Barney Google eyes.
I would king it in the living room,
As any schoolboy would,
Loving their envy, pressed to find
A friendly way to draw the blind.

Those runs, those flights
Make the celebration in my spirit . . .
The shining tuba's *oompah, pah,*
The crashing cymbals, the clarinets,
The thumping bass, the rippling race
Of the fingered keyboard (I can hear it);
The blue salute of the saxophones,
The purr and romp of bronze trombones.

Hold that tiger . . . Hold that tiger . . .
Hold that tiger . . .

For My Irish Grandfather

I am stung now with a different shame than then,
That day in front of Kresge's five-and-ten
When my urchin friends and I ran into you,
Staggering, unshaven, your crushed felt hat askew.
You swooped down with unbounded love to hug me,
Then stopped and rocked in grieved uncertainty.
You must have sensed my recoil, my debate,
Young as I was. (Was it seven or eight?)
Lips tobacco flecked, blue eyes clouded and remote,
You fished in the baggy pockets of your coat

(That coat so oversized
The sleeves fell past your fingertips). Your eyes
Found sunlight. You held up a dime,
(One you had just bummed, maybe) black with grime
And chew tobacco, and tendered it to me.
I ran and left you gesturing helplessly.

They say the whole town knew you, Tommy Dwyer,
That you had a voice like one of heaven's choir,
That silver voice my mother used to call
Your "sad and tragic downfall."
In those depression years, in the saloons,
They plied your weakness. One would importune,
"Have another drink Tommy. This one's on me."
And another, "Sing us your beautiful *Mother Macree*."
Whole seasons you would disappear.
When I'd ask mother why, she would look severe.
"He's riding the rails," she'd whisper. "Who knows where?
Let's pray God's mother keeps him in her care."

In laurel time I think of you the more.
That's when you'd show up at the door.
Mother would argue you to a hot tub.
My father, when you were sobered up and scrubbed,
Would cut your hair and shave you, find you shoes,
And one of his old suits. For a month or two
You'd be a different man. Then you'd be gone
As suddenly as summer moving on.

I wish I could have known you in your heyday,
When your eyes were like the May and every payday
You courted pretty Bridget Rooney
With ballads of the times, all Juney-moony;
Before the years of drudging the coal mines,
Her early death, the booze, the brooding bread lines.

I keep a priceless memory
Of an hour or two you spent with me
When mother left me in your care one day.
You made up games in a grandfather's way.
I'd run and hide behind the chair.
You'd pretend to look for me everywhere
Til you suddenly spied me. Then you sang,
(How tenderly your tenor rang)
"Peek-a-boo,
I see you
Hiding behind the chair.
Peek-a-boo
I love you
Hiding behind the chair."
Did you remember, hopping a freight in the bitter midnight air?

The last time I saw you alive we cried.
It was when mother died.
We never knew how you heard the news.
You appeared out of nowhere, like sorrow's muse.
I sat in the living room all alone
With mother. (She lay as if carved in stone.)
The front door opened slowly, slowly.
You stood there, bowed and bald and holy,
Your felt hat crumpled in your hands,
Your too-big overcoat strangely grand.
You ignored me and moved to the coffin and stood
A long time looking, still as the wood
Of the crucifix above her head,
One with the silence of the dead.
Down our cheeks ran the drops of our shared loss.
You made a gigantic sign of the cross,
Shouting, "Jesus, Mary and Joseph have mercy
On my darling, my girl, my little girl . . .

She forgave me all my sins
She took me in
When I had nowhere to lay my head.
She's with Christ and his angels and saints." You spread
A kerchief over your nose and blew it.
Then (young as I was, I knew you'd do it)
You started to sing.
Your voice had the lilt of an angel's wing.
"My wild Irish rose . . .
Sweetest flower that grows . . ."
From dining room, kitchen, from the street outside,
Family and neighbors gathered, wet-eyed.
"You may go everywhere,
But none can compare . . ."
My memory fails here, and my art,
With you singing her beauty, your hand on your heart.

Windows

From the sanitorium's third floor,
Mother, deathward in her isolation,
Waves through the dormer to her boy below;
Throws kisses which, in retrospect,
Pierce my spirit like pieces of jagged glass.

Framed in the suburban picture window
Like Botticelli angels, my young wife and babes
Wave, throwing me kisses. I wave in return
Through the window of my '51 Chevrolet,
Backing out of the driveway into . . . now.

By misted casements now I wave to you,
Throwing you kisses,

Watching you tall, on your own,
As you stride resolutely down the front walk
Toward the glittering crystal towers of your dreams.

A thousand brazen windows catch the sunset
In memory's dusky citiscape. I curse
All of those hard transparent barriers
That separate us from the reach of love.

I want to smash glass.

Aunt Anna

. . . the sad heart of Ruth, when sick for home,
She stood in tears amid the alien corn . . .
—*Ode to a Nightingale*

It must have been like landing on a moon,
So alien and so far, it seemed, from the small town
You had never been away from—that March day
We moved into the house in Washington.

The bare parlor floor was piled with crates
And cartons left unopened by the movers,
Precious trove you had transported into exile—
Old linens, pictures, your hand-painted china.

You were sitting in a covered, high-backed chair
Left by the movers near the wide front window
Bereft of blinds or curtains, in full view
Of the naked street, the lamp post, sullen houses.

It was dusklight and the city's fitful noises
Sounded all the more forbidding in the stillness—

A siren's scream, a streetcar's lamentation,
The hoot and chunk from nearby railroad yards.

I see you under that high, old-fashioned ceiling,
Looking small and lost, huddled in the shadows,
Outlined by the window's dying light
Like a figure in a Rembrandt etching, crying.

Did you panic at keeping house for your four brothers?
At raising two small children for the eldest?
Did you weep for Sithee's grave untended? Friends,
Girlhood dreams you left behind in Shenandoah?

My sister and I wept with you, reaching hands
Over the arms of the chair to pat your shoulders,
Feeling urban darkness closing in around us
Like the mystery of how all days, all residences end.

Finally you wiped your eyes, stood up and strode
Through the dark house to the kitchen. Piece by piece,
You lovingly unpacked your dishes, your mind made up
To make this empty, friendless place a home.

For My Lebanese Grandfather

Blue brilliance of sunlight
On the sidewalk in front of Sithee's house.
Is it Sunday morning?
My father is speaking
To the man I know is his father.
He is taller, larger than my father.
He wears a dark suit, with a vest,
A gold watch fob
That flashes in the sun.

As my father speaks, his father studies me
With black penetrating eyes.
I am waiting for him to smile.
Jaddu,
This is my only memory of you.

Christmas at Sithee's

In glorious panoply,
With shining ornaments and colored lights
And icicles of tinsel,
The cedar tree towers
To the parlor ceiling. At its foot
A Lionel train, tiny Pullman windows lit,
Whizzes around a magic track.

For nearly ten years,
Ever since Alex's death,
(He was the youngest of her seven sons)
She said *No* to Christmas trees.
Alex's train was packed away
Deep in the cellar. Now,
Because my sister and I
Are living in her house,
She has relented.

Father whispers, "Go tell Sithee thanks.
Give her a big hug."

BARBARA BEDWAY

Death and Lebanon

Ohio

Mashaya ruins the night for everyone, both aunts say it has to stop. After dinner they find her sitting on our bed already in her nightgown, dark circles under wide green eyes. Aunt Philamena says tell us, *habibti*, what do you see? Tree shadows? Branches against the windowpane?

The dark hair swings no from side to side.

Something you hear, then? The backyard dogs howling, your old aunt here snoring? Maybe Mr. Truskaloski upstairs hacking out his lungs? No?

No.

Mashaya, child, something makes you scream.

Sitting in our bedroom window I watch the bonfire in the yard across the alley. With my cheeks against the cold pane of glass I see our neighbor wrapped in shawls bringing food on a plate to her dogs. They leap up in their chains. The high-pitched barking goes on and on. If our aunts weren't watching, Mashaya would be in the window with me, watching that fire in the tall metal drum.

You tell me, Ajunya, Philamena says, what can I do now?

At home I am Ajunya and Marcia is Mashaya, but only at home. In the Miner's Supply my aunt calls me Angie; it's Marcia who stocks the shelves. To her customers my aunt speaks Polish, Russian, a little Greek. Her sister Hikmet gets by with just Italian. Everyone here came from somewhere else but my sister and I are the newest: two years here from the Lebanon, because of the events. I was nine and Mashaya eleven when we came with our sitti, called grandmother here, to live with her daughters in America. At night I sit in our window and think of Beirut: the flashes of light, the ten-second count to the artillery's boom.

Ajunya, are you listening? *Look* at your room. What can I do that I haven't done? What?

We live with bare walls and a bare floor; all pictures, mirrors, crucifixes got put away and their ghosts with them. Because of Mashaya's dreams our aunts hang up every piece of clothing, never move the furniture when they clean; leave the dresser top, the floor, the chairs bare of anything that in the night could become the head or neck or arm of a stranger. Mashaya told them: his nose is twisted in the crucifix, his eyes shine out of the mirror. Sometimes there is no stranger but something else. Still, Philamena has to open the closet door to poke for hiding strangers, then shut it so the hanging clothes can't shape themselves into the wrinkles on an arm, a face, the back of a huge hand.

Well?

Xaala, I don't know.

Mashaya, look at me, even your sister can't tell what it is, she sleeps right next to you. At least she's trying to. Everyone has to sleep, child. Mashaya, can't you *look* at me?

Philamena slaps her reddened hands against her black dress. She is so tired from these interrupted nights that her heavy body sags and her legs and ankles swell. Aunt Hikmet, thin and belted inside her own black dress, tells her beads in the doorway.

Mashaya, Mashaya.

Philamena hugs my sister, whose face disappears in the dark woolen sleeves. Outside the bonfire is low. It will die before Mashaya can watch it.

Aunt Hikmet brings her rosary into our room. She kneels on the rugless floor and we face her. I hear the crack of my sister's bony ankles. She smiles at me and tucks her nightgown under her knees.

Philamena leans on my shoulder and groans to her knees. Beads click. We pray.

We pray hail marys for the dead: for our mother, who died having me; and for our sitti, whose life gave out once she got us, safe and sound, to America. We pray for who's not dead but dying, the old women Hikmet visits in their homes every week, nuns and widows giving out after years of a life in Christ. We pray for the Lebanon and all the true Lebanese, the believers in Christ, who must not give out until peace comes to the country at last.

Amen, Hikmet says, while my sister's lips are still moving. She's forming silent words to someone, to God or whoever it is, to keep our father from giving out in the Lebanon.

IN BED we listen to the sound of our aunts' slippers scuffling down the hallway. We count one minute and hear the creak of their beds. Mashaya reaches for her shoebox from under the bed and I pick up the rosewater bottle by the bedpost. We rub the rosewater into our skin and we sniff each other.

That's good, Mashaya says, and hooking her long hair behind each ear, she bends over her dusty box. Some nights she needs to look and some nights she leaves it alone, but for sleeping she always needs the rosewater smell and the sight of its thick blue bottle.

I hold the flashlight pen while she sifts through her treasures from the Lebanon. There's dirt and broken glass and Sitti's hypodermic needle for her insulin. In a rubber band Mashaya keeps strips of posters she tore off the walls of Beirut. She has eyes and hair and lips and shoulders from a hundred different boys, boys whose families plastered their pictures all over the city to honor their sons dead in the events. The boys might have been kidnapped or died fighting in the streets but it's Mashaya who keeps them, their creased smiles and folded eyes.

Hold this, she says, and hands me a strip of wide forehead.

Somewhere in the box she thinks there is a whole face but we haven't found it yet. Once our sitti said we were close, we almost had it, but the eyes looked in different directions.

Let's give up, I tell her. Nothing looks right tonight.

Hold the flashlight closer.

The pieces are getting too crinkly to see.

You're not even looking.

I'm tired of looking.

Then we'll never find anything.

She puts back the lid and folds her hands on top of it. I tug at the blanket and wait. She won't look by herself. Sitti helped when I wouldn't but Sitti died months ago so it has to be me now. I know I should search more but my eyes are too heavy, they close when I tell them not to.

Can we sleep now? I ask her.

I never sleep. She leans down to slide the box under the bed.

You do sleep. You have to. You dream.

I dream with my eyes open.

The dreams began after Sitti died. For the week she was sick Mashaya sat beside her next to the trays of pills and needles. It was summer, the hot air thick with unfallen rain, but Sitti was keeping us indoors. She watched and worried in her bed damp with sweat. She yelled *y'allah, y'allah*, get inside, and pointed toward the ceiling where she said she saw a locusts' swarm. Hikmet ran for the doctor but Mashaya closed the window and started to shake. Sitti called her Melania, our mother's name, and pulled off the cloth Mashaya tried to press to her forehead.

Melania, she said, her gray hair loose and damp across the pillow, get inside. Locusts are the teeth of the wind.

Beirut

Papa and his cousin Faisz sit at the kitchen table, talking in French about guns. Both prefer to speak in French. They say the true Lebanese are Europeans by way of the Phoenicians. We have no relatives in France but Papa is proud to have two sisters-in-law who live in America. He sends us there once a year for a month, where he forbids us to speak any Arabic.

Sitti laughs at the two men. She calls them *mughnuuni*, crazy ones, and scrubs her pans viciously. Mashaya dries them and hums to herself over the names and numbers of guns we all know by heart: Katushka, Kalishnokov, Duska; American M-l6s, Czech M-58s.

I know Papa is sad he has no sons to help him defend the Lebanon. He is handsome in his olive-green army uniform of the *phalanges libanaises*; his high black boots, the beret atop black hair cropped close to the scalp. He has a plan to get to the teenagers firing a 122-millimeter gun from the Cercle de la Renaissance sportive. The boys fire round after round into the Christian section, then they strut—Faisz gets up to show us their strut, with his hands high on his hips—they strut free as birds across the Avenue de Paris and jump for a swim into the Mediterranean. Faisz says sometimes they pick up rackets for a quick game on the tennis courts nearby.

There are battles all over the city and my father has chosen his. He and Faisz fold up their paper and diagrams and pick up their M-16s.

Au revoir, Papa says, kissing Sita.

Ma issalame, she answers, facing her dishes.

Papa slams the door.

Remember, Sitti tells us, untying the clean white rag from around her grey bun and sinking into a chair, just remember. The French say *merde* for shit but believe me, it still smells the same.

She turns on the radio for Sharif Akhaoui's daily report. He used to give rush-hour traffic reports but now he tells where the roadblocks are and what bridges are safe to cross.

Today, he is saying, you would be mad to go out. The gunmen are everywhere, every street is dangerous. Do not go out. Do not even try to.

Sometimes we listen to Akhaoui for hours while Sitti stares at the radio. Today he is naming street after street. No pharmacies opened, no bakeries. *Do not go out*. People telephone him with new sniping in Ashrafiyeh, with kidnappings in Ain al-Rummaneh. He repeats every ambush, every kidnapping.

Sitti keeps one hand on mine and an arm around Mashaya. No one touches the dial. Akhaoui's voice gets higher and louder. He screams by the end of the day.

MASHAYA'S JOB is to set the trash on fire. Just before curfew at seven o'clock she runs out to the street with a few drops of kerosene and lights the tips of the garbage. While the fire is spreading she tries, quick as she can, to pull out what she wants: broken bottles, bloody scarves, twisted pieces of metal. She won't touch moldy bread and she hates the daytime, when flies stay round the piles of trash and keep even the cats away. I don't like the nights when the sky glows red from tracer bullets and we hear rats in the cellar where we sleep on a mattress by the stairs. The rats make a soft, scuffling sound that doesn't worry my sister. She says if you can hear them they're not near you yet.

When our neighbor Mr. Helou left the city, he took a wide glass jar filled with dirt from his home in the mountains. Mashaya keeps bits of crumbling stone from the porch outside in a shoebox beside our mattress. What she pulls from the trash she lines up in a corner and shows me before we sleep. She loves hard things with jagged edges, blackened in parts by fire. In the dark she gives me a sliver of glass and I do what she wants me to do. My fingers curl tight around it; she squeezes my hand with hers. When I open it up my hand is bleeding.

Mesquina, poor thing, Mashaya says, and taking back the sliver of glass she covers the cut with her mouth.

SITTI SAYS we are going to America. It's early morning and we're sitting in the kitchen where it's still dark. Yesterday the lights flickered out and for the first time did not come back on. When the telephone is working, Sitti is busy calling, making her plans. We have to get to Cyprus and we need gold. While she's talking, Sitti drinks her arak with vodka because there's no water and there's no bread either. She won't let us go to the bank building downtown and take water from its oriental fishpond, as certain neighbors have done. But she hands us dried figs to suck on while she cradles the phone to her ear. I chew and chew to make the most juice I can, but the taste is still bitter smoke from the garbage fires and dust from the April *khamsin.*

All week clouds of yellow dust have blown across the city, settling onto the still bodies left in the street and seeping past the newspapers taped over our broken windows. The dust keeps Mashaya moving from room to room, shaking herself and kicking at the choking air. She stops when we hear roosters crowing outside; she says we could be in the mountains if we shut our eyes, listen to those roosters and the quiet of no cars moving in the street. By the living room window we shut our eyes and hear Sitti yelling from the kitchen.

It's too early but already there is the crack and whoomph and boom of the fighting from the city center. We hear gunmen scuttling over the walls and into the empty streets. They wear thick ski masks and run with their guns pointing to the sky. Sitti slams down the phone and shouts for us to get into the cellar. She stays on the top step because she's never able to make the climb back up from below. With both hands she helps herself sit down near the wall. Missiles fizz through the air. Sitti's voice is tired and hoarse.

I think we have a boat for this weekend, she says. Girls, can you hear me? That's two days. You can stand anything for two days.

YOUR BOAT is Anthony Quinn's yacht, Papa says, stepping into the kitchen as Sita slams the living room door and stays behind it. You'll go out with *le tout Beirut.* Tell them, Faisz, tell them what a boat that is.

Faisz says that is quite a boat. It's going to have a swimming pool and possibly two. The boat leaves from Jounieh, and in Jounieh all the shops are open and the streets are clean. People dance by candlelight in the Four Seasons Hotel.

I ought to be recuperating in Jounieh, Faisz says, holding up his bandaged hand. He and Papa have dark bristle all over their faces and they smell like the smoke of hashish. It's quiet again, still as mornings used to be. Papa comes back only in the quiet. He's brought bottled water and bread from Damascus. The wooden part of his rifle gleams around the sticker of St. Theresa holding a cross.

When you come back from America, Papa says, Jounieh is where we'll live. He hands each of us a gold coin with a reindeer on one side and tells us to hide it from Sitti.

This is to help you come home, in case I can't get there myself you'll have money to get your own tickets.

Pierre, Faisz says, what are you doing that for? They could get stopped and searched on the way to the boat, someone might think they have more somewhere else.

Mashaya starts crying into Papa's shoulder. His uniform is rough but she stays there with her head down and tugs at the buttons. Papa says we won't get stopped, it's taken care of. Faisz reaches for me.

Do you know why you have to go away, *habibti*? he asks, gathering me carefully into his arms. It's because of war, you have to understand war. Everyone looks dangerous now, even children. We were on sentry duty this morning, your father and I, and we saw an old man in slippers alone in the street. Your father looked through his binoculars and said he *seemed* empty-handed, but your father had to shoot him anyway. Now, do you know why he did that?

Mashaya burrows into Papa's uniform. She says nothing and I don't want to.

Tell them, Pierre, Faisz says.

Papa is trying to smooth the thick tangles in Mashaya's long hair. His wiggling fingers try to work their way through the clumps, but can't.

I know where the man lived, Papa says. He wasn't going to make it anyway.

Be serious, Faisz says, stroking my arm with his bandaged hand.

Papa says, I am.

PAPA SAYS we were needed for a maneuver.

He came into the basement with his flashlight and put his face next to ours. He still smelled of hashish and his reddened eyes were large. Mashaya jammed the lid onto her shoebox but our father was not looking there.

Hurry, he said, everyone has to help. Even old women like your sitti are helping but Sitti's asleep, she's had too much *arak* today.

At the top of the stairs we looked in on her, asleep on Mashaya's bed.

She's out for the night, Papa said.

We stumbled in the dark to the front door and Papa lit a cigarette with one precious match. In the flare I saw Mashaya with her hands in fists staring ahead at the door. There were two soft taps. Papa stooped to kiss us.

This lady is Mr. Helou's aunt, he said. You do what she says and you'll be back before curfew. Ajunya, stop smiling, there's nothing funny about this.

I did feel my mouth stretched wide but I wasn't smiling. I tried to believe my body was nothing, that I could get through the streets like air breathed out of a chest. My chest felt so tight it seemed only the thinnest breath could escape.

Papa opened the door and gave us to the old woman standing there. She had thick hands like Sitti's and dressed like her in a black dress and a rag around her head. She carried a small shovel and told us to say nothing until we got where we needed to be. Papa touched her shoulder and said he had to meet Faisz. He picked up his gun and disappeared into the dark.

The old woman led us down two dark streets where nothing moved. A match flared in an alleyway but no hand seemed to hold it. We stopped at a building site near the corner. Mashaya let go of my hand. More women with children came out of the side streets and alleys; everyone holding shovels, trowels, dustpans.

Do this, the woman told us, pulling a sandbag from the pile of them and holding it out in front of her. We each took a side of the bag while she shoveled dirt from the site into it. I heard her breathing hard and praying in French under her breath. My hands shook and I dropped the bag twice but Mr. Helou's aunt muttered I know, I know, and picked my side up for me. Mashaya's hands were still as she stared at the thickening bag. When it was filled we laid it aside and filled another, then another, until our arms were aching and our breaths were loud in our ears. Two boys pushing a wheelbarrow helped us toss our bags in with others.

Now run, the woman told us. It's one street down and one street over.

People we couldn't see were scurrying into the alleys and buildings. Mashaya and I ran, holding each other's slippery hand and stumbling over the rubble. Behind us we heard the crack of a rifle but we were standing up so we ran on. I thought of invisible things, of a breath that breathes on and a look without eyes. Then my chest was so tight I could think of nothing and held tighter to Mashaya's hand.

We got one street over and our house was easy to find. Sitti had put a forbidden candle in the window, and was waiting.

Who told you to go outside?

She pinched me, pulled me through the doorway and yanked Mashaya in by her hair.

Who? Your father?

She cursed and slapped Mashaya, who started to laugh and fell down on her knees, laughing harder. Sitti slapped her again and cursed our father, the Lebanon, and Jesus Christ. An explosion too near the back of the house stopped her.

Y'allah, y'allah, get downstairs.

She blew out the candle and groped for our hands. Mashaya was still laughing.

SITTI IS SO CONFUSED this early morning. While the taxi waits she rushes around the kitchen and bedrooms, swiping at dust with a rag and fluffing up the pillows. She curses the squatters who took over Mr. Helou's house, then says it can't be helped. But they let their goats wander along the balconies; they cook their meals on the floor. Enough, enough, it doesn't matter. Get your sister, it's time to go.

After five minutes she finds us in our bedroom, where Mashaya is stuffing strips of paper into the sides of her suitcase. Her blue sweater is grimy and stained and it smells like smoke from the fire she set this morning. She won't brush her hair and she won't take off that sweater.

What, child, is this?

Sitti picks among the folded clothes in the suitcase, finding dirt and broken glass and pieces of twisted metal. She takes Mashaya's face in her hands and looks a long time into her eyes.

Mesquina, poor thing, she says, but Mashaya pulls away. She runs past me and I brush at the ashes that settled onto her hair.

Don't touch me, she says. I'm burning.

Ohio

Saturdays Philamena works in the store and Hikmet takes my sister to the counselor. I make tea for Mashaya and pour in lots of milk. She stirs it, the spoon goes round and round.

This time, if the counselor says Mashaya must give up her box, she won't go back again. If the counselor says that all refugees feel that way at first, attached to some physical thing, she'll tell him we're not refugees, not like the Palestinians, we know we are going back.

Hikmet from the porch yells *y'allah, y'allah*. Mashaya shrugs and brushes past. She leaves her rosewater smell.

Alone in the kitchen I push back the curtains and put three plates in the sink. By the window I say my prayer. *Beirut*. God, let it be like this:

The first time Papa comes back from maneuvers, I say, Don't come in. I say, Father, if you come in, the kitchen chair where you sat with your maps won't sit still for you anymore. If you come back, the table will collapse, the edge where you rest your hand will bend and the legs fold under. Don't try to come in. The door won't let you, the knob that you twist won't turn in to us, won't give us away. God, let Sitti be in her place at the sink and Mashaya will be at the window. Let everything here be what belongs, water in jars and bread flat and white on the table. God, God, let here be where Sitti does not die, where Mashaya stands wiping our plates in the light of the open window.

Why We Are in the DAR

MAMA MADE TABBOULEH, and that took courage. The ladies of the DAR did not know those tastes mixed up together, the crunchy bulgur wheat and the lemony mint dressing. By now Mama can make it just as our Lebanese grandmother taught her to: she so finely chops every bit of parsley and scallions and tomatoes so the red tomato mingles with confettied green and white onions and presto, you've got a Christmas dish, Mama says. But she will not mound the tabbouleh in the center of a plate and surround it with torn bread and lettuce leaves for scooping, because to some that would be exotic and primitive and not at all sanitary. To be considerate we've put out white and green mints in a bowl by the tabbouleh, because the DAR ladies are not likely to munch on parsley leaves as our grandmother did, to sweeten their onion breath.

A tureen luncheon means we must also cook up those little Swedish meatballs that the ladies love, and the yellow "perfection" salad all Jelloed up with shredded carrots and cabbage and crushed pineapple wiggling within. The ladies will bring covered dishes and a setup of their own, so as not to make too much trouble for the hostess, who is my mother today for the first time and she says God willing the last.

The Christmas decorations are up no thanks to Uncle Bashir, who promised to help now that Papa is away but he's too mad at Aunt Melania to think straight. He has gone and visited the funeral director uptown and warned him for the umpteenth time that when he, Bashir al-Hadiri, is laid out in the Dulkoski Funeral Home, his only sister is not to be allowed in, no matter how pitifully she begs; she *must* be deprived of the final comfort of viewing his mortal remains. And that is her punishment for saying that his oldest son, my cousin Assad, should not wear white suits summer and winter, he looks like a blackberry in a glass of milk.

My sister Louise is good at winding ropes of pine along the banister and she makes fancy red bows out of ribbons saved from Christmases before we were even born. There's so much to do Mama has us staying home from school with headaches. But we are not worried on that account. Mrs. Roth, my fifth-grade teacher, says our mother writes the best excuse notes—she said you could excuse or forgive the Hadiri girls absolutely anything, given their mother's perfect penmanship and expressive paragraphs about even the common cold.

Well, for God's *sake*, my mother exclaims, setting out the water pitcher on the desk where the Regent will preside, we have no *flag*. The ladies of the DAR salute the flag first thing in their meeting which is after lunch and usually Mrs. Winston brings the tabletop flag no bigger than my Barbie doll but she will not be here due to diverticulitis. Call Virginia Reberson, Mama instructs Louise, who is bowing everything that can be bowed, she has circled the punch bowl with ropes of pine and draped the chairs and mirrors and doorways and though Mama says it is a bit much I believe it could be in a magazine.

"Look at that snow," Louise points out the window, one last rope of pine hanging across her arms. "This may be the last time we ever see snow," she says cheerfully, and I know she is already planning her complete, year-round Florida wardrobe with pale yellows and pinks to set off her suntanned skin. Mama says she herself is going to live in Bermuda shorts, but if I want to hide my scabby knees and still stay cool, well, I can always settle for pedal pushers.

I am dragging folding chairs up from the basement which is really my father's job but he is in Florida sending us postcards about the job interviews that he has to go on since Mr. Carlsbad the school board president said he should not be rehired as a teacher because he is a direct line to the Pope. Mama says that's a fine way to treat a decorated war veteran of the First Infantry Division, the Big Red One: No mission too difficult, no sacrifice too great. Well. Mama says Mr. Carlsbad can kiss our suntanned behinds; soon we'll be in Florida where the weather is simply too sunny and pleasant for folks to make a fuss about keeping Catholics out of the public school system.

Mrs. Celestia Carlsbad herself is coming after all, how can she have the nerve, Mama says. Last year she was Regent and opened meetings with a gavel that her father, Judge Waldron, used to scare the bejesus out of immigrants like my grandmother, who sold a little Jake's Leg to feed her nine children during the Prohibition. Sent her to jail for a year, which is not so big a shame as you might think. Well God knows people were lucky to have someone like your grandmother to go to, Mama told us. People came to her because the whiskey was good and if it wasn't the best at least people knew they wouldn't die from it. There were boys went blind from bad whiskey, and what did the Women's Christian Temperance Union and Judge Carlsbad care about *them*?

This is just the place and time to tell that my mother's mama was president of the WCTU, but only for one year.

Still, it hurts my heart to think of my grandmother, we called her *Sitti*, the Arabic word for grandmother, to think of her way down in Alderson, West Virginia, at the federal prison and my nine uncles and aunt, then children like myself, sent off to the county home with only beautiful red-haired Aunt Melania taken in by relatives. Even today I do not like it when someone tells me not to make a federal case out of something because federal anything is a serious matter and will have consequences far beyond the county jail.

Virginia Reberson said she will bring her flag, Louise reports, and I see Louise has changed into her black straight skirt and blue mohair sweater, which so perfectly matches her blue eyes and sets off her perfectly flipped light brown but she says dark blonde hair, that I feel wounded even looking in her direction. Mama tells me fifth grade was an awkward year for her, too, but I am date-colored like my father, with coal black hair and brown eyes, so I will never have eyes matching a color that I love. Look at Natalie Wood, Mama will always say, but brown eyes are not the first thing I think of when I see Natalie Wood, and her hair, by the way, flips perfectly in *West Side Story*, which Louise and I have seen eleven times in theaters from here to Columbus.

Waiting in my bedroom closet for me to change into is a red corduroy jumper with a white-yam poodle on it. Can you imagine Natalie Wood in that?

Maria of *West Side Story* would surely not have been able to get into the DAR, Daughters of the American Revolution, its chapters standing in the same relation to the Mother Society as the Posts of the Grand Army of the Republic stand to the head of the army. It says this in the booklet Mama has sent for, and she has followed directions to track down what is needed for her to join, based on PEDIGREE and PATRIOTISM, the DAR. She has proved lineal descent from a Patriot of 1776. Today in the membership she will write the name of the far-back relative who is getting us into the DAR, Mr. Gideon Baruch Eli Wolcott, born 1756, died 1801. She will also write her name, Mrs. Eugenia Lee Wolcott Hadiri, but it is that Hadiri that is the main thing, the name that my mother wants to see inscribed in the membership book of the DAR.

"Honey, go change into your jumper now, and do something with your hair, it looks like you combed it with a fork." Mama is rushing by in her housecoat with her makeup on, already beautiful but only half dressed. It's eleven-thirty and at twelve o'clock sharp the ladies will arrive, snow-haired Mrs. Letitia B. Waldron and vicious Mrs. Celestia Carlsbad, Lily Irene Jackson who is not so bad in the talking-to department, she has a granddaughter that babysits us and never once inquires as to what religion we are being raised in, mixed up the way we are. Mrs. Augustus Adams Guild will need a footrest, and when I bring it to her I must refuse the quarter she will offer me and agree that a Catholic in the White House demands vigilance from us all.

Daddy is a Catholic and some people are vigilant about him. The school board will not hire him again, due to his being a direct line to the Pope. Plenty of Presbyterians and Methodists can coach so why bother with someone who takes orders from Rome. Is what the school board says, we hear. Louise and I do not take orders from Rome, because our parents are going to let us decide what religion we want to be when we come of age, which is sometime far in the future, possibly 1969. Still, it is worrisome in summer to watch your friends coming home from Vacation Bible School with coloring books and mimeographed sheets of songs that will help them get into heaven when you yourself have been reading Nancy Drew and listening to *Oklahoma!* on the reel-to-reel.

I wish to God, Mama says, whenever we point this out to her, there were Unitarians somewhere close by.

Oh why now does the phone have to ring, says Mama with a run in her stocking and the nail polish bottle in one hand and that tiny black brush in the other that she's dabbing on the run behind her leg. "Get it, Phoebe, will you?" and I do and it's Dad and I shout out about the tabbouleh and the ladies but he says I'm beat let me talk to your mother.

Mama unclips one pearl drop earring and leans against the kitchen wall, cradling the phone in her ear. "How's it going, honey?" She is silent for some moments. "Oh, Yusef, no. Stop right there. Don't even consider it." Mama puts one hand over the phone and tells me to run up and get her dress off the bed. But I'm not so fast going up the stairs and I hear her repeat, "Yusef, we agreed. You cannot work for your brother. It's out of the question. *Out of the question.*"

Louise is half way down the stairs with Mama's sheath across her arms. She puts a finger to her lips and sits down on the stairs. I say not a thing and join her too. My mother is saying, we both hear her clear as day, "Yusef, Yusef, listen to me. You're a *teacher*, we're moving so you can *teach*. You don't have to be a gofer for Sheik Bashir. Well, I'm sorry, but you know how he treats you. He'll always put his own son ahead of you. What do you know about the real estate business? Don't. Don't do this."

Louise looks at me, rolls her eyes and shrugs, but I know she cares, her mouth is in a frown. Maybe she's thinking that her dark blonde but really light brown hair will not be lightening in the Florida sun. This year, anyway. Not me. I'm thinking I just don't want to hear Uncle Bashir asking me another first communion question, or see the Redman sisters down the lane standing at our front door, asking could they look at the A-rab that lives in this house. Everybody must be so tan in Florida they won't know the difference, tan or Arab.

Mama hangs up the phone with no good-bye that we can hear, and a few seconds later there she is, at the foot of the stairs, mascara in streaks down both her cheeks. She takes her dress from Louise and sinks down on the bottom step with her head against the banister.

"So, girls," she says, "so girls." Her eyes are closed and she is rubbing her forehead, rubbing and rubbing it in circles with the palm of her hand. "Well, now we know, don't we? If we ever doubted. Blood is always thicker than water." Louise nods knowingly, but I don't see the point. Mama could just call Uncle Bashir and tell him to mind his own damn business. He can't get any madder at her because he's already said that when he's dead he doesn't want her coming to the funeral home or the funeral, since she flat out refuses to convert. I start to remind her of this but we hear the crunch of gravel down the lane and see Mrs. Waldron's big black Buick pull up with a carload of the ladies, every one of them wearing a wide-brimmed hat.

"You two go help them with their things," Mama says, climbing up the steps to her room. "Tell them I've got the tiniest little headache and I'll be down in a minute." Her bedroom door shuts softly and here we are. I am still not changed and my hair's not combed but Mama didn't seem to care so I don't either. "Come on," Louise says, sighing in the same way Mama does. She stands up and brushes off her skirt. "I'll write our name in the membership book, if she won't come down." I nod. And if Mrs. Augustus Adams Guild gives me a quarter for her footrest, I'm going to take it and never say a word.

Turning Lebanese: A Family Story

IN THE SUMMER OF 1977, I visited a tiny village on Mount Lebanon fragrant with the scent of mint and roses, and wondered why my grandmother had never wanted to come back, not even for a visit. Seventeen years earlier, her children had offered to buy her a plane ticket, and when she firmly declined it the matter was dropped. Yet every spring she asked to be driven to a wide field a few miles from her home in Adena, Ohio, where a slender stream sprang out of the hillside. There she picked mint and held up the sprigs for her children to smell. "*Mit al-Lubnan*" ("like Lebanon"), she said. She wondered at the sheep in America, with their truncated tails, and told her children about the sheep with large, fluffy tails that grazed on the slopes of Mount Lebanon. My father found her a picture of one in an encyclopedia entry under "Syria." She was content to look at that.

When thousands of Syrian-Lebanese arrived in this country at the turn of the century, as she had, and were referred to as "Turks" because their passports bore the stamp of the Ottoman Empire, the irony was lost on their new countrymen. My grandmother believed that if a Turk walked into her kitchen the food would spoil. She said that when the Ottoman tax collectors came to her village the blood ran in the streets. Her happiest memories seemed to be of cooking for the cardinal, whose ample larder filled her with awe. Though Lebanon was proclaimed an independent republic by the time her family could afford a plane ticket in 1960, she seemed to doubt a fundamental change in the country she remembered. "In Lebanon," she told us, circling her stomach with her hands, "only the bishops are fat."

There were so many versions of Lebanon told by the relatives who visited my grandmother's house. I heard that Lebanon was not Arab at all but Phoenician, that Lebanon was only a mountain, but the most beautiful mountain on earth. I heard that the reason the family came first to the West Virginia side of the Ohio River was that the people of Mount Lebanon always look to settle with water in front and hills behind—escape and sanctuary, necessary to the *ahl-al-jebal* (people of the mountain), which they had remained since the seventh century when their ancestors fled the Orontes River Valley and persecution by other Christian and Islamic tribes. But by 1960, my grandmother had long ago left both hills and water. When the 1908 flood in Wheeling, West Virginia, took two of her children's lives, she moved with her husband across the river and inland to Adena. When her son chose to marry a Protestant, she told her new daughter-in-law: "*Ma'alesh.* It doesn't matter. There is only one God, the same God, for everyone."

I arrived in Lebanon with little knowledge of the country save what my grandmother had told me. I recognized the smells and tastes of the country because of her kitchen; I recognized the rooms in the houses filled with long couches and settees from her living room, arranged to be welcoming to guests. What I did not recognize was the appropriate answer to the question from my hosts, shopkeepers, and friendly students at the American University of Beirut: *What are you?* I'm an American, half Lebanese.

But what are you? Your religion? Your rite? Your village? Your family? Without answers, I was a stranger there.

There was everything and nothing of what I expected in Lebanon. After a civil war with roots in seventh-century fears and twentieth-century politics, few Lebanese felt safe looking beyond the tangle of clans and religions for the answer to *what are you?* "I am against my brother," says a village proverb, "my brother and I are against my cousin; my cousin, my brother, and I are against the stranger."

Years ago, when my grandmother was offered her ticket to Lebanon, I had begged her to go and take me with her. It was so hard not to persist: She danced the *dabke* at weddings; she blessed our leave-takings in Arabic. Why would a Lebanese not want to go back for a visit? Her answer was to take me on the front porch with my school notebook and pencil. We sat on the long divan and she wrote down the numbers one to ten, saying each out loud, holding up the right number of fingers. We went on with the lessons she hoped would help her, at the age of seventy-two, to count and make change in English. She was the stranger, too.

In Her Own Hand

USUALLY WHEN SHE ASKED, she was sitting in the yellow recliner in front of the television set. Maybe we'd just watched *Queen For a Day*, her favorite, and finished cracking all the pistachio nuts on the TV tray between us. My Aunt Phoebe would still be in Bedway's Market next door, and Aunt Lillie, cooking supper in the kitchen. We *had* to be alone, or she would never ask. Soon my father would be coming from his office on Main Street to take me home to Cadiz, his heavy footsteps tramping onto the enclosed front porch with windows facing Hanna Avenue. Then my grandmother, whom we always called *Sitti*, the Arabic word for grandmother, pointed to the paper and pencil on a nearby desk and said what sounded like "Gibbet me." It was time for her English lesson. She was seventy-two years old.

My two older sisters used to give the lesson, and I felt a solemn awe, at the age of eight, that Sitti would ask me, too. I brought her the paper and pencil, and we slid the bowl of pistachio shells to a side of the tray. I printed my name first, in gigantic, tilting capitals that took up half a page. It was her turn then. Long minutes went by as she put down the four letters of *Mary*, her name in English. I tried again, smaller capitals, straighter sides; she reprinted hers exactly as before, but bearing down harder on the pencil lead. The late afternoon sunlight had faded by the time we were satisfied, but we turned on no lamps. The black-and-white television set continued to flicker, and its voices covered our silence. When we heard my father's footsteps on the porch, we stopped. It seemed our names on paper were her secret, and she folded them away into the pocket of her dress.

The brick-paved road that signaled to sleepy children we'd reached Adena from Fox's Bottom still rumbles beneath passing cars, but there are no longer Bedways in the green-shingled house on Hanna Avenue. Once there were eleven, and the nine children grew up to be my seven aunts, my uncle Toni, my father, John. When I was five, I played a jump-rope game to name all Sitti's daughters, a skip each for Angelina, Phoebe, Genevieve, Lillie, Elizabeth, Adelaide, Geraldine. I never knew my grandfather, who arrived from Lebanon at the turn of the century and peddled bolts of cloth and housewares up the red-dog paths to the Ohio Valley mining camps. The floods of 1907 convinced him to move his family inland from the Ohio River's shores, and he opened a grocery in Adena. For a while certain confused citizens of the town thought the dark-eyed, dark-haired family in the big, black car were gypsies traveling light.

We were a bit mysterious, I thought, even at the age of five. A stay with Sitti meant *labneh* and olives for breakfast, and *marcouq*, the flat Arab bread we called "shovel bread" and rolled up to dip into hummus or salads or ate in the dull American way, with butter. A stay at Sitti's meant the words of a foreign language were always spoken to you or over your head-strong consonants, catches in the throat, words that settled on us, like the gentle *habibti*, a sound that meant we were loved. Sometimes Aunt Phoebe called a salesman or a complaining customer *majnoon*, and we made our own translation. On hot summer nights we heard teenage boys drive mufflerless cars through the single traffic light. My aunts shook their heads while Sitti smiled. *Kul deek ala mazbaltu saiyah*, she said—something like "Every rooster on his dunghill crows."

If late at night you couldn't sleep, you'd find your way to the kitchen. And if you finished the stuffed grape leaves, or diminished the *labneh* by half, there was nothing to fear in the morning. My aunts and Sitti were grateful a child had a good appetite. *Alakel ad al mahabba*, the Lebanese say: "The food is according to the love."

Years later I studied the language Sitti brought to Ohio from Mount Lebanon, and learned that that familiar word for crazy, *majnoon*, also meant "touched by God." But much of her vocabulary remains mysterious, and especially certain words I never actually heard but whose power I still remember.

When we left Sitti's house for the drive home after Sunday visits, our last glimpse was of her in the doorway in her dark-blue dress, hair in a bun, her right hand making the sign of the cross as she blessed us in her language. What was she saying? What were those words? In our pockets there were no papers with names in *her* language. She prayed as she watched us children waving from the back seat, facing her until we turned off Hanna Avenue, afraid even into adulthood to miss the sight of her pronouncing the words that got us safely home.

JOSEPH GEHA

Where I'm From—Originally

"YOU'RE NOT FROM AROUND HERE, ARE YOU."

The man had put it like a statement, but I recognize the question that was being implied. By that time, having lived "around here" for over a dozen years, I also knew that if I didn't answer as expected, I'd be leaving the door open for the outright questions that were certain to follow: "*Where are you from?*" and "*No, but I mean, where originally?*" Asked openly, I ought to add, in a friendly spirit. Even so, I still wasn't used to it. I tried a smile.

"That's right," I said, and volunteered nothing more. I was just asking for trouble, of course.

"So, where are you from?"

I turned and faced the man fully now. "Toledo," I told him. Which I knew perfectly well wasn't at all what he was asking. He looked to be a nice sort, a youngish grandfather. Why was I being so contrary? All he was doing was making small talk. It was a sunny autumn day and here we'd found ourselves two adults among children—my daughters, his grandkids—in line at a county fair carrousel in Iowa. The white crispness of the short-sleeved shirt he had on, along with his hairless arms and clean, pink-tipped fingers, made me think he was maybe a dentist. That, and his no nonsense persistent manner.

"Originally?" he said, as if to specify.

I answered "Ohio. Toledo, *Ohio*," pretending to specify, too, since there was a Toledo, Iowa, not far from here. I was behaving badly. Was it my fear of dentists? My frayed nerves from being with the kids all day? It was not as if this man's curiosity wasn't understandable. After all, I didn't look like I was from around here; "here" being a part of the country that was more familiar with a blonde Scandinavian/Irish/German mix than with the olive skin and black curly hair common to people from Lebanon.

Nor could he know that I heard the question a lot "around here," the last time only a few days before. I'd taken my daughters swimming, and a little blonde girl they'd made friends with at the pool kept glancing at me out of the corner of her eye. I was in a bathing suit, and I'm fairly certain it was the body hair. "Your dad's not from around here, is he," she stated just as I dove under water. Surfacing, I heard, "No, I mean *originally.*"

In '71, before the war in Lebanon, I visited Zahleh, the town where I'm from—originally. Although I'd bought my clothes locally, I was easily recognized (from my manner? my gait?) for an Americanized Lebanese. Even so, I still felt I fit in. The people looked as if they all could be members of my family. I could see where my sister got her classic dark beauty. The men looked like my brother, my father, me. I saw hair that grew in the same curly whorled patterns as my own. I remember one small boy in particular, dashing past me and glancing behind in a familiar lopsided, just-got-in-trouble grin that instantly brought to mind my own face as a child shortly after we came to America, me grinning and saluting for the camera on the pavement in front of my father's newly opened grocery on Monroe Street in Toledo.

I felt the same grin forming on my face as "the dentist," having helped his smallest grandchild onto a pastel pony, stepped down off the carrousel to join me once more.

"No," he said, taking right up where he'd left off, "no, I mean *originally.*" He squinted a pale eye at me as if to underscore his persistence.

"Ah, you mean *originally*. The country of my *origin*, you mean!" I was taking it too far, and I considered relenting. Back in the sixties I used to save bus money by hitchhiking to my classes at Toledo University. I didn't find it strange that on the basis of my looks the driver might begin talking to me in a foreign language (Greek, Yiddish,

Italian, and Spanish—eventually I learned to identify them all). In Toledo, with its ethnic mix, this experience wasn't unusual. My parents used to do it, calling out *Ibn Arab intah*? to any olive-complected fellow on the corner or in the car next to us at a stoplight, while my brother and sister and I slid groaning to the backseat floor, out of sight of the stranger's puzzled shrug.

Now the dentist waited, and I could feel my grin widen as his eye unsquinted for my answer.

Which I delivered straight, deadpan: "Norway."

He didn't call me a liar. Instead, he simply nodded his head. This was Iowa—"heaven" in the movies—and not only are the people nice, they have a hard time believing anyone else is not nice.

But, being an Iowan myself after all these years, I couldn't leave him like this. Besides, Iowa's a small world; what if I needed dental work some day? (I pictured myself in the chair, helpless, and him in his business whites, pliers in hand: "Norway? I'll give you Norway!") So I took it all back, beginning with, "Not really."

What I didn't tell him was that most of my life, child and adult, had been an attempted escape from my Arab roots, and that these innocent questions—from dentists, from my daughters' playmates—were reminders that I hadn't yet blended into the Great American Melting Pot.

MY FAMILY LEFT LEBANON and came to America at the end of World War II, when I was still a toddler; we traveled by ship and underwent quarantine and processing at Ellis Island. It wasn't until I started first grade that I began to speak English. So I remember feeling different at an early age, and not liking the feeling; I was teased for my accent, for the garlicky smelling food in my lunch box. I remember schoolmates calling me "Dirty Syrian," chasing me, and yelling at me to go back where I came from. (They didn't know any better; being kids, they were slow to extend to humans the empathy they lavished on puppies and goldfish.) When they eventually did know better, many of them would become the first friends I ever made. I remember, too, how American women made a fuss over my thick curls, pausing in department store aisles to pat them fondly with their white-gloved palms. Of course, I was fully aware of how cute those curls were. But I also remember wanting those curls to be blonde. Because Americans, real through-and-through Americans, were blonde. They had blue eyes. And nobody would ever think to tell a blonde-haired, blue-eyed American to go back where he came from.

During the first couple of years of school, my accent faded, and I remember helping it along, mouthing Peter Piper and his peck of pickled peppers over and over on the long walk home. (More than a tongue twister for Arabic speakers, given that the language has no *p* sound.) Perversely, this accomplishment seemed only to make me all that much more aware of my parents' heavy accents. Fixing a self-conscious gaze on my mother and father, I was ashamed at the way they haltingly massacred English in front of Americans (who, from my view, were an impatient, finger-drumming lot), but I'd be absolutely *mortified* whenever they backslid into Arabic. They couldn't open their mouths around me, neither in Arabic nor in English. Either way, they couldn't win, those two.

After school, I wanted to eat only American food. I insisted that my mother make hamburger for dinner; and she—being a good sport—not only gave it a try, she figured to do hamburger one better. And so, what I ended up getting was more like lamb-burger, with garlic and parsley and vinegary onions ground into it. Couldn't she see that I didn't want better than hamburger? What I wanted was not to be different.

My newfound friends weren't much consolation; they never seemed to notice differences so much, or if they did, they invariably took my mother's side. For reasons that are obvious enough to me now but which I couldn't at the time fathom, my mother's cooking was famous among my friends. They loved being asked to stay for supper, even though this invitation meant being served something as strange as lemon chicken stuffed with pine nuts and pilaf and ground cinnamon lamb; sweet greens cooked down in olive oil and garlic, then mashed and rolled into well-salted, paper-thin bread; almond butter cookies or baklava for dessert.

I HAD BEGUN WRITING FICTION while working nights in the stockroom at Sears Roebuck and attending the University of Toledo on partial scholarship.

Luckily, the first teacher I showed any of it to—Gregory Ziegelmaier, a young playwright who was new to the English faculty—proved to be both kind and generous in his encouragement. From my first course with him, he urged me to begin taking my writing seriously. Sometimes I used to drop by his office just to chat—about writing, usually, or the advantages of one program of study over another. And because he seemed interested, I soon found myself telling him about my family, about my parents having had less than three years' schooling between them; about my father's being so superstitious he kept a piece of what he called the True Cross wrapped in a bandage under his armpit, claiming that if he lost it he would lose all his luck; about my mother's uttering startled blessings whenever I chuckled over something funny in a book—she never understood how, outside of demonic possession, anyone staring at an inanimate object, a book, could suddenly be moved to laugh out loud. Another time I told him the story of how my father had tricked the steamship officials when my sister came down with typhoid the day before we were scheduled to sail from Beirut, rouging her fever-yellow face and tickling her to alertness as we ascended the gangplank; and about how my whole family got stuck on an escalator in our first days here—the stairs in America just wouldn't stay still! And the childless Jewish couple who "adopted" our family; the trip to the art museum (where, we were told, they have pictures on the walls and music) that ended with all of us listening to piped music on the lawn of a gas station that was celebrating a grand opening, its plate glass windows painted with cartoon characters.

My teacher enjoyed these stories, and I had to admit that I liked telling them. So why, he wanted to know, wasn't he seeing any of this in my writing? Taking my writing seriously meant, of course, taking my experience seriously, too, including my immigrant heritage. But what he didn't understand was that to include such material would be to identify myself with exactly what I'd been avoiding all my life.

So, while my writing skill improved under his guidance, even my better stories remained imitations in the mode of whatever writer I currently admired.

MY FIRST TEACHING JOB was over seven hundred miles away from home, at a college in Springfield, Missouri. The people there were friendly, welcoming—in fact, they were downright sunny. Strangers trimming hedges chirruped hellos as I bicycled past their tidy yards. The mailboxes all bore standard American names like Anderson, Stone, Douglas, Brady; if I looked hard enough I'd probably find Cleaver, too. Word had it that the wife of Gene Autry—the cowboy hero of my childhood—had once attended school here. The campus itself, like the town, was a sea of freckled good looks. Who'd have thought that this country had such a concentration of blonde-haired adults? (I hadn't yet been to Iowa.)

I'd located the real America, as only television of the fifties could have imagined it, and I was determined to belong.

So why, after a few weeks, did I find myself giving in to the urge to grow back the beard that I'd shaved off months before my job interview? Sure, beards were common enough then, then being 1968 and the dawning of the Age of Aquarius. But this was also the Deep Midwest, where college men still wore crew cuts and flattops. What was I up to, growing a black curly beard? Well, this much was clear: if blending in was my aim, I seemed to be having second thoughts.

In fact, I was having a whole chain reaction of second thoughts, all triggered by the most minor incidents. For example, one day in my first month there I remember standing at a supermarket counter and waiting while the checkout clerk searched for an item on her produce price list. Finally, she indicated the item, a bulb of garlic, and asked me in her soft Missouri twang, "Whatcha call this?"

"You mean garlic?" I asked.

She nodded and thanked me. A small thing, memorable only because at a different grocery less than a week before another clerk had asked me the same question about a bunch of parsley. "This is parsley—right?" she'd said.

I was amazed. How could somebody not know parsley? Swiss chard I could understand. Endive. Even watercress. But ordinary parsley? And garlic! What sort of pot was I melting into here? Instead of being eager to blend right in, I found myself holding back, realizing that I did not want to be different, after all—but on *my* terms.

Meanwhile, during session after session at my writing table, my mind kept straying to images of Monroe Street in morning sunlight, and my brother a small boy on its pavement sweeping wine bottles from the entrance to our father's store; hearing the mutter and coo of pigeons and looking up at the flat tarred roofs for the arrival of the homeless man we called the Pigeon-man who used a fishing rod to snag pigeons and sell them to my father for food. I saw the apartment above the store, and myself, dark-eyed and olive-skinned, looking like exactly what I was, an Arab boy in a Gene Autry cowboy hat, peeking from behind the blue velvet armchair at the window, watching my mother serve Turkish coffee to the aunt who wore two pairs of glasses on her nose at once, and the uncle who was so simple that even my brother and sister and I used to look at one another and wink.

Now in Missouri, living far from those streets, and as if freed up by the distance, I found available to me the landscapes of my past—people, situations, places—all that I'd rejected while breathing the actual air of those landscapes.

FICTION, as I tell my students, presents us with the opportunity to walk in someone else's shoes; and picturing the other guy—in this case the Arab American immigrant—as a complex person with human frailties as well as human virtues defeats the possibility for sentimental simplifying: good or bad, black or white, us or them.

Such a lesson is especially important today, when the politically hot Middle East has been made even hotter, when Arab American businesses are fired upon and torched, and college-educated students in Ames, Iowa, chant "Death to all Arabs!" out their dorm windows.

These feelings are understandable; it's difficult not to get carried away at the sight of classmates and neighbors marching off in desert camouflage. And yet, "All Arabs" includes me, includes my daughters; the words alone do damage.

To say that gunmen and arsonists don't know any better may or may not be stating the obvious. But the chanting students? As understandable as their feelings are, and despite their college educations, I must conclude that they, too, simply don't know any better. Just as I had to conclude years ago when I was mocked for speaking with an accent and thinking my thoughts in another language. Those students, smart as they are, need to get out of their own shoes for a while. Reading stories can help them to do that. Most fiction, if it's any good at all, asks that the reader use at least some measure of empathy—that particularly human faculty whereby one can appreciate what an experience must feel like for someone else. The reluctance to feel empathy can express itself in intolerance for the unfamiliar, in self-preoccupation and narcissism. At the very least it hinders maturation; it's children who stomp on anthills, the emotionally stunted who douse cats in gasoline. Empathy, on the other hand, has a maturing effect and leads us into the world.

SHORTLY AFTER my collection of short stories came out, I was invited to give a reading at a bookstore in St. Paul, Minnesota. I'd never been to the Twin Cities before, and knew no one from there, so imagine my surprise when a total stranger, an older woman from the audience, approached me afterward with a familiar "Hello, Mr. *Jeha*," giving my last name its Arabic pronunciation. What really floored me, though, was her adding, "You're one of Elias's boys, aren't you, the littler one they called Zuzu."

I hadn't heard myself called "Zuzu"—the Arabic diminutive for Yousef—since I was five years old. (Entering first grade, I remember how I'd insisted that even at home I be called Joe, an American nickname.) It was a shock, hearing the first name of my childhood pronounced by a total stranger.

Who, of course, turned out not to be a stranger at all, but a distant cousin who used to visit Toledo regularly years ago, and she remembered my family when we first arrived in America. Her smile, and the sidelong glance that came with it, I recognized from my father's side of the family. So now, in a city where I knew no one, I found it was, ironically, my turn to be asking the question: "Where did you come from?"

"Here."

"No, I mean originally."

"Originally," she replied. "I was born in St. Paul, a mile from this spot. I've lived here all my life."

Here? Here looked blonder than Iowa and Missouri put together! And the odd thing was, the more we chatted, the more it began to make sense; why couldn't she be one of my people as well as from around here—*originally*? Why not, indeed? After all, who said America must be a melting pot into which we drain and disappear? The nineteenth century, that's who. The Great Melting Pot has always been a nineteenth-century notion, and I'd just as soon it stayed there, along with the Know Nothings and Manifest Destiny. I prefer instead an image I've come across more and more in recent years—that of the mosaic. The American Mosaic. Common sense tells us that the American immigrant experience resulted not from melting down the uniqueness in each separate one of us, but from arranging those pieces and joining them together toward the design of a larger, more complex picture, one that makes use of differences to create richness and power and harmony. The achievement of which is the promise of Ellis Island. And in the stories I've written, the struggle for which is what America is all about.

Stepping Out

ON A SATURDAY EVENING, not six months after his wife left him, Nate Yakoub finds that he's run out of panty hose. Again he examines the final remnant that Jeannette had left behind—stretched to cobweb thinness and stiff with dried wax—before replacing it in his shoeshine kit. Well, then. So he has to go back to buying his own, that's all. He'll just have to go back to doing everything the same as he did before he was married, almost ten years ago.

And yet, in the midst of his resolve, he has to sigh. Because it won't be the same. Being single isn't the same as being single after having been married.

He can see that just as he can see himself right now, silly in his undershorts, peering into the mirror on Jeannette's side of the closet where the light is always better. His chest hairs are turning white. Thirty-six years old and getting dressed for a date. Thank you, Jeannette. He can just imagine the upward curl of her lip. She used to tell him that his thinning hair looked distinguished, she pinched his pudgy middle as if it were cute, then on the morning of her thirty-fifth birthday she woke up and realized she'd "grown" out of love. It isn't fair. He never did anything to deserve this. You "fall" in love, and "grow" out of it?

He shouldn't do this. "If you think too much you'll go crazy," his mother would say, one of her Arabic proverbs, *La'at tetfikir kteer, inta . . .*

"Whine, whine, whine," Jeannette would say if she could hear inside his head.

Call it whining, or call it spinning your wheels, which is how Glen Broylan at work likes to put it. The fact remains that after half a year Nate still can't figure it out.

He finishes dressing, then puts on his trench coat and steps out onto the porch to wait. His car is in the shop again, the lemon Jeannette had bought the year they met. Right before the divorce was final, he'd suggested they trade, that she take the new car—a consideration typical of him, frankly—and in the morning it was gone. Not even a thank-you message on his machine.

Six-thirty, almost, it's just starting to get dark. Tonight the clocks will be moved ahead to Daylight Savings Time, so tomorrow it'll be brighter at this hour. Colder too, judging by the clearing twilight. A departing overcast rose-rims half the sky. Picture-perfect. Looking up, Nate imagines dinner, but not with Claire. He sighs. She's a nice enough person, Claire, but no, not with her. Instead, a someone he can't quite envision because he hasn't met her yet. She would offer him something to drink from a stemmed glass, then step out of her high heels, leave them there in the dining room to come lie barefoot beside him in front of the fire.

During those first months after Jeannette left, Nate never considered dating. Alone, expecting her return, he discovered that he kept a tidy house, unusually clean in fact. He installed an extension phone in the basement, one in the kitchen, and another within reach of the shower—he wanted to be able to answer before Jeannette could change her mind and hang up. Now the whole house rings and beeps and chirrups whenever there's a call. Until he gave in and subscribed to cable TV—something Jeannette had wanted him to do for years—he used to sit night after night, alone, in silence, in a meticulously swept and dusted house, paging through the magazines Jeannette left behind, even trying to read some of the paperbacks that she laughingly called trashy, but which had kept her propped in bed for hours. He did what he figured other men like him did, the abandoned and the reluctantly divorced: he waited for her to come to her senses.

But eventually the greeting messages on her answering machine changed, turning girlish and flirty: *Hi, this is Jeannette. I'm sunbathing right now and can't come to the phone,* or *Whatever I'm doing, I'd rather be talking to you!* She sounded happy. She would never come to her senses.

And so, Nate finds himself reduced to a night like this, waiting for a date with a woman he is already imagining out of the picture, in a town where he doesn't have a single relative, a town so deep in the center of the United States, so far from mountains or oceans or big city attractions that his older sister has come out to visit only three times in twelve years, and his younger sister never once. Neither one of them ever divorced.

Jeannette's leaving surprised everybody. Her family loved Nate. When they first heard the news of her leaving they actually called *him* to sympathize! Why? Because Nate Yakoub—he would remind himself, trying to allay his sense of failure—had been more than a good husband. Jeannette herself used to say it: he was a mother-in-law's dream.

"HEY, YOU DIDN'T DRINK, YOU DIDN'T CHEAT." Glen Broylan would tip back in his swivel chair and smile knowingly, as if it were some telepathic marvel to be able to read the thoughts of people in the middle of divorce. Older than Nate by nearly ten years, Broylan is a division manager at Agri-Tech, Inc., in effect Nate's boss, and he wears his graying hair in a buzz cut. "You didn't gamble, you didn't forget anniversaries." He would recite the list with casual indifference. "You didn't hit." For nine years the two of them have shared a windowless office in the management wing of the company's bunker-like administration building, a time that is longer than the last two of Broylan's three marriages put together. Usually Nate would just go on pretending interest in the numbers on his computer screen, privately amazed that three separate women on this planet would actually marry Broylan.

"You didn't tell secrets, you weren't stingy, and, hey, there were no problems in the bedroom. Hoo-boy, I'll bet right at the end there the sex even heated up."

Once in a while, Broylan surprised you. Maybe there was something to this savvy he claimed to have because, as a matter of fact, all during those last months Jeannette hadn't been able to get enough, the more the better. Once they'd even managed a quickie in the kitchen, right on top of the morning *Register.* Okay, then—Nate flipped off his computer and swiveled to face Broylan—then why?

"Why? Wake up, guy. She already 'told' you why."

"You mean you believe it? That 'grew out of love' business?"

"Why not? Hey, it's just one more way of saying 'boyfriend.' Face it, guy, the cage door's open—she opened it—and what you have to do now is step out."

But there wasn't a boyfriend, not in the beginning anyway. Jeannette said so when he asked, and Nate had believed her. No, what had first flashed through his mind as he'd listened to her go on about how she "grew out of love," was the suspicion that it was his fault, that he had somehow not been American enough for her.

The thought surprised him. Transferred here to company headquarters in the middle of the Corn Belt, Nate hasn't heard the familiar old country accents for nearly five years, since his mother's funeral in Toledo. Lately he's felt like mourning her all over again. That day he watched his wife pack, following her around the bedroom like a dummy, he kept thinking of his mother, how much she'd wanted grandchildren.

Jeannette's face in the vanity mirror had looked serious, determined to follow through. She was wearing her beige suit with the vented jacket, tailored for travel. He tried to get her to laugh. "What'll people think," he said. "I mean . . ." He took his shine kit down from the closet shelf to show her what he meant and to invoke the intimacy of something she used to tease him about. " . . . I mean, a guy *alone* asking for panty hose at the drug store?"

"Here then, for the last time—" She whirled to face him. "Just so you'll stop your whining!" She flung something high up and across the bed at him.

Nate ducked, but what struck him on the neck was soft, a pair of wadded-up panty hose. The legs had flowered open and gently draped themselves against his neck and shoulder. He didn't remove them. These kinds of things happen in fights, and sometimes they make you laugh. But when Jeannette didn't see the humor, Nate began to feel embarrassed, standing there like that, waiting. Waiting for what? For her to laugh, sure . . . and, laughing, take hold of the pantyhose to lasso him in.

Instead she simply looked at him, simply, sadly, and then she shook her head. That was the moment—even before she lugged her suitcase past him and down the stairs—that he felt her truly gone. Pulling the pantyhose off his chest, he felt before he heard the front door slam.

AS NATE SLIDES IN ON THE PASSENGER SIDE he is surprised to see that Claire has on a dress. She is chief safety officer in charge of quality control for all the labs in Testing and Development at Agri-Tech. Most days she strides the corridors of the research wing in white coveralls and a hard hat. Not that Nate was expecting her to be in work clothes, of course, but he hadn't imagined her in anything so feminine, either. Patterned in rich paisleys, the dress is ankle-length and billowy, like silk.

"Hoo-boy, I like the dress," he says. "Is it silk?" Hoo-boy? After nine years in an office with Broylan, it's a wonder he doesn't start looking like him, too.

Claire pauses, one hand on the gear shift, and takes him in with a wry smile. "Thanks," she says. "A little silk, probably. But I think it's mostly something like rayon."

"Anyway, it still looks nice," he says.

She seems to like that. She likes *him*, he can tell. Still smiling, she checks over both shoulders before backing out of the driveway.

Although this is their first official date, Claire and Nate aren't strangers—in a small town it's hard for lives not to cross: she used to be in the same women's reading group as Jeannette; and Nate has a nodding acquaintance with Claire's ex-husband, a professor at the college, since they go to the same barber.

A dinner party last month found Claire and Nate the only two unattached guests. A set-up, of course, mutual friends meddling. Like a good sport, Nate played along, acting the part of Claire's escort for the evening. Luckily, she could not only carry the conversational ball, she could run with it. His role amounted to little more than sitting next to her at coffee while she talked about work and about the trials of home ownership—the bungalow she'd just moved into had a smell in the fireplace and a "mouse problem" that she hoped she was finally rid of. But it was food—especially exotically prepared dishes—that Claire could have gone on about all night. "You're Lebanese?" she was delighted to discover. "Well then, you must know all about grape leaves!" She called last week to invite him to a Middle Eastern meal she was preparing to celebrate the fortieth birthday of her friend AJ, the current girlfriend of Glen Broylan. Because Broylan had wanted to show off AJ's house, a large, newly completed place that had been awarded her as part of a divorce settlement, he'd insisted that they bring the meal there. "It's a date, then," Claire had said over the phone, and it took Nate some moments to realize that that was exactly what it was—his first date since the divorce. He was stepping out.

And now here Nate is, listening to Claire's pot lids rattle familiarly on the back seat floor, the car filling up with the aromas of cooking. When Nate was a boy the old Chrysler used to smell like this after visits to his grandmother; all the way home he and his sisters had to perch their feet between dripping grocery bags and hot, loose lidded pans. "Mm," Nate inhales deeply. "Let's see. Garlic. Clove. Olive oil. Cinnamon?"

"Yes . . . yes." Claire nods after each guess. "Very good." Her hair is a darkish, used-to-be blonde, held at the back with a small gray satin bow. AJ, Broylan's girlfriend, keeps her hair much blonder. Too blonde, in fact. She works in the same wing at Agri-Tech, upstairs in Invoice Processing, and it was a glimpse of her strikingly blonde hair that had first caught Nate's attention as he was passing by her compu-station. He had to back-step for another look. She was sitting with widened eyes, totally absorbed in the screen, a middle-aged woman with hair bleached almost white and skin turned pearlescent by the glow of electronic spreadsheets. Except for the hair, she was surprisingly ordinary looking, and he couldn't quite reconcile her with the AJ who played such a prominent role in the blunt fantasies that Broylan liked to share aloud after he started dating her.

Claire makes an abrupt left turn, and Nate, at that moment unbuttoning his trench coat, has to brace one hand on the dash to keep from rolling into her. There used to be a high school tactic of purposely cutting too-sharp a turn to slide your date up against you. It was looked on as sort of a test back then, when sitting up close made a girl one kind of date and sitting only a few inches farther away made her another kind. Here and now, though, Nate isn't sure whether he's ready yet for either.

Claire concentrates on the road, her silver earrings swaying with the motion of the car as she makes another sharp turn. "Whoa, cowgirl," Nate says. There is an artificially jovial tone to his voice that surprises him. It sounds like somebody on TV.

"Relax," Claire says, and pats his knee.

It is nothing more than a light, good-buddy tap, yet it feels far better to Nate than it ought to. Probably because, married, he'd got used to being touched. Touching is a part of being married, even badly married.

"My ex-husband said I always drove like a man," Claire says, laughing. "He meant it as a compliment."

She is friends with her ex-husband. This amazes Nate, maybe because of his Mediterranean blood. Claire seems too nice a person to nurse grudges. She isn't magazine cover pretty, but he notices that in profile her front teeth buck out slightly in a way that he's always found attractive in women. Something else attracts him—the actual physical presence of her next to him here in the car; maybe that earring, swinging with the momentum of her driving, was chosen with him in mind. He is attracted, too, by the focused attention as she leans in toward him. He would like to return her touch on the knee. Instead, he looks down at his feet.

His shoes are Italian, Fieramoscas. They shouldn't need breaking in, but Nate's extra wide feet weren't made for shoes like these. But so what if he needs a shoehorn to get into them, he likes his shoes to look good. While dressing for tonight, he imagined after supper the four of them—himself and Claire, Broylan and AJ—seated Japanese style around a low coffee table, playing *Pictionary* or *Baby-Boomers*. In such a situation people notice shoes. Especially if you're asked to remove them because the carpet's white.

A nice shine says something. His father had said that in America it was a sign of success to walk in a sharp-looking pair of shoes. Saturdays as a child, Nate used to play cowboy astride a swiveling barber chair, while his father got a shave and a shine. Baba would be leaned back, knees up, a black cigar poking straight up out of the mound of shaving cream that hid most of his face. "Sir," the barber called Baba, and "Mister." The shoeshine boy spread on the black polish with his fingertips. He used a brush, then a rag that clapped rhythmically, like hands to music. Last, he slid a woman's nylon stocking tightly back and forth across each toe. Nate loved the way Baba paid the shoeshine boy, flipping the coin at him in a spinning arc—right out of the movies. The boy always caught it one-handed, with a snap you could hear. Privately, in Arabic, Baba called the boy Il musq'een, the poor fellow. The boy looked only a little older than Nate, and the sneakers that he wore winter and summer were cut open on the sides to let his toes spread. Mahou ayb, ya America? Baba sometimes said under his breath, asking America whether she was ashamed. But afterward, walking home next to his father, Nate watched Baba's newly shined shoes taking step after confident step, as if there on the American sidewalk was where they always belonged.

Today men wear brushed suedes or jogging shoes or Hush Puppies, or those high priced "walkers" with the dull orange finish, like bum shoes. Nobody anymore seems to appreciate the hard luster that only buffing with nylon can put on a pair of sharp-toed black shoes.

AJ STANDS IN THE FOYER and chatters away about her nickname with the exuberance of a schoolgirl. "It stands for Amy Jean," she admits, "but don't you *dare* call me that!"

"Not me," Nate protests somewhat more good-naturedly than he intended. He finds himself actually flirting back with her. More and more lately, his own feelings baffle him. Isn't it just five minutes ago in the car that Claire gained his undivided attention with a simple tap on the knee? He's heard of this kind of thing, divorce making a person susceptible. At the foyer closet he starts to take off his coat while balancing a covered dish in one hand, and gets the other arm of his sports jacket caught in the trench coat's sleeve. It takes the help of AJ and Claire both to untangle him.

Broylan, staying back from the confusion, begins to laugh. Fixing him with a look, Nate walks over and thrusts the eggplant casserole into his hands. What is it women see in a man like that? Apparently, what had been true back in high school is still true today: women have lousy taste in guys.

"Come on in." AJ takes the casserole dish from Broylan and leads the way up several steps to a cozily arranged dining alcove. Following, Nate watches the pump-pump of her snug behind. Beneath a cluster of black balloons strung from the chandelier is the cutout of a lumpy, wry-faced cartoon woman, her speech balloon asking, "What—40 Again?"

"Great house," Nate says, taking in a two-story wall of windows. The plush-carpeted living room overlooked by the dining alcove is as expansive and as minimally furnished as the lobby of a public building. There is even piped-in music. Standing still to listen while the others go on ahead, Nate can just make it out, a rhythmic whisper high in the sky-lit ceiling. Its faintness deepens the room's sense of lonely distance. How can two people call this a home? Like a couple of BB's rolling around in a shoebox. The place must have cost at least a couple hundred thousand dollars, not counting the lot. No way of knowing for sure without coming out and asking. Jeannette would've asked. She'd also want to know how a college teacher, even one who teaches engineering, can afford to build such a place. Nate wouldn't know how to answer her. Outside consulting? Or something totally incomprehensible to him like tax and futures investments? But whatever the answer, he'd wait a beat and say, "Crime."

Corny, but Jeannette would've laughed. Would Claire?

Going back out to help carry the rest of the pans and covered dishes in from the car, Nate glances back at the modest front of the house. A shuttered door, two low windows hooded by awnings, and the rest of it garage doors. A poker face. From the street nobody could possibly guess at the luxurious inside.

Later, a tour shows that the house also includes a wine cellar with a built-in temperature controlled humidor for AJ's ex-husband's stash of Cuban cigars, a bathtub carved from Italian marble, a bedroom wall of beveled mirrors. The fireplace in the master bedroom has a hearth the size of a small stage, and stretched out across the hearth, like a miniature polar bear rug, there is a white German shepherd. The dog barely raises its head at the entry of strangers into the very inner sanctum of the house. AJ recites its full name, which is long and aristocratic and divided by a "von."

After the tour, Nate feels lethargic and vaguely annoyed. Acting impressed tires him out. Besides, he can't help feeling like an intruder, he and Claire and Broylan, all of them intruders tramping through the house of some poor musq'een who isn't here anymore. Other men eyeing his ex-wife's ass. Patting his ex-dog on the head. Doesn't anything belong to anybody anymore?

SEVERAL TIMES throughout the meal, Nate tells Claire how wonderful her cooking is, and although she rewards each compliment with progressively lingering nudges of her knee against his, the praise is nonetheless genuine. The food not only tastes good, it also tastes surprisingly authentic. But this he does not tell her, thinking she might sense the disappointment he is also feeling: imagine, his mother's cooking, the storied feasts of his grandmother and aunts, all accurately reproduced from mere recipes in a cookbook, and for the enjoyment of people who can't even pronounce the names of the dishes, *baba ghanouj*, *ful m'demmis*, *waraq enab*.

"And what do you call this again?" Broylan keeps asking. "What's in it, I mean."

"Diced camel hump," Nate says, casually, reaching for another diamond-shaped piece of *kibbeh b'il sanniyeh*.

AJ stops chewing. "You better be joking."

"He's joking." Claire gives him a jab of her elbow.

The narrow crescent-shaped table where Nate sits between the two women must have been especially designed for the alcove. Broylan seems isolated, having to sit across from them like a counter clerk. Maybe that's why all the questions. At a distance beyond the alcove—the whole downstairs seems nothing but one big distance—an art deco style wood burner, chromed and sleek, stands within a brick-bordered circle of raked sand. Occasionally throughout the meal Broylan's self-satisfied gaze strays pleasantly to the orange flicker within the stove's isinglass window. Then he would return to the meal, take another bite, frown.

"What's in here, this green stuff?" Broylan asks.

Before Nate can respond, AJ reaches over and gives his knee a warning tap. "Don't you *dare* say anything gross!"

"It's endive." Nate shrugs. "You cook it like spinach—panfry, never boil." He hasn't cooked any of the meal, but as resident Arab, he feels a certain obligation; in primary school, kids on the playground used to ask him to say something in Arabic. *Kilu kharrah*, he taught them, *Eat shit*. "The rest is just garlic, lemon juice, olive oil."

Broylan acts interested, dabbing fastidiously at the corners of his mouth as he listens. "Hoo-boy," he makes a pained face. "This over here must be that dip that makes you blast off!"

Nate glances over at AJ. Poor thing, had her ex-husband been so terrible that Glen Broylan is an improvement?

Seeming to read something in his look, AJ places a hand furtively on Nate's knee. At that exact instant Claire has, by coincidence, reached beneath the table and put her hand on his other knee.

Broylan's eyes light up. "Hey, tell them the Arabic for farts. Nate says there's words for different kinds of farts the way Eskimos have different words for snow." He leans forward on his elbows, smiling at Nate like a fond, wine-addled uncle.

Then Claire, with the undisguised flourish of one who's had enough, leans forward, raises her glass to AJ, and announces a toast: "Life begins at forty!"

There is a silence. Broylan looks confused. Has someone changed the subject?

Are pickings *that* slim for divorced women? Nate wonders as they toast AJ. The thought saddens him. Then he pictures Jeannette winding up alone, maybe having to date a Glen Broylan, and this saddens him even more. But *La'at teftikir kteer,* his mother's proverb says, Don't think too much, or you'll go crazy.

LATER, Nate pauses over his dessert and, during moments of silence, begins to picture the four of them sitting there, silently eating. A crazy thought. Maybe it's the wine, but what he feels is that he is sitting there seeing himself sitting there. The crazy part is knowing that he should be *in* the scene, not watching it from the outside, because crazy people did that.

He begins to eat, and immediately feels sorry at the sight of himself chewing his food and swallowing it. Eating always makes people seem so vulnerable, trying to nourish themselves. Especially these people, in the very act of surviving, himself among them. Embarrassed just thinking of his former married smugness, he wonders whether the others have felt it too, AJ chewing meekly as if she never really liked food, Broylan wolfing it down, Claire taking the tiniest bites, chewing and swallowing—as a little girl she probably ate all her vegetables in tiny bites, broccoli and spinach, and he sees her that way, the little girl she once was. Did she think any of this would happen to her? Looking around the table he sees them all as children again, himself one of them, silent for this moment, chewing their food to grow. He imagines Jeannette as a child, too, Jeannette whose hair was always in ringlets in the old photos at her parents' house. Six months. Had he gotten so divorced in only six months?

"YOU MEAN YOU AREN'T SURE YOU'RE RID OF THE MICE?" Nate had asked, but he didn't care, really. It was something to talk about on the ride home. What he was thinking of at the moment was to get home and take his shoes off, maybe catch the end of *Saturday Night Live*. But the moment they'd pulled out of AJ's driveway, Claire had begun acting concerned. "Sometimes, you know, I think I can still hear them," she'd said. "This tiny scraping sound in the walls. It's gotten to where I hate to come home to my own house. Alone, I mean, at night. Because what if it happens again, what if I turn on the light and see one?"

So, okay, Nate agreed to come in with her. And now, leaning with one arm braced over the commode in her bathroom, he, too, hears something. Or thinks he does. Repeatedly, he interrupts his stream of urine to better listen to what seems to be coming from within the baseboards themselves, a faint, scratching sound.

Finishing, Nate gazes upward, focusing idly on the diamond pattern of a bath towel stretched over the shower curtain rod. Beyond the tile is the bedroom where Claire, if she can hear him, must think he's suffering from a prostate condition with all his starting and stopping. In movies and sitcoms nylons are always hanging over the tub to dry, and the guy in the house—the father or the beleaguered husband—is supposed to get terribly upset, as if nylons drying in the bathroom cause some sort of essential inconvenience for males. Which they don't, as far as Nate is concerned. Behind him, there are four pair of panty hose draped on the grip bars and on the shower rod. He washes his hands and wipes them on the tiny guest towel. Now, while Claire is in the next room, waiting for him to check out the house for mice, he looks again at the panty hose.

But first he must tell himself that he isn't some kind of weirdo. Because what's weird about wanting a good hard shine on your shoes? And what's weird about getting back what was taken away from you?

He listens a moment for the scraping to begin again. Then, quickly, without even pausing—as he'd intended—to decide on the most faded or worn out pair, he pulls down a pair of panty hose and wads them deep inside his trench coat pocket. Hoo!

When he opens the door, Claire is waiting for him in the hall, smiling. She has changed into a robe that shines flush against her skin. Her hair, brushed down, catches highlights from the bedroom lamp behind her. He feels as if he's walked onto the cover of one of Jeannette's paperbacks: guy in a trench coat with a slinky woman leering at him from a doorway. Very American, only it's him now standing there in a trench coat, Nate Yakoub. And what would Jeannette think of the way this other woman is looking him up and down right now?

As if in answer, Claire's smile widens and one eyebrow arches in surprise. He feels a light tugging at his coat. Looking down at himself he sees that she has hold of the belt of his coat. He starts to say something, but with her free hand she places a finger to his lips; no need to explain a thing, her smile tells him. She takes a small step backward into the bedroom, then another, pulling the belt taut. She's drawing him toward her, step after step, just as he had wanted Jeannette to do. He smiles now, too, but Claire gives him no time to consider his gratitude, no time to think of anything except the physical certainty that he must step closer each time the belt draws tight. He must, or else lose everything again.

SAMUEL HAZO

Understory

It's not that sometimes I forget.
I'm told that everybody does.
What troubles me is how
        whatever I've forgotten trebles
        in importance the more I keep
        forgetting it.
                        Some word . . .
                                        Some place . . .
Today a student from the Class
        of Way Back When
        seemed certain I'd remember him
        by name.
                I tried and tried
        before I had to ask . . .
                                Though students
        and ex-students are my life,
        I must admit that I remember
        most of the best, all
        of the worst, many who have left
        this world, and not that many
        of the rest.
                It leaves me wondering . . .
Is memory a beast that sheds
        its baggage as it goes?

Are facts by definition destined
for oblivion?
Or is it absolute
that what I can't forget no matter
how I try is all that's worth
remembering?
I know a mother
of four sons who mixes up
their names.
Ollie is Bennett.
Bennett is Drew.
Drew
is Christopher.
Facing one,
she travels down the list before
she pleads, "Tell me your name,
dear boy."
Outsiders realize
they're all one boy to her,
regardless of their names.
She knows
them by their souls.
That reassures me.
For JoAnn Bevilacqua-Weiss

The First Sam Hazo at the Last

A minor brush with medicine
in eighty years was all
he'd known.
But this was different.
His right arm limp and slung,
his right leg dead to feeling
and response, he let me spoon him

chicken-broth.
Later he said
without self-pity that he'd like
to die.
I bluffed, "The doctors
think that therapy might help you
walk again."
"They're liars,
all of them," he muttered.
Bedfast
was never how he hoped to go.
"In bed you think of everything,"
he whispered with a shrug, "you think
of all of your life."
I knew
he meant my mother.
Without her
he was never what he might have been,
and everyone who loved him knew it.
Nothing could take her place—
not the cars he loved to drive,
not the money he could earn at will,
not the roads he knew by heart
from Florida to Saranac, not the two
replacement wives who never
measured up.
Fed now by family
or strangers, carried to the john,
shaved and changed by hired help,
this independent man turned silent
at the end.
Only my wife
could reach him for his private needs.
What no one else could do
for him, he let her do.

She talked to him and held
his hand, the left.
She helped him
bless himself and prayed beside him
as my mother might have done.
"Darling" was his final word
for her.
Softly, in Arabic.

Ahead of Time

Her letter, mailed from Saranac,
is dated 1926.
My mother's
writing to my aunt.
It's two
years since she told her father,
"Dad, I'm marrying Sam
and not the man you had
in mind."
That's decades more
than half a century ago.
My mother and my aunt are dead.
I'm well past sixty when I share
my mother's letter with my wife.
It stills us like a resurrection.
Later I read it to my son
and to his wife.
They tell me
how alive it seems as if
a woman neither ever knew
is speaking in this very room
to each of us.

The letter's full
of questions I can answer,
but the time for answering is over.
I realize my life's already longer
than my mother's was by almost
thirty years.
The letter in my hand
is older than the two of us.
The more I read, the less
there is to read until
I reach the bottom of the page.
The last sentence ends
with a hyphen.
There's no page two.

JOE KADI

Writing as Resistance, Writing as Love

whose world?

Hunched over on a small chair in the library's corner, I'm invisible in my physical surroundings and on the pages I'm devouring. It's my usual Saturday morning extravaganza—read until nauseated, stagger back to the house with an armful of books, snatch every free moment during the week, dive in.

Books shone brightly on the desolate landscape of my childhood, in ways both profound and basic. They provided fantasy, escape, a reality in stark contrast to the one around me. I especially loved reading about children with happy home lives and positive experiences with a friendly, bustling outside world. But equally profoundly, books, and the children who inhabited their pages, betrayed me by ignoring my world. Where was I? Where were workers? Arabs? Rarely to be found. And if found, never a good word. Stupid janitors who couldn't think, idiotic truck drivers who couldn't write, dirty Arabs who couldn't be trusted.

And still I read, still I coveted shelves full of books, still no one could offer a better present than a book. Still I carried a deeply buried and mostly jumbled desire to carve my own niche in this world. Yet I couldn't imagine anything other than renewing my library card year after year, reading someone else's stories—entering this world of words and books on someone else's terms.

Similar feelings plague me today, after working as a writer for several years. Is there a place for me? Claiming writer status remains so difficult I can barely say the words. If I manage to, I fight the impulse to cover my mouth with my hand, the exact same motion made by toothless family members. Fear and shame prompt their gestures, and my impulse. Who ever heard of someone from a general motors city, destined for secretarial work (if a great deal of luck came her way), thinking, *saying*, she can write books? Who ever heard of a working-class Lebanese writer?

daring tongue maneuvers

I pace back and forth in the living room of the ugly apartment my lover and I rent. We pay too much money for it and the creepy landlord never fixes things when they break. I'm getting small shocks from the shag rug and the radio's turned up. Every day I change my mind. I'll never turn on the news because the American media has taken lies and distortions to new levels in this particular imperialist venture taking place in the Persian Gulf. No. I'll keep the radio on all the time because it might alleviate my feeling of utter helplessness a tiny bit.

This day, tuned into public radio, I hear someone introduce Edward Said very distinctly: "Edward Said is an Arab-American intellectual." This astonishes me. Edward Said has ten minutes to talk about American imperialism and anti-Arab racism? Miracle of miracles. But then the full impact hits and I don't hear anything Said says. Someone, a talk show host on national radio no less, used "Arab" and "intellectual" in the same sentence. And not as part of a comedy routine. The words catch in my chest and something tears wide open. Arab-American intellectual. Can it be possible? Do these words fit together? Can the combination work?

I've always understood the power of words. Certain words can be crunched together into a hard ball and flung with lightning speed. They can knock you off your feet and leave you gasping for breath. It happened to me with the word Arab. People enjoyed hurling word combinations at me—Arab whore, greasy Arab, crazy Arab—and bowling me over, day after day. I never believed anyone who said,

"Sticks and stones can break my bones but names can never hurt me." Names did hurt me.

Then, a turning point, a revelation. Words hurt; they also heal. Words jostle my insides, wake me up, jump-start my brain. Someone can place "Arab" side by side with "intellectual" and say it over the radio and the earth moves. And if I can keep my understanding of the power of words front and center while I devise my own wild mixtures, maybe I can open up worlds for people like me, maybe I can offer my writing for healing and resistance.

the importance of silence

The ropes around my ankles and wrists cut into my skin, but the tightest gag cuts across my mouth and tears into the corners. Before tying me up, my father tells me, "You're so bad. You're so bad." Over and over. After he stalks out of the room and slams the door, I try to figure out what I did. I wrack my brain, but nothing comes to mind. Time crawls by. Has one hour passed, or five, or ten? Finally, my father decides—relying on some internal method I can never discern—he should undo the knots. I crawl into bed and hold myself every bit as tightly as the ropes did.

Silence is critically important. Or, more precisely, *my* silence is critically important. I knew that from day one. Inordinate efforts, overt and covert, went into shutting me up. Teachers rewarded quiet children. My mother told me if I didn't have anything nice to say not to say anything at all, and she meant it. The priests who routinely ripped my body and mind apart held knives to my throat and told me they'd kill me if I ever said a word. My father tolerated me best when he had me muzzled.

All systems of oppression—from child abuse to racism to ableism—function most effectively when the victims don't talk. Silence isolates, keeps us focusing inward rather than outward, makes perpetrators' work easier, confuses and overwhelms. I didn't know this as a child and teenager. I just knew I had to be quiet. The few times I managed to croak something truthful, I experienced repercussions, swift and brutal, that left no doubt about my oppressors' intentions.

Coiled Tongues

Which tender body
shall be carved up
served on a platter
to Monsignor tonight?
Male or female?
White, yellow or brown?

Wavering at rectory door
I watched my father's car
grow smaller.
Catholic obedience
always goes too far.

Before Monsignor devours flesh
he dresses it properly
manipulates each limb carefully.
Do clerks blanch
when selling garter belts
and black nylons
to fit 10-year-old bodies?
Are store managers
appreciative accomplices
who insist Monsignor
take generous discounts?

Mouth a final blessing.
"You Lebanese girls are so pretty."
His voice slimed over my ribs,
anchored in.
Some words cannot be exorcised,
even with flames.

Monsignor savors flesh more
when flavored with lies.

"Yes, I liked it."
I memorized the force
of white fingers
picking my bones clean.

Years later
I remember the children
whose eyes slid under the pew
whose tongues tangled
when Monsignor walked by.
The VanDerHagen girls
the Beneditto boys
the Lee children.
I envision priests
marking the names in ledgers
systematically recording each feeding.

Years later
at a party
someone tells a "joke":
A newly-ordained priest
celebrates with
a lavish table.
"If this is poverty, Father,"
asks a guest,
who could have been me
who would have said it grimly
"If this is poverty, Father,
what does chastity look like?"

Times change.
Time changes.
Bony and bloody remains
on platters
metamorphize slowly,
gather force.

Now
when he poisons the room
with his presence
our eyes will rivet instead of slide
tongues coil instead of tangle.
"What does chastity look like?"

The man with the backward collar
will chew fingernail, grip chair tightly
as this new reality strikes full force:
No bodies here
for carving, serving, devouring.

Memories withstand long decades.
Sins cast long shadows.
Take heed.
Broken children coil long tongues.

Moving from Cultural Appropriation Toward Ethical Cultural Connections[1]

MY GRANDMOTHER trudged from the hills of rural Lebanon to the shores of the Mediterranean, carrying clothes and a derbeke.[2] She and the drum survived several weeks in the steerage compartment of a large boat. No small feat. And now she's dead, and the derbeke sits on a shelf far away from me. But I ended up with my sittee's determination, which I've needed to navigate through the stormy waters of drumming.

After experiencing so much anti-Arab hatred growing up, I cut myself off from my culture as soon as I could. I tried hard to assimilate, with the attendant craziness and confusion; but thankfully, my journey into political awareness and action brought me back to my racial/cultural heritage, and in particular to its music. Hearing familiar rhythms, I found myself thinking about—and wanting—a brass derbeke with a chrome finish and intricate engraving. Just like the one my grandmother brought from Lebanon.

So my lover and I embarked on a grand search to ferret out my derbeke. It took a long time, partly because I didn't know where to look, partly because white people's interest in drumming hadn't fully impacted the market. In January 1991, a year after the search began, Jan and I marched in Washington, D.C. to protest the slaughter of Arabs in the vicious outbreak of U.S. imperialism known as the Gulf War. During that weekend, alternating between grief and numbness, we chanced upon a store specializing in musical instruments from around the world. I found my derbeke.

The end of my search? No. Just the beginning. Now I needed a teacher and a community that would offer technical assistance and political respect. I attended drumming workshops, but each proved as problem-laden as my first, where I found an overwhelmingly white group of women who apparently hadn't given much thought to the issue of playing congas or derbekes. I'm using the word "play" loosely, because even as an unskilled beginner I could tell these women didn't know the traditional Arabic techniques and rhythms I knew simply from listening to Arabic music. Further dismay resulted when I questioned two women and discovered they didn't know the name of their drums; they had just been drawn to the derbeke for some unknown reason and made a purchase. They spent the workshop banging happily on their drums in ways bearing no resemblance to proper derbeke-playing style.

I sat through this drumming workshop, and subsequent ones, with a familiar mix of anger and fear. Anger at the casual (mis)use by white people of important aspects of culture from various communities of color, fear that such groups would prove the only resource available and I would simply have to put up with crap in order to learn. These disheartening experiences led to another year of my derbeke gathering dust as I grew more certain I'd never find what I needed.

But after much searching, I found a wonderful teacher, Mick Labriola, as well as drumming friends/acquaintances I connect with politically and musically. Because of this, and because of my deep determination to forge ahead in spite of obstacles, drumming has proved an incredibly positive experience. I've re-connected with my roots. Experiencing how much beauty and importance Arabs have given the world has helped me feel pride, as opposed to shame, about being Arab.

Then there's anger and grief. My initial experiences at drumming workshops proved common. I continually see derbekes in white people's homes, played by white musicians, banged on at drumming circles. Many players don't even know the name of the instrument, or where it comes from. They don't play properly, and they don't know traditional Arabic rhythms.

But none of this seems to raise any concern, as more and more white people jump on the drumming bandwagon. Why drumming? Why so popular? Because it's a powerful activity? Because it's a wonderfully communal instrument? Because it allows people to learn about other cultures through music? Most days I think these explanations provide a more positive interpretation than the situation warrants, especially when I notice the apolitical spirituality of the New Age movement embracing the concept of "getting in touch with inner rhythms" via the drums of people of color; white people dredding their hair and buying African drums; people "playing" an instrument without knowing its name.

Within these actions, I sense an imperialist attitude in which privileged people want to own segments of other people's cultures. To me, it's cultural appropriation, a subject I'm confused about and infuriated by. I have many questions and ideas, but few answers. The complexity of the subject lends itself more to books (*not* written by white people) than single essays, so be forewarned; I can't tackle everything. I've tried to streamline this by focusing it around drumming, and in particular derbekes, since issues and questions relating to drumming carry over to other types of cultural appropriation.

I've thought long and hard about defining cultural appropriation. Culture includes any and all aspects of a community that provide its life force, including art, music, spirituality, food, philosophy, and history. To "appropriate" means to take possession of. "Cultural" appropriation means taking possession of specific aspects of someone else's culture in unethical, oppressive ways.

While helpful, this basic definition simplifies rather than deepens. It doesn't examine various aspects of cultural appropriation. To do that, I'll analyze what happens when white people play derbekes incorrectly.

It seems to me those white people use derbekes perceiving them as generic, no-name drums unencumbered by hard political/historical/cultural realities, never asking themselves the questions that would uncover these realities, such as: whose music is this? What has imperialism and racism done to the people who created this music? Do I have a right to play this instrument? What kind of beliefs do I hold about Arabs? Ignoring these questions and ignoring Arab musical traditions translates into cultural appropriation—white people taking possession of Arabic culture by commandeering an important instrument and the music it produces. The derbeke and its playing style are important pieces of Arab culture, with thousands of years of history attached. To disregard that and play however one chooses whitewashes the drum, and by implication Arab culture. When stripped of its historical legacy, the drum is placed outside Arab culture, suggesting that Arab culture and history aren't worth taking seriously; even though Arabs have created something valuable and life-enhancing in our music, that doesn't matter. White people can and will choose to perceive the drum as ahistorical and culturally empty—a plaything that can be given whatever meaning the player chooses.

To perceive a derbeke as a plaything is to carry the privileged attitude that has wrought devastation all over our planet: "Everything is here for me to play with and use." Whether peoples, lands, or cultures, it's there for the grabbing. This take-take-take attitude pushed white colonizers through whole peoples and lands on the Asian, African, and American continents. Although brown, black, and yellow people filled those continents, white people perceived them as empty.

That kind of colonization continues, and new forms have evolved. The colonialist attitude has affixed itself to our music, clothing, religions, languages, philosophies, and art. I overheard a white shopper in a music store examining a derbeke. "Cool drum. I'll take a couple." He perceived the derbeke as an empty vessel waiting to have meaning infused into it, as opposed to an important cultural symbol/reality embodying centuries of meaning.

I don't believe every white person who buys a derbeke holds that attitude, or that no other issues or desires are mixed in. But I do believe large and small vestiges of colonialist ideas live in many places, and it frightens and angers me. These ideas and their practice have already destroyed so many of our people and may well destroy more. Many white people don't know they possess such a mindset, and unthinking, unexamined ignorance can cause irreparable harm.

These political questions must be raised, along with the psychological effects of cultural appropriation. Many times people of color gloss over these, possibly because we don't want to admit the extent of our pain. I want to try.

Cultural appropriation causes me anger and grief. Anger about flagrant disregard and disrespect for me and my community, about unexamined privilege and power, about cavalier white people who use important cultural symbols/realities and turn them into no-name items. And grief, which stems from a hopeless, powerless feeling that I/my community will never get the respect and consideration we deserve, that no matter how hard we struggle, no one hears our words or heeds our demands.

Along with those responses is one that so far hasn't been examined in our thinking and writing about cultural appropriation; for me this causes deep pain. Cultural appropriation cuts away at and undermines my basic racial identity.

It's been hard for me to create a clear, strong identity as Arab-American. It's been hard for me to believe I really exist as such a person, when dominant society categorically trivializes, diminishes, and whitewashes Arabs. I've struggled with this for years, and recently my identity has been strengthened, thanks in part to my derbekes. They help me realize I come from somewhere, my community exists, and we've created wonderful cultural expressions over the centuries.

When, as happens frequently, I come across the attitude that clearly says the derbeke is an empty vessel, I begin doubting myself and my community, doubting our very existence. I fight constantly against internalizing the message—if the derbeke means nothing, if it comes from nowhere, I don't exist.

It's impossible to examine increased derbeke sales or the increased numbers of white "shamans" without discussing multiculturalism. Strange things are happening under the guise of "honoring diversity," because multiculturalism, as defined and practiced by white people, is partly responsible for the increase in cultural appropriation. While I'm not opposed to *authentic* multiculturalism, I do believe unauthentic or artificial or perverse multiculturalism simply feeds and reinforces imperialist attitudes. Examples of this abound. Young white schoolchildren aren't taught to connect ethnically with other cultures; they're taught to take whatever they want from other cultures and *use* it. White adult consumers snatch our various arts, wanting the stuff but not caring if its creators are systematically destroyed.

Given the brutal racism endemic to our society, it makes sense that much of what passes for multiculturalism is actually covert and overt cultural appropriation, actually a form of cultural genocide. As dominant white society casually buys and sells our symbols/realities, their cultural meaning is watered down and their integrity diminished. Today items from various communities of color are all the rage, but I'm not happy to see the walls of white people's homes adorned with African masks, Asian paintings, and Native ceremonial objects.

Behind the rhetoric and hype about multiculturalism and honoring diversity lurk the same attitudes of entitlement and privilege that form part of structural racism. For the most part, these white people haven't done the work necessary to become allies of people of color. They know little or nothing about current global struggles of people of color, as we define and articulate them. They don't engage in acts of solidarity around specific issues such as Native self-determination or Palestinian liberation. They don't read books by radical authors of color.

Further, these white people haven't analyzed a monster related to racism, that is, classism and the global capitalist system. All of us need to be clear about how and where and why the capitalist system fits into the picture. We need to ask critical questions. Is "multiculturalism" the latest capitalist fad? Who's in control? Who's benefiting? And who's making money, now that it's popular to hang Native dream webs on bedroom walls? Could it be people of color? Hardly. As more and more people of color are forced to live on the streets, white entrepreneurs are getting rich selling our art, music, and spirituality. Watching them profit as they exploit and appropriate our cultures, when for years we experienced hostility and scorn trying to preserve them in a racist society, is truly galling. I grew up with white people belittling and "joking" about my family's choice of music and dancing; now I can watch those same people rush to sign up for "real" belly-dancing lessons. Taught by a white woman, of course.

Economics impact culture, as the belly dance example shows. The particular combination of racism and classism that has popularized belly dancing taught by white people has several implications for Arab-American culture. Arab dancers who can't make a living teaching may be eventually forced to give up their serious studies of traditional dance altogether; this is one factor that eventually leads to cultural genocide. If a certain type of belly dancing becomes popular and another particular strain never catches on with white teachers, the latter could slowly disappear. Again, this factors into cultural genocide. For every cultural form happily adopted by the dominant culture's racist and classist system, another falls by the wayside. Some expressions discarded by dominant society will continue to thrive among marginalized communities, some will be lost forever.

Further, class exploitation crosses over with racism in certain ways, and thus many people of color are working-class or working-poor. Consequently, we can't afford to buy the now-available music, paintings, instruments, and books from our cultures. We can't afford travel to our countries of origin. Observing white, middle-class people engaging in these activities adds yet another layer of anguish and complexity to these issues.

Recently I talked over the phone with a white, middle-class man who has traveled extensively in various Arab countries, attended Arabic language schools, and now speaks Arabic fluently. Upon discovering I was Arab-American, he began speaking Arabic to me.

As is all too usual, I got so choked up with rage I couldn't think clearly. I said curtly, "I don't speak Arabic," and hung up. Next time, I have a response all planned out: "Gee, if only my grandparents hadn't experienced so much racism and been so isolated! Then they wouldn't have tried to assimilate. Then they would have taught us to speak Arabic. Which would be so helpful these days, now that multiculturalism is in. For those who can afford it, which of course precludes most people of color. Oh well, I hope you're having a splendid time with it all."

The discussion of cultural appropriation between white people and people of color is critically important, but I want to push further. If we keep the focus on relationships between colored and white, we come up with an overly simplistic analysis that ignores the fact that many people of color are just as inattentive to these issues and thus act inappropriately toward each other. It implies the only groups worth discussing are *the* white people and *the* people of color, two broad categories which are sometimes helpful but also present problems in terms of understanding the complexities of race. These simplistic categories feed into the myth that people of color constitute a monolithic group unscathed by differences of skin color, immigrant status, gender, ability, sexuality, language, class, and religion. Further, reductionist categories support the lie that we can only be discussed in relation to white people, that our only important relationships exist with white people.

A simplistic analysis of cultural appropriation minimalizes and trivializes what we as people of color from different communities do to each other, glossing over the fact that we can and do commit acts of cultural appropriation, and thus hurt each other badly. I've had the painful experience of watching other people of color using derbekes as no-name drums. Our racial identity doesn't rule out unjust acts toward each other. If I were drawn to an African mask in a store and bought it without knowing where it came from, what it represents, and who made it, would that be acceptable? Of course not. I'd be committing an act of cultural appropriation as surely as any white person who did the same thing.

Our existence as people of color doesn't mean we know much—if anything—about other communities of color. It doesn't mean we've done the hard work of freeing ourselves from stereotypes and lies about other racial/ethnic groups. I've heard, time and again, the same kind of anti-Arab racism out of the mouths of people of color that I've heard from white people. Unless people of color do the same anti-racist work we want white people to do, we can't become true allies and friends.

However, I don't equate the actions of people of color with those of white people. There's a difference between a white person and a person of color playing derbekes incorrectly. The white person's actions feed into structural racism; they're part and parcel of the systemic oppression by white people of people of color. The person of color's actions stem, I think, from a mix of structural racism and horizontal violence in which the dominant white power structure keeps us carefully divided from each other, duplicating their mistreatment, and ignorant about the many ways our lives connect.

Even with this understanding, it still hurts when a Latino uses a derbeke as a generic drum. In some ways, because I so badly want and need solidarity from other people of color, these actions hurt more. I don't expect as much from white people, so I'm not as shocked and hurt by their actions. But betrayal from other people of color cuts deeply.

Betrayal appears in varied forms, and I briefly want to mention sexism. Many men of color bring a problematic and divisive note to discussions of drumming and culture by insisting women can't drum because it's not "traditional." I have two responses to this. First, there's historical documentation from many cultures, including Arabic ones, of women drumming in earlier times. Second, even in relation to preserving our cultures, I find the label "traditional" almost irrelevant. If women didn't drum in the past, why would we want to carry on with that aspect of our culture? Are the men who propose this anxious to continue every traditional cultural practice, from the most inane to the most misogynist?[3] Plenty of manifestations of sexism and misogyny in Arab cultures need to be kissed goodbye.

As a person of color, I want to do more than react to oppression by white people. It's important that, as a subject and moral agent with power in the world, I state what I want and what I consider acceptable. For starters, do I want to share cultural traditions?

There are several reasons I do. First, when healthy cultural connections occur, it's personally and communally affirming. Someone has taken the time and energy to understand and appreciate the derbeke. She's taken me and my community/culture seriously, and shown respect. This affirms me and helps strengthen racial identity.

Second, I'm enriched by participating in an authentic multiculturalism that involves having friends, listening to the music, learning the histories, and being allies in struggle with people from various cultures. This type of multiculturalism has, at its root, respect, thoughtfulness, a political analysis, and openness.

Third, in practical terms, I don't know how to separate. I was born of an interracial marriage. I live in a racially mixed community and belong to organizations and groups that cut across cultures. I've read and listened to and integrated perspectives of people from different racial/ethnic communities. How to undo this mixing? Forget the books, the stories, the poems, the music that have become part of me? Give up friends? Return to my places of origin—which isn't physically possible, and where I may not feel at home for other reasons? It seems foolhardy to consider this.

I support the idea of sharing across cultures, but I also believe some things should never be shared. For starters, sacred instruments, rhythms, and rituals. Yet, unbelievably, this has happened, continues to happen. Several years ago I attended a music festival where two white women planned to perform with a sacred instrument from a community of Australian indigenous people. Although an Australian aboriginal woman was present and voiced objections, it didn't matter to the musicians. At the last minute, outcries from a larger group prevented the show. I don't know if these two musicians used the instrument other times, but given the depth of their resistance to restriction of their "artistic freedom," I wouldn't be surprised if they did.

Of course, I question whether those women should have been performing at all, since their show consisted of playing instruments from various communities of color. I'm tired of seeing white people get the praise, money, and publicity from public performance. However, I can't deal with these questions and issues here. The topic needs an essay of its own and quite possibly its own book.

Back to making and preserving connections across communities. How to make such links? And what to call them? Words carry critical weight in liberation struggles. Naming ourselves and our desires is vital. The term "ethical cultural connection" embodies my ideas. It focuses clearly on culture, on the lifeforce of a community. "Connection" speaks to a freely-chosen bonding experience between two people or two groups. The adjective "ethical" clarifies the type of connection—one based on respect, justice, and integrity.

Ethical cultural connections are comprised of respect for the community involved, a desire to learn and take action, an openness to being challenged and criticized, a willingness to think critically about personal behavior, and a commitment to actively fighting racism. These cornerstones remain the same whether I'm getting to know one Native person or buying a carving from a Native museum. They apply to people of color and white people.

I've come to the conclusion that I'm not opposed to non-Arabs playing derbekes if it's done with respect, knowledge, and seriousness, and if these attitudes manifest themselves in concrete action. I want drummers to learn the derbeke's culture and history, and the proper way to play. And to take this knowledge a step further by actively countering the imperialism, racism, and genocide Arabs experience today. It's not enough to celebrate cultural difference by learning language, music, or history, when people's whole worlds are at risk.

Of course, this raises a critical question. How do I know if someone's doing those things? By watching? Maybe the person plays the derbeke correctly, maybe he knows Arab rhythms. But that doesn't tell me how much he knows and cares about my people.

I can only know for sure if I talk to the drummer. That's the only way any of us will know. Typing out guidelines or policing cultural events won't do it. We need to talk—across cultures and classes. I've spent days and days and days writing this essay, and months pondering it, and I've been unable to think of any other way to know where a person stands. My analysis doesn't help in isolation. It helps as we communicate across all racial groups—Asian (including Arabs), Latino, Native, African, and white.

And talking to one person won't cut it. I'm sure any white person interested in assuaging her conscience could find enough white-identified Arabs to assure her whatever she does with the derbeke is okay. There are many such people in all communities—people who for whatever reasons have become so alienated from their roots and their communities that they casually approve of the worst kinds of cultural appropriation. At the music festival I mentioned earlier, participants discussed cultural appropriation several times, and it appeared the women of color shared a clear and unified response. That is, until a well-known woman of color, a superb drummer, announced from the stage that anyone who wanted a drum from whatever culture should buy it and play it. So much for solidarity.

I don't want white people seeking out white-identified people of color to give them the stamp of approval. I want white people to talk to many people, including political activists. I want discussion around power and privilege, about who benefits from cultural appropriation and in what ways, about who will decide how cultural connections happen and what makes them ethical. I want discussion about actions and the meanings they carry.

In these discussions, participants need to take emotional reactions into account without letting them dictate the whole discussion. I'm so sick and tired of watching non-Arabs thoughtlessly pound away on derbekes, I might not notice when someone's doing it right. I might not even care. I'm entitled to my anger, but one person's emotions can't set the tone and agenda for these discussions.

I believe politicized people of color and our white allies must start framing discussions with helpful guidelines that make sense to us. Discussions must be cross-cultural and focused on tough questions about racism, classism, unauthentic multiculturalism, power, and privilege. And I suggest we include the ways in which personal experience can help frame critical thinking on cultural appropriation.

Looking at the five derbekes that now grace this home, I'm struck by the connection between my drumming and my political thinking. The deeper I go with one, the deeper I go with the other. The political analysis I push myself to do translates into more meaningful drumming. Playing the derbeke helps deal with the pain I experience around vivid examples of cultural appropriation. I offer this personal example not as a "feel-good," quick, on-the-surface remedy for oppression and cultural genocide, but rather as a somber statement of possibility. We can plumb the depths of the worst in our society while participating in meaningful cultural activities that ground us and keep hope alive.

Notes

1. Many thanks to Jan Binder for her help with this article.

2. A *derbeke* (pronounced der-beck-ee) is a traditional Arabic hand drum. I've seen several different spellings, but this is the one I prefer. The drum is also known as a *dumbek* (pronounced doom-beck)—there are varied spellings for that word as well.

3. Another problem with this attitude is that it feeds into the dangerous lie/myth that cultures are static and unchanging entities.

PAULINE KALDAS

Cumin and Coriander

THE OIL SPLATTERED as she slipped another falafel patty into the frying pan. One drop stung her cheek and she brushed the pricking sensation by rubbing her shoulder against it. Faten was almost finished. The stuffed cabbage was done, the vegetable *tagen* needed just a few more minutes in the oven, and the spinach phyllo triangles were all set on the counter. Once she fried the rest of the falafel, she would be able to pack up and go to the next house.

Mr. David's kitchen was large, with lots of counter space and a new oven that worked easily. The gas was hooked up so she didn't have to worry about replacing the *butagaz* cylinder. The American University in Cairo had built this new building in luxury style. Mr. David's apartment had a huge terrace, almost as large as the apartment itself, with a view of Zamalek's landscape of old villas. Sometimes, Faten would take a minute to step out onto the terrace and let her eyes roam over the city. Despite the growing population and the many new buildings, most of the villas had been able to salvage at least a small garden with orange or guava trees and perhaps some flowers. There were also several new boutiques like Mobaco, Concrete, and New Man, where the upper-class and foreigners shopped. Faten preferred being in the kitchen, the feeling of space around her as she maneuvered, a circular dance from refrigerator to counter to oven.

She took out the last falafel, still crackling from the hot oil, and placed it on the paper towel along with the rest. It was almost two o'clock. She was running late and would have to hurry. She wondered if she should spend the two pounds on a taxi to go downtown or if she should wait for the minibus that cost forty piasters. She looked at the money Mr. David had left for her—forty pounds when he owed her only thirty-five, twenty for the food and fifteen for her salary. He was always generous. She would take a taxi. This morning she had been late because she got into an argument with the taxi driver who stopped for her. He had arrogantly insisted that she pay him four pounds when she knew that two was fair. Finally, he waved his hand, encircling the whole area of Imbaba, and stated with assurance that any foreigner he picked up would pay him no less than five pounds. She muttered under her breath, "God save us and protect us," and told the man to go on and find his foreigner; she did not want to delay him.

Faten took the vegetable *tagen* out of the oven and placed it alongside the rest of the food. Then she covered everything with tin foil since she knew Mr. David would not be home for a while. She was grateful to be working for him. He was a young man and not married. He never complained about what she cooked or how she cooked it. Often, he would not give her a list for the next week and accepted whatever choices she made for him. How lucky, she thought, the woman who would marry him. Not like Mr. John, who insisted she use less and less oil. Now he only left her two drops to cook with. And when he was home, he would hover about her. How did he expect her to make the phyllo or the eggplant with no oil? The food came out dry and brittle, nothing to soften the palate, to make one desire it. She wanted to stop cooking for him, but she was reluctant to give up any of her jobs. She didn't know what might happen tomorrow.

She still hoped that she might be able to take her daughter, Houria, out of the public school and put her in the private school with her brother, Mahmoud. *Houria*—it meant freedom. When her son was born, her husband filled out the birth certificate and afterwards told her the child's name. Then, she became "Om Mahmoud," the mother of Mahmoud. She had not expected anything different for the second child. Instead, her husband came in after she had given birth. The room was still spinning, and the walls seemed fluid, waving back and forth with the motion of a belly dancer. He held her hand and smiled. "Well," he said, "do you have a name for our daughter?" She immediately said, "Houria," without thinking it through. Her husband looked a little surprised, but he nodded and said, "It's an old name but good." The name, which meant freedom, had been popular during times of war: 1948, 1967, 1973. What brought it to her mind now, she wondered, when there was peace?

Her husband had insisted on sending Mahmoud to a private school, even though they didn't have much money. After her husband died, she worked hard to continue paying the school fees. Maybe now with the new jobs she had gotten, there might be a chance of transferring Houria. She had been lucky. Maybe her husband was still watching over her. The only job she could find after his death was working as a maid for an Egyptian woman. Then an American professor moved in next door. Faten started cleaning for her. One day, Miss Carol came home with bags of groceries. Faten asked her if she would like her to cook anything. When Miss Carol asked if she knew how to cook, Faten paused at the peculiarity of the question, finally replying, "I can cook anything you want." Miss Carol recommended her for other jobs, cooking for the foreign professors at the American University in Cairo. Soon she had enough to fill her days, often cooking for two people a day. She quit cleaning for the Egyptian woman and became a full-time cook. The pay was better, and she could be in the kitchen by herself. Most of the foreigners never disturbed her. A few of them gave her a small radio to listen to while she cooked, and sometimes she would sing. But summers were hard since most of them traveled, and she could only hope they would give her something extra for that time.

Faten slipped off her long *galabiya*, now spotted with grease and tomato sauce. She reminded herself that next time she would take it home to wash, but she knew she would probably forget. She pulled the long black skirt on over her head, then the sweater over her thin chemise.

She went to the small bathroom and started to tie the black scarf over her head. She caught her face in the square mirror above the sink: her nose took up a little too much space and her face seemed so round. But she was surprised by the blush on her cheeks—it must have come from the hot kitchen. Her lips were full, drawn with precision. Once, one of the women she worked for had told her she was beautiful. Faten stared at her, puzzled. The woman continued, complimenting her smooth brown skin, her clear complexion. "The beauty of your face," she said.

Her husband had thought so too. He would touch his hand to her face and tell her she was as beautiful as the moon. She would smile hesitantly then slip his hand away, feeling embarrassed as if she had been caught in an illicit act. He was gentle, more than she had expected. She did not mind staying at home, taking care of the house, the children. The market nearby was good with clean, fresh produce, not the shriveled tomatoes and rotten fruit in other parts of the city. A breeze traveled through their small balcony, and sometimes, as she swept, a slip of wind would caress her arm. Then, so many times, at the beginning of the month when her husband got paid, he would come home with small gifts for the children and something for her, a scarf bright with a pattern of orange and purple, or a purse, or, once, even perfume. How she raved at his extravagance, buying such gifts when they could barely afford the school fees. He would wave her away and say, "Woman, don't you deserve something in your life?"

Yet, there were days when he returned home quiet, his shoulders stooped, refused anything to eat, and just sat on the balcony smoking a cigarette. "This country," he would say, "does not respect the man who works." She didn't understand and could only tell him that everything would be all right and bring him a cup of tea with mint.

Faten saw again the face in the mirror. She shook her head and reprimanded herself. "Look at you, in your late thirties, a widow with two children and you're thinking of your beauty." Why, she wondered, had her parents named her Faten, after the actress Faten Hamama? Surely they hadn't wished her to become an actress—what a disgrace that would be. It was the word *Hamama* that always intrigued her: a strange name meaning a dove. She imagined a white dove flying into the clouds, losing its outline.

She finished wrapping the scarf over her hair, now streaked with a few lines of gray. She had to hurry and get to Mr. Nicholas's and Madame Kristine's. Since she was running late, she hoped they would have nothing unexpected for her. So strange they had been. That first time she went, Madame Kristine made her sit down and insisted on giving her a cup of tea, then she had gone on and on in her bit of broken Arabic about how they never had a maid or a cook and they wanted her to be happy and to tell them about whatever she needed. She smiled, trying to grasp what she could of the words. Then they started leaving dishes in the sink, which she had to wash before she could cook. And sometimes she was asked to do the laundry. Last week, she spent the whole day there cooking phyllo, grape leaves, tahini, macaroni, and more because they were having a party.

Faten went back to the kitchen, put the money in her purse, then checked the list of food she was making for them. Fava beans—she would have to pick those up on the way there at one of the kiosks then spice them at the house.

She folded the list and placed it in her pocket. Then she walked to the door and picked up the two shopping bags of food she had bought that morning. She stepped out of the apartment, put one of the bags down, and pulled the door shut, turning the knob to make sure it had locked behind her.

When she arrived, Madame Kristine opened the door with a large smile. She ushered Faten into the kitchen and chatted as she watched her set out the food. Then she walked over to the sink and opened the cabinet underneath it. She smiled, pointed at a plastic tub filled with an assortment of dirty plates and glasses, and said, "Thank you, party food was good." Faten stared at the pile. No one had bothered to rinse the dishes, so there were particles of food and smudges from people scooping with their bread. She looked up at Madame Kristine whose smile had become engraved. Faten nodded, and the woman left the kitchen.

Faten closed the cabinet door and began cooking. She could hear music from the living room, something loud with lots of strings. It moved quickly, and she wondered how anyone could make out the words. She cooked silently, trying to get everything on the stove at once. Only the beans were left, but she didn't feel like making them. So often, the cumin and coriander with the garlic would fill her nostrils, and she would have to stir or beat something hard to keep the images from taking shape.

As she mixed the spices in, she again remembered the day her husband died. The children had been particularly energetic, and it took a long time to get them to fall asleep. Finally, she had been able to make herself a cup of tea and sit on the balcony, looking over the rooftops—so many with makeshift apartments where families made a home. The smell of manure and slaughtered goats reached her from the camel market. Some people came with their camels from the Sudan hoping to sell them; others sold goats and sheep that they slaughtered right there. The place had become a tourist attraction, and officials were talking about charging an entry fee. Such things the foreigners wanted to see. When she told one of the couples she was working for that she lived in Imbaba, they had said, "Oh, the camel market." "No camel," she answered and went into the kitchen.

Her memory continued. She had finished drinking her tea on the balcony. It was getting late. Her husband was still not home, and she decided to go to sleep. When he returned, she was already in the midst of a dream. She never remembered what that dream had been, but it was something urgent and immediate that he woke her from. He shook her awake and said, "Woman, it's not even midnight. What are you doing sleeping? Come on, get up and make me some food." So she had heaved her body out of bed and gone to the kitchen. He insisted she heat up some fava beans and add the cheese and *basterma* meat he had bought. They sat at the table together because he wanted her to stay with him. He started eating and asking about the children. At the third or fourth bite, he brought his right hand to his left arm and started rubbing it. "My arm, Faten, my arm hurts," he said. As she went to him, his head fell onto his shoulder, and that was all.

Faten shook herself a little to come out of the memory. She was looking for a bowl to put the beans in but couldn't find one. Then she remembered the dishes. She opened the cabinet and saw several dirty bowls. She stared, and her shoulders rose with one heavy breath. Then she lifted the tub of dishes, placed it by the sink, and began to scrub.

The Top

LIGHT FILTERED THROUGH the thin slats of the closed window blind, creating a pattern of long, narrow stairs on the opposite wall. Shoukry stared at it as he sat at the round linoleum-topped kitchen table waiting for his wife to bring him a cup of coffee and some toast. The pattern shifted with the direction of the light until it started to fade and his eyes lost its movement.

Walking quickly toward him, his wife set down the demitasse of Arabic coffee and a plate with two pieces of toast sliding back and forth precariously. "Here," she said, barely parting her lips. Before he could ask about butter, she had bustled away. He sipped the coffee and ate the toast as it was, occasionally glancing up at the wall to see if the pattern might return in a different form.

"I have to go in early today," she said, grabbing her pocketbook and sweater. "If you come home before me, there is hamburger in the refrigerator. You can put it in the oven."

"Amira, what about Amira?" he asked.

"She has a meeting after school."

~

The desk in his office in Egypt had been very large. Even if he bent forward and stretched his arms to either side as far as he could, feeling the tendons on the inside of his elbows pull and strain, his fingertips would barely grip the edges. The desk chair was cushioned, and it twirled around. The men who came to see him sat on a straight-backed hard wooden chair. They would lean forward, their hands vigorously explaining their request. He would relax, fit his body into the chair's contoured shape and let it rock a little with his movements. Never would he move his body closer to the man in front of him. Even when shaking hands, he would stand upright behind his desk, so the other man had to bend forward to reach his hand. It was this precision of his movements, he believed, that had earned him the respect of his colleagues and the men who came to see him. That was why he was called Ustaz and Pasha.

He was in charge of issuing permits for the construction of new apartment buildings or adding more floors to old ones. With the population growing so fast and so many enterprising young men eager to gain some of the profit, his office had a long list of appointments that stretched six months ahead. About once every month, he would refuse to give a permit because the new government building codes had not been followed. The rest of the time, he might overlook certain discrepancies if he were offered some compensation in return. He would debate with the man across from him that the codes were really too strict given the rising cost of building materials. In his mind, he justified his actions by convincing himself that he was adhering to a set of revised codes based on his own better judgment. He thoroughly enjoyed discussing the building projects with the builders and felt himself to be an expert, often giving advice on the drawings laid out for him.

❧

"And why not? Are we less than anyone?"

"I said no. Our lives here are good and we will stay here."

"Why don't you look around you? Everyone wants to leave this country and its misery."

"What misery? I've reached a high position in my work. And here we are living in an apartment that is beautiful and large. What more do you want?"

"I want what all people want. I want a house for myself with a garden and a fancy car. I want to go out to enjoy myself and to see the world. I want my freedom, not this society that suffocates our desires."

"The world is in your home in front of you, your husband and your daughter. We are your world."

"You're just afraid. A coward."

"That's enough. You've given me a headache."

"Look at my sister's husband. He doesn't even have a college degree like you. And they've only been in America for six months, and now they have a house and a car. Think. You, with your college degree and your experience, how far you can go in America! This is a country that gives opportunities that one can't imagine."

"Enough. Enough. Just what do you want from me?"

"At least think about it, Shoukry. Lots of people are emigrating now, especially after the '67 war. And all of them, in a short while, achieve a high position, and they have things we can never reach here even if we work till we die. This country is closed. Abd el Nasser doesn't want to let anything in. And he's fighting everyone's battles. Everything that is of worth in the country he lets go. There's no future here."

"Let's thank God for what we have and not look too far. My work is good. There is no need."

"If we were going to America, think how people would see you. They would look at you as if you were a king. This America is heaven."

"All right. All right."

"Will you think about it?"

"Yes. Yes."

"Why don't you get the application tomorrow from the embassy? We can just look at it. We won't lose anything."

~

Fifth floor, please.

Ninth floor, please.

Tenth floor.

Top floor, please.
Good morning, Sir.
Good afternoon, Miss.
How are you today, Shoukry, the fifteenth floor.

LIKE A CONTINUOUS CIRCLE but flat, never curving out, no interior space inside the lines. Confined in this elevator, pushing buttons, taking people up, down. The high metal stool to lean against, occasionally rest the weight of the body, back stiff, supported by a thin slip of air. Surrounded by tongues inside lips dancing out sounds that merged into a flat rhythm, repetition of *th*. Alone, pressing tongue between teeth into a wind-blown whistle.

And his wife, *his* wife. She didn't even have a college degree. Now working in an office with her own desk. Thinking she's somebody. Lying, lying to everyone. Making it all up. Filling out the application with her sister at her shoulder instructing. Say you graduated from Cairo University. Tell them you worked at the National Egyptian Insurance Company. They won't know. They can't check. Put an x next to filing. It's easy, just putting things in order by letter. You'll get the job.

Interviews. Straining to determine when the word ends and another begins. The sentence stopping. His turn to speak. Lips in jigsaw pieces to form the shape for the word to pull it out.

Then she says, "I got you a job. You'll be in charge. Practically your own boss."

❧

"Where's Amira?"

"A friend picked her up early this morning. She's going on a weekend ski trip with her school."

"And why wasn't I told? Don't you need my permission? I'm her father."

"I signed the permission slip for her. You were asleep and she had to take it in that day."

“And did you find out anything about this trip? Are there boys going too? Don’t you think about your daughter’s reputation? You want her to ruin herself?”

“Oh Shoukry, calm down. It’s a school trip. Don’t make a fuss over nothing.”

❧

In the elevator, sometimes, the smell of flour, bread, the baking of crust, would whisper through his nose. He’d twirl his tongue around the crevices of his mouth searching for the taste of that holy bread, the *orban* he ate as a child. Going to church with his parents in Coptic Cairo, walking through the cobblestone alleyways to the Hanging Church where his father was a chanter. At the end of the liturgy, the smell of incense swung from the priest’s gold chalice as he walked down the aisles between the rows of pews. The smoke would flood Shoukry’s nostrils and mix with the floury smell of the *orban* just being brought out.

On the way home from church, women placed themselves throughout the alleyway with baskets of holy bread for sale. Dressed in sheer layers of black that became opaque, each one enticed him with her song. He would beg his mother for a piaster to buy his very own *orban*, round and whole with the pattern of crosses engraved in its center, instead of just that small bite the priest handed out. Only on holidays would she give him the piaster, and he would eat the bread slowly and possessively, trying to redesign the crosses with each bit that he tore off to put in his mouth.

But in the elevator this craving came over him like a shadow until he was sure that if he could only trail the smell he would find the *orban*. Sometimes when the elevator door opened, he would stick out his face and sniff, trying to catch the direction of it. But people would rush in too quickly and he would lose its trace. Once, he was concentrating so hard, the door almost closed on his nose, and he heard the echo of laughter around him. Still, he would creep his tongue over his lips in hopes of catching a hint of its taste.

"Shoukry, you look a little tired. Why don't you go home early today?"

The house was quiet. For a while, he sat on the sofa and waited for his wife to return. When he got hungry, he went to the refrigerator. Leaning against the door, he looked inside. A little milk on the top shelf, an almost empty jar of mayonnaise in the door and, on the middle shelf, an eggplant. It had a long neck then it curved out, smooth and round. All of it was a deep layered shade of purple. "Too big to make stuffed eggplant," he thought. Just then he heard the key in the lock and quickly closed the refrigerator door and returned to the sofa.

His wife and daughter entered with bags of groceries. He could see that his wife had a beaming smile on her face.

"When will you start?" he overheard his daughter asking.

"In two weeks. I'll be the supervisor of my own department, and I'm going to have my own office. They're giving me a very good raise."

His wife turned to him as she put the last of the groceries away. "Well, Shoukry, aren't you glad? I got promoted today."

In the dream, he was a young boy just coming out of the church. The sun was hazy that day, relieving the usual heavy heat of the summer months. It must have been after his father died since his mother was wearing black. She was talking to one of his aunts, and they walked together ahead of him. While kicking a small stone and following its path, he spotted the round worn piaster. Just as he picked it up, he saw a woman selling the bread and went toward her, stretching out his hand with the coin. Smiling, the woman handed him the bread and spoke some words of blessing. He heard his mother calling and began to run. While running, he looked down to see the *orban*, but his hands clutched only air. He woke with a small scream stuck in his throat. Still expecting to see the bread, he looked but found nothing except his fingers in the same position as in the dream.

~

It was after having the dream that it became difficult for him to press the elevator buttons with his right hand. He would reach for them, but his fingers refused to separate, and his arm wanted to remain secured to his side. Now he had to turn his body slightly sideways so he could press with his left hand.

"How are you feeling, Shoukry? Maybe you should see a doctor. You don't look too well."

People's stares began to bother him, and sometimes he would begin to explain about the craving, about how the *orban* had disappeared. But before he could seek out all the words, the person would get off the elevator, leaving his words half-formed.

~

One day, another craving came over him. Strong and overpowering like the smell of vinegar, the taste of *koshari* settled on his lips. His mother would make it during Lent when they could only eat what didn't come from an animal. Rice, lentils, and pasta with a few chickpeas and the spiced, almost tart tomato sauce, but most of all the thin, crisp-fried onions he always demanded more of. The taste kept scratching at his mouth until he almost went frantic stretching his tongue for it.

It had to be here, somewhere close. If only he could get out of the elevator, he would find it.

The beeps calling the elevator down stung at his ears, but he kept going up, up to the very top where the tourists went, in one movement that felt like could be flying, until finally the elevator stopping flat with a drop. He put the key in to keep the door open and stepped out.

The sun's brightness flooded his eyes and he squinted sharply to be able to see. A gust of wind came around him, and he smelled dust and heat, but no *koshari*. He sniffed harder, but the smell was gone. He walked to the railing and looked over the Boston skyline, buildings sprouting out of the ground as if they were ancient trees.

He wondered at the elevators in these buildings, if all of them had someone like him who pressed their buttons and ran them through the length of the day. His eyes focused again on the breadth of the landscape, and he began to walk around, keeping his head turned to see the city revolving.

When he had made a full circle and returned to his original spot by the railing, he could hear buzzing and hard pounding coming up from the elevator. The banging increased in his ears. There was the elevator standing with its door open. He stared at it then looked around and saw the neon EXIT sign next to it. He opened the door and began to descend the stairs. His feet were sluggish, but as the spiral continued, he gained speed and a rhythm guided his feet down till it became a repetitive tapping. He held the railing with his left hand and felt the smoothness of it slide against his palm. Soon there was only a swirl of white from the walls and the tapping as he wound around, unhinged, from the ground all the way down.

A large crowd of people had gathered, including at least two groups of tourists. His head was still going around, and it was difficult to keep his feet still once he was standing in one spot. He saw a man hurrying toward him, his face red and his arms gesticulating wildly. He must calm him down, he thought.

"It's all right, Mahmoud. Don't worry. I'll put the paperwork through, and you'll be able to build those apartments in no time. Just be a little patient. There's no need . . ."

But the man was now shaking him and screaming, "You bastard, you foreign idiot! What do you think you're doing? Going up there for a breath of fresh air! Where the hell is the elevator? What do you think this is, an amusement park?"

Shoukry tried to understand, to answer him, until a woman came up and began to pull the man back.

"Stop shaking him," she said, "Can't you see he's crazy? He's not even speaking English."

Shifting Spaces: 1990–1993

WHEN WE WERE LIVING IN EGYPT the last time, in the early 1990s, we used to walk almost everywhere. We often went to Alfa Market to do our grocery shopping. Alfa Market was a twenty-minute walk away from our Garden City flat, going by Kasr el Aini Hospital, a complex of orange bricks and white cement, where my cousin Mona did her residency. We had gone to visit her one day, our shocked expressions hidden as we watched the patients walking up and down the hallways with no supervision. One man, his head round and balding, wearing a green dressing gown, browsed through a tray of medication. We peeked into the rooms to see patients sitting on the floor sharing the evening meal brought by relatives.

A trespasser coming to ogle the natives. No clear distinctions: *Egyptian—Not Egyptian.* Fear chiming through my body. Safety? By conjuring up those aseptically clean hospitals in the United States, strict regulations. Embracing home. Distancing home.

After the hospital, we pass the Manial Palace, an assortment of villas including King Farouk's hunting lodge. Now a modern five-star hotel where I can run from the pollution and the clothing restrictions—no shorts, nothing sleeveless, and the sun's heat pouring sweat down your back. Could I wear a galabeya, loose to my ankles, designed in flowers, the traditional dress now associated with being lower-class? I wasn't raised into the ease of wearing one. I'd feel disjointed maneuvering through the streets in it.

The Manial Palace Hotel with palm trees caressing a round pool. For forty pounds: spend the day with buffet lunch stretching across four long tables, wearing your bathing suit. No veiled women swimming, long skirts twining their bodies. My body exposed in their stare—the family at the Marsa Matruh beach whispered as I quickly slipped on a loose dress after swimming. Is this my Americanness: the heavy breath of balancing rocks?

An oasis with an arranged jungle of plants cleaning the air so you could forget about coughing up black phlegm, relax on lounge chairs, breathe easily. A space to be with other expatriates, as if I were American.

~

But in other places, so oddly disjointed. Social gatherings discussing the peculiarities of Egypt and Egyptians, techniques for survival. An American woman living alone complains how fruit and vegetable merchants give her the worst produce when she requests only a quarter of a kilo.

I explain: they don't like to sell less than a kilo. Egyptians live in large households, few people buy so little. Perhaps establish a relationship with a particular merchant.

Her response: a defiant toss of the head. An assertion she has a right to buy as little as she likes.

Then put up with the spoiled produce! But I keep quiet.

Feel the edges of space pressing me.

Not a spokesperson for Egyptian culture. So much I don't know but learning from a different location—an Egyptian, not a foreigner memorizing her lessons. Yet, conversations place me on the dissecting table except, twenty-five years in America, allow my Egyptianness to be overlooked.

MAUREEN'S PARTIES on the roof of her AUC apartment downtown. Overlooking the entire city, pattern of rooftops, rising and falling. The citadel in the distance lit up. The tallest building with the neon *Sport Cola* sign. Closer, a makeshift home on top of a roof, two men talking, a duck, a cat. The city revolving, my arms wide to embrace it.

Looking out over the roofs, Barbara says, "Cairo is just like a big village."

Jolted back.

To travel this distance, be here, live, and still see only what you imagined before you came?

rooftops clamoring for space
night air seeps through a maze
I'm tucked into a refrain of images

~

After the Manial Palace, we walk over the Giza bridge. Sometimes in the evening, a bride and groom stop to have their picture taken under a halo of moonlight. The Nile laid out behind them, red and yellow feluccas drifting open sails toward the wind, and the Meridian and Gezira Sheraton hotels creating a landscape of lights over the water.

So many weddings—Adham, Mira, Ashraf. After her wedding, my cousin Mira, who was moving to Asyut with her husband, stood in the bedroom trying to squeeze her twenty pairs of pants, ten belts, thirty scarves, fifteen fancy dresses, along with shoes, skirts and shirts, into two suitcases. I was called upon for American ingenuity, made decisions, assured her Asyut was only an hour flight; she could get the rest later.

My Aunt Amal's apartment in Maadi, up a half-circle of gray cement stairs, was small for her husband, herself, and three daughters: two bedrooms, a dining room, small kitchen, bathroom, and a tiny living room like an entranceway where we usually sat. But the space left behind when I immigrated in 1969 was still there. I neither had to be invited nor ask to step back into it. Even in the middle of summer, heat penetrating the walls, one tiny window in the room, I stayed for hours, forgetting the time.

WHEN MIRA CALLED to tell us that her father, only in his fifties, had died suddenly of a heart attack, my breath stalled. I looked at my husband, knew he was remembering Christmas at St. Mary's Church, walking through a maze of cobblestone streets in Old Cairo, where my uncle was a chanter. He was a lawyer by profession but the music of the church was his true passion. I was sitting with my Aunt Amal and her daughters. My husband had to sit on the other side with the men. In the middle of the liturgy, my uncle walked back, took my husband's arm and led him to the front, making a place for him with the other chanters, wearing their white robes with red sashes and gold crosses. He was the tallest among them, but he hummed in the language still new to him as my uncle smiled proudly.

At my aunt's house after the funeral, we felt awkward, not knowing what to say, how to react.

He always greeted us wearing light blue pajamas or undershirt, at home sitting in his chair. With family, there was no embarrassment. How formal: his picture framed in the dining room, wearing his lawyer's suit.

We didn't know what to bring so we brought oranges and peanuts. Emad and Mira and her sister, Manal, laughed at the strange offering and we all stood in the kitchen eating, still able to smile a little.

They pressed clay
Shaped space.

Once over the bridge there is the tall building, plants draping its entrance. The Omam restaurants on the top floor—Japanese, Indian, Italian, Moroccan. Luxuriously decorated and expensive by typical Egyptian standards, a hundred pounds for a meal for two. But we had gone there several times. Our AUC salaries made that possible. Left behind our part-time jobs in Rhode Island, living paycheck to paycheck, gathering our change at the end of the month to buy Chinese food. Arriving in Egypt, we became wealthy.

OUR FIRST WEEK IN EGYPT, a friend took us out. As we walked in the upper-class suburb of Mohandessein, a young beggar girl began to follow, trailing my dress (bought in America, orange and green, circles and triangles). Ignore her. Persisted at the edge of my dress, not even asking for money, looking up: as if I were some kind of princess.

Our friend managed to make the girl go away. The sidewalk moving. I looked ahead wishing *to twirl around, catch the girl in my arms, pirouette the air.* Only to descend, and the longing of her vision persists, my creation, indelible.

IN OUR AUC GARDEN CITY FLAT, a plumber came to fix something and brought his son. The young boy, six or seven, stood, transfixed in the living room staring at us. Our friends Maggie and Ayman and their daughter, Tia, were there. We told the boy to follow his father, but he wouldn't budge. Through his eyes, the apartment, magic carpets to ride, bouncing on clouds. We had created the moment of his poverty.

Space crowded
tapestries, rugs, vases piling my mummified corpse

A woman asks where I work.
"I teach at the American University in Cairo."
Replies, "You're not really living in Egypt."

WHERE was I? Egyptian colleagues. Egyptian students.

AUC in the middle of Tahrir Square, originally one of Khedive Ismail's palaces with delicately carved mashrabiyya windows. The center of the city. The most prestigious university in the country. Job ads specify a preference for AUC graduates. But the first time I step on campus with its manicured lawns, tennis courts, and courtyards with fountains, I wonder if I'm still in America. The students in European clothes, young women wearing miniskirts, young men on a fashion runway in their jeans. I puzzled at how they got through the city streets dressed like that.

Drivers bring them to school, pick them up at the end of the day. Surveying the city from the back window of a car, they don't feel the air tightening around their bodies as they maneuver through the overcrowded city. Where was I, participating in this space of Western images, gaining respect because I had lived in America?

~

Alfa Market was one flight up in the tall building. A new supermarket like Sunny's and Tamco's. Not a Super Stop & Shop but nevertheless with shopping carts and aisles.

On one side, toys and housewares. Barbie dolls dominating, prices starting at a hundred pounds. Contained in sparkling spaces, an array of paraphernalia.

Young men from Upper Egypt, military duty, holding guns and standing guard in front of embassies, cultural centers. Ten-pound monthly salary. Sometimes clicking the safety at a passing foreigner.

In the food section, products multiplied: Oreo cookies, pancake mix, corn flakes, saltine crackers. I had vowed never to buy any of them but when I got pregnant I was grateful for the saltine crackers.

Alfa Market still sold the olives, feta cheese, and pickles, but instead of being piled in cylinder containers or tucked behind the counter, they were displayed behind the glass case, neatly arranged into patterns of colors delicately sparkling. It was still wise to give the man who sliced your cheese a tip, but he had learned to subdue the sense of urgency.

One day I saw a woman, heels and tailored skirt, with her servant trailing in a dark galabeya, carrying a child, pushing the cart. Where was I? The space between them. *The young girl who took care of me when I was a child—I cried, not understanding why she couldn't come to Alexandria on vacation with us.*

Who would I have been if I had stayed?

So oddly matched these products. *Could I take a box of pancake mix for my partner, dance a waltz to drum beats, an olive at the tip of my tongue?*

ൾ

Back into the street with our shopping bags, over the bridge trembling with our footsteps. My husband's brown complexion and features identified as Egyptian—"a weight lifted off my back"—not a black male in the suburbs followed by police cars. Nothing to distinguish him. I look like so many other Egyptians. *Horns improvise a discordant melody as we walk, mirage images in a neon lit landscape.*

JACK MARSHALL

Deal

These vast lawns landscaped for show
and seclusion along this prime stretch
of South Jersey Shore, at night elegantly
lit by tall, tapering swan-necked streetlamps;
these grand gingerbread houses are rumored
paid for with coin bags full of slot-machine quarters—skimmed
cream from new casinos, Atlantic
City just down the boardwalk.
Glass-walled, bubbled-roofed, up go
honeywood homes built big as luxury
liners. From their windows, owners can see
their ships carrying their cargoes in heavily
insured, cubed containers inching the horizon.
On this blue-chip shore front
colonized by new-rich, first-generation Syrians
whose parents were forties welfare-recipient
immigrants in Eastern and Bay Parkways, Brooklyn,
my widowed mother—uprooted from living more than fifty years
across the street from her once-handsome, proud brother
now a paranoid hermit—
my mother, now more than ever through cataract-clouded
eyes unimpressed by the view, sneers, "Big
deal!"

Prolonging my yearly visit from summer's magical daylight savings into suspiring fall's magically reversed standard
time, I need to make the quick miracle
drug, which money is,
and have taken a job working for a scowling
boss who wears an embroidered yarmulke on his head
to mark his humble place beneath the heel of the most high
Allah Elohim. Like Him owner of a time corporation,
he sells shiny jeweled pieces of sun
that tarnish by the gross on wrist and throat and drives
his Russian- and Spanish-speaking women clock pinchers
numb.
Fingers, having to set, stiffen
around a moment, the very heart of time, stalled, then drive
themselves faster in the cold, bleak,
thirty-thousand square-feet shed—stone floor, steel roof—just to
keep from freezing; and even if there were any
heat, it would only rise to the rafters anyway.
Among dials gone dead and quietly wild—
cat pulsing batteries', modules', quartz crystals'
brief lifetimes running down all
around us, he tells me he believes in a life
after death, that his piety ensures
a place there for him. God is his good-
luck charm, long-term banker, and hustling
export agent in Hong Kong, guarantor of never-ending
credit. It is for more of this
each night on the chartered bus home he prays,
then with his pals plays poker with renewed brio.

In my mother's small three-room apartment,
her illegal immigrant Haitian nursemaid,
Carmella, having read her Bible fanatically
squealed for the blood of a blond

masked wrestler on the all-day TV, chirps her Creole pidgin
and asks me how she can record a message on the same tape
her mother and three children have sent from Port-au-Prince.
She has not seen them in over a year.
Lying on her stomach on the bedroom floor, she plays
the tape over and over, legs lolling side
to side, back and forth, listening
to them in turn speak, in unison sing to her as she
sings along. Behind a shaky, arthritic hand, my mother
jeers, "*Mittle shwayt keleb*"—Arabic
for "Like a bunch of dogs"—she calls
children calling their mother, a mother calling her child-
like daughter herself a mother. I too must call
up hand-signed pidginese to answer,
"No record *pas que* tape erase," to which she nods
that helpless, uncomprehending smile,
as when my mother in her own broken
but not inaccurate English tells her
the brand name of the sugar substitute
she wants from the grocer, Sweet 'n' Rough.
After the high-pitched, tropical-plumed
chant of her children's voices, I hear
Carmella's mother repeat a gruff, cautionary
"*Mal . . . mal . . .*" and wonder
what about, and watch her eyes
widen, brow wrinkle, with rapt attention.

Living this past year with my mother, she's given her
each morning the prescribed
injection of twenty units of insulin for her diabetes
and does again: slow swab, quick shot in the thigh,
Mom curses, Carmella gives her laugh,
as when she holds out one
each of the five kinds of pills—each

a different color—with a glass of water
Mom must take before bed; and though she's full
of excuses as I was as a boy,
there's Carmella, nursemaid monitor
of the medicine cup, both hands held out.
Later from my room I hear
Mom scold and tease, and Carmella's mischievous
laugh, and it somehow pleases
and saddens me at once to imagine
this going on before I arrived, wondering
how long it will continue after I leave.

G–D

Is how we unspelled it back then, taboo—
Loaded, defused for secular use,
While the rabbis, all beard and black cloth, hovered

Overheard, gall-breathed, stick-wielding
Watchdogs shadowing the pages we scrawled on
Omitting the one—

Forbidden o—
Void vowel, hollow
Between consonantal poles, short—

Circuiting powers of the unutterable
Name the eye does not reach and words turn back from

Together with the mind.

—

Those raised, ready sticks—broad as two-by-fours—
Pried from the backs of hardwood chairs, struck
Open palms, clenched fists, deep stinging

Whacks if you lost your place in the reading of the sacred text.
One summer day, dodging a random blow, a headstrong boy
Leaped out of the classroom window to the ground

Two floors below, picked himself up with a curse
We'd utter only under our breath

And hobbled off, never to return.

—

Ancestral, perennial, penitential,
Bred-in-the-blood diet
Of denials, feeding

On exile's endless
Minus sign, subtraction
Of all feeling but the mute

Recognition: before the first step is taken,
The end is reached; before the tongue moves,

Speech is finished.

—

I can even now hardly bring myself
To spell it whole, so fiercely
Did those scowling fanatics guard against the invisible

From taking form.

—

Ha-shem, we said in Hebrew, meaning the Holy Name.
But in English the veiled vacancy more visibly
Renders the withheld power of what is not there.

Chaos—down to the microscopic
Mess of atomic elements and molecular mayhem—is ordered
Creation compared to that minuscule black

Slot housing wormhole loops and branches bridging
Worlds lost to us down micro-networks of space and time,
As many as there are

Motions, motion creating forms, forms
In motion, constantly
Deforming, reforming

Singularities just below a horizon
All depth but not yet
Given birth to a wealth of light.

—

What might you have said
Had you been allowed to
Speak? What might you have thought

Had you been allowed to think?
And, forgetting what you were supposed to
Know, what knowledge might not flow

And, like all pleasure and science that heals, fly
In the face of Tables of the Law?

—

Unapprehensible, unapproachable
Creator of the universe permanently

Out of the galactic lariat
Loop that filling in would cinch and knot: the nothing-
If-not-worlds-wanton

Original ovum
Circled by astral tadpoles
Drilling to the core . . .

Though no Rimbaud, this I know:
O echoes,
Enlarging space, its mother—

Moaning *A* beginning to brim
Molecular messengers already
Full-grown bodies on the nuclear lattice . . .

Hung by a thread, the same moment
Opening them to the tame household deities
Opens to the whirlwind

Gods that have no name.

Arabian Nights

These two not breathing now once lived
in a house that has no number anymore,

no window looking out on an avenue
only a window can look steadily on . . . and then,

with clarity, on mostly confusion. No more
third-floor walk-up bricked-in now

above the Mobil gas station, below a neon Pegasus
riding thousands of nights into an afterlife for old autos.

In this photo they smile so easefully
from so far, the past seems

not to have happened yet. So long
ago, before I was born—I can hardly believe

how beautiful they are! Clear
looks in their eyes I keep

looking into and through, I follow
my mother's across in steerage so close to hullside,

she said, you could hear a shark, scavenging for garbage,
being ground up in the propeller;

my father's I follow through sweeping dust
out of piled Persian rugs carpeting the enchanted

lace-curtained clip joints of Fifth Avenue.
His faded immigration photo

showed a swarthy young Arab with a wary look.
This studio pose I've found

shows them in a regal calm I never saw, lost
how or when I hardly have a clue, I wonder,

have their still proud, unruffled foreheads,
his wavy pompadour, her petal-lipped mouth, been retouched?

From his right hand tucked suavely in hip pocket
a black silk strip unrolls

down his rented tux, a yard, of
good luck he'll use up

just in staying alive. In her arms she holds
a dozen large calla lilies in full bloom.

KHALED MATTAWA

Selections from the Ibn Hazm Epistolary

From Cordoba

God made souls in the shapes of spheres then cut them into halves. And when God made the body he placed only half of a sphere within it. That is why we are born without speech, weak and defenseless. And that is why a child is curious, attaching itself to all that may fill the gap in its chest. In adulthood, the person that finds the other containing the other half of his soul develops an attachment based on that old splitting occasion.

Of course, people's reactions to this encounter depend on the sensitivity of their natures. Some are puzzled, some ecstatically joyous, some horrified, but all are deeply moved by it at the expense of everything else.

Thus love is a welding of the shattered beings of this creation. So tell your friends that the catalyst for love burns and becomes part of its ruins. And in closing remember that the secret of bliss is not effusion, but a series of contacts and departures.

From Cordoba

You look at grains of iron on a flat surface, and they are like a tribe that has found its farming grounds and pasture and settled. However, once you bring a piece of magnet near them, you can easily move them from one side of the earth to the other. The lover who's found his beloved is all packed like those grains under the draw of the magnet, enclosed onto themselves. He is not a person, but a herd of passions guided by the impulse that momentarily triumphs over others. All is urgent, the moments of stasis and waiting are as desperate as the movements themselves.

It is difficult to know whether we enjoy this state or not, and we can never answer such a question. We are elated and we are pained because we are in the grasp of the terrible forces that brought this world into existence. The struggle of love is thus a confrontation with the question whether it is better to live or not to have been born into this mortal world in the first place. Only those among us who have truly lived and loved know that there is no answer to that question, and they know that our inhaling and exhaling are the echoes of our wavering between these two answers.

From Cordoba

The soul too in this world of clay becomes earthbound. If it finds difficulty letting go, it may not enter love. And then if it does enter, what will it find? Love is not a fall, it is a leap. If you feel you're falling despite yourself, you are falling in all the senses of the word. Rather you should feel as if letting go, but toward a destination. Those who love quickly are falling into blindness. They can easily gather themselves because all they held within them was hollowness. They write callused poetry. They address their amours with battered words.

Then there are those who claim to love more than one lover. They are tearing themselves up in order to reach their various destinations, their concurrent loves an ongoing process of scarring, their souls assemblages of torn parts. I remember visiting the palace of my friend the Prince of Seville. In one room that the prince decorated with thousands of mirrors facing each other in every possible manner, I remember seeing my image multiplied a thousandfold. Every mirror I stared at reflected itself on other mirrors. And since the room was full of images multiplied a hundred times, I saw myself divided in my peripheral vision. I could not see a straight image of myself unless I brought my eyes so close to one of these mirrors that I was almost blinded by the strain of my effort. This is the state of the lover of many loves.

From Granada

All fictions lose their story lines, all ruses come to an end. All break-offs are a construct of hate. Thinking bewilders here, the disaster reaches its ripening. What did she want, what will he approve of. No change can change things. No catalysts. The chests of hope depleted. We took our love into a corner, as if embarrassed by our intimacy, as if we thought no one would believe us. Why did their presence disturb us so. We've left each other with ruins and with them we are building labyrinths.

From Jativa

If the lover cannot dissuade the beloved, if the thought of her only brings fatigue, then let him resolve on oblivion. Let him examine his soul, and consider the misery and privation it is suffering, let him labor to satisfy his desire in whatever manner he can.

I have said before that each one of us contained one of two halves of a soul. But to think that one is the lesser of the two halves is love too. To think of the discovery of flaws one did not know one had, the constant deferral to the loved one, the avoidance of conflict, the surrender, to think these are dishonor is wrong. To love is also to ask if one is worthy of love. On the other hand, if one thinks that he or she is the better of the two halves of the soul, it cannot be love he is feeling.

From Cordoba

Nothing in the world matches two lovers who have escaped intruders and gossips, and who have ceased to be apart from each other, who were saved from ennui, saved from enmity, who were compatible in manners, and who have matched each other's love, and whom God has offered sustenance, good work, and a quiet peaceful era, and whose union is in accord with God's pleasures, and whose friendship lasts until that drowning no one will escape. This is a gift few attain, and a need not found by all its seekers, a state that overcomes the passing of youth and the loss of kin. I have known a couple that has possessed all this, and yet on whom no sun rose without a quarrel. But both were stamped unto each other. One day one is the boiling ore and the other is the clay into which it is poured, no drop ever wasted. Love is then a root of pity and a branch of it as well, and thus must be unperturbed by motives and measurings.

And that is my wish to you. I am afraid our correspondence may not go on for long. I've heard that a large army has arrived at Tarifa and is on its way to our city. I am certain we cannot fight them off.

From Almeria

Fidelity is to keep her secrets, her public and private, large and small actions should all be important to you. You should conceal her bad points, cover her faults, announce her best aspects, see her actions in the best light, trust her desires, and help her fulfill them. When she is excited you should not be languid, when she is weary, you should not be imposing. Fidelity demands that we prefer charity to justice, no conditions imposed, no goals established.

From Almeria

The world oppressing you and the love that spurns you. To the first you must be harder than iron, sharper than swords, not answering to what would lower you, never assisting in your own cowering. In the second, you must be softer than cotton pressed until nothing of you seems to remain. Delve into humility. Bend and soften with your tongue words and sighs enlarging the rage directed against you so that you can quell it. Echo pity when it rises, or when whispered, into deeper resonance and meaning. Lend art to what was being shaped, firm up and wall all that is about to seep or scatter.

Love is not of this world. Otherwise why would we seek it. Do not be your old self. Make a better self to live in. Even seducers who shatter us with their betrayals, the rage they boil in us, is really a measure of our hope. When seducers flee from the face of the earth, consider the earth and all its inhabitants dead. And love is dead too when there is no rage. In the beginning of love, quarrels are liquid and warm like blood. They are signs of health. When they are cold and bitter, they are calculations, the applying of oil or grease to rusty hinges, a way to ease a door into opening for love to depart.

From Valencia

There is a breaking off when the beloved begins to treat the lover harshly inching away in favor of another fancy or when tediousness sticks to his sides he sees death before him when he utters his desire for parting he gulps the choking draughts of despair. Look at those two, the man breaks off talking, the woman off in silence. If they have no lovers to run to they walk into failure tediousness strapped to their sides they park their cars, open the doors they turn on the switch their houses blazing with emptiness.

From Cordoba

After many weeks of resisting the impulse, I finally visited the ruins of our home in Balat al-Maghith. I did not go earlier because I could not bear recalling the days that passed in that distant mansion, the joys I knew there, the months of my young years I spent with beautiful girls, whose company could immediately fire the most sedate of men, and soften the heart of the most ardent. Walking around it, I imagined those women now lying beneath the dust, or dispersed to distant parts and faraway regions, scattered by the hand of exile, torn to pieces by the claws of expatriation. I heard owls hooting and screeching overhead. Back then night followed day with bustle and movement, coming and going of countless feet. Now day follows night there, and all was forever hushed and desolate. These sad reflections filled my eyes with tears and my heart with anguish. My soul was shattered as if by a jagged rock, and the misery of my mind waxed ever greater. So I took refuge in poetry, and carefully uttered the beautiful sounds of the words.

From Fez

There are times when the lover says NEVER, thus giving up on the beloved. Of course, his longing burns him; he tosses in sleep, cannot stand the company of others, their voices like beasts howling at his ears, the songs of birds sound like cutting of stones or the hammering of nails. He seeks darkness, and when he does finally sleep, his dreams open a vista unto the rest of his life or the lives of others that he does not want to let go of. Though a rich and sustaining domain the joy and comfort these dreams give him does not spill into or affect the anguish of his waking hours. It is an exclusive domain; he has to dip into it to get its rewards. As such it embodies his wish to die and connect with the world of the hereafter. Yet at the same time it is his even breathing while asleep, ebbing and flowing to the tides of the sea of being, that release the poison from him and free him at last.

Of course, even detachment, even with acts of strong will, the lover may ignore his best judgment. One day he may find himself heading, nay pacing quickly or even running while others look away, to reunite with his beloved. Tears will fall from their cheeks and cleanse their souls. They reunite and may in fact bring their bond into a happy union. But oh that NEVER, that fire which he branded his heart with. Of its ashes, he, knowing or unknowing, builds a room that he will keep onto his own. A place he will never allow his beloved to enter. A tomb of his embittered self, which he alone can revisit. A small heart made of scabs beating alongside his heart.

D. H. MELHEM

Preface for Walt Whitman

One's-self I sing, a simple separate person,
Yet utter the word Democratic, the word En-Masse.

Poem of my life
from you I extrapolate a country
as your particles assemble and cohere
on my palette of rainbow mountains
that range a geography of waste images
to compose
a simple, separate person
who has dreamed America
a long, hard time . . .

28.

bright world in morning light
touch these blind scrawls to write
the dawn still young in me
inscribe my tongue

to ocean   rain to come
rice in the sky   wheat from the sun

like pine cones on a raging forest floor
heart   heart   break open

53.
Hudson Continuum

Man walks to the river, shouldering
a long pole. Fishing rod?

A sewage dump, you say. But I cling
here, skin against glass, window of my sight
my soul leaping like a hooked trout upstream,
gills opening their pale dawn.
I can catch the sun in my mouth that sings
ribbons of light to you
I remember the brisk river
I rode as a child
into the salt wedge of my spirit that,
wild and silvering, touched roofs,
went whooping into the air.

Look at her! Look at her!
my space thought. She is one of us—
she is none of us. She is
herself, as we are,
particles of now.

then/now
part one

IT IS WARM in Grandma's kitchen. Throughout this, her second apartment in the New World, the fiery steam heat rises with dawn and dinner from the coal-stoked furnace in the basement, but the kitchen is warmed all day by the cooking and washing. My mother, my grandmother sit at the white enamel kitchen table, kneading dough, shelling peas, measuring pine nuts into the chopped lamb and onions, soaking the crushed wheat for kibbeh, filling dozens of meat pies, stuffing chicken and squash and green peppers and eggplants, rolling stuffed grape leaves and stuffed cabbage like cigars, making dumplings for yoghurt soup among cans of sesame oil and boiled butter, peeling scores of potatoes for baked lamb necks and shanks and roast chicken, boiling rice, browning rice and onions, adding rice and tomatoes to large pots of marrow-bone vegetable soup, sitting and chatting over familiar tasks that are done must be done will be done every day without respite, my mother, my grandmother at the kitchen table with me between them on a stool in the corner where I watch and listen, tasting dough and stuffing, rewards for being content to observe and accept, with my silence, their love.

Waiting for them to acknowledge me, I absorb the strange names of relatives and friends I shall never meet, Beit this and Beit that, houses remote as the house of Atreus, incidents and characters recalled and savored as I anticipate the mention of meaningful names dropping from the flow of Arabic between them: aunts and uncles who live in the house, my mother's sisters and brothers.

And I bear witness to a daily translation of two women's lives into pots and pans, the circumscription of kitchen walls, with heat rising amid the smells and rhythm of effort, into patterns and patience, interchangeable days carried by movements worn to such precision that hand and object extend each other. How many times does the body yearn beyond clothesline and tar roof? Dough sticks to fingers; clock hands restrain.

Bookladen on Friday
we board the Franklin Avenue trolley
and pass under elevated tracks
to the library.

Inside
I sit on a child's chair
that dips into forests
and fly with griffins and gods
into the mystic certitude of words.

My mother
pensive, content
reads in the next room
where her presence beckons
mysterious volumes.

Half-filling a chair
beside her
we study
Dante's *Inferno*
I, mainly
Doré.

Along the aisle, my mother
at your skirt I feel your cool fingers
our free hands clutching
their books.

say french:
who knows what lebanese is?
or syrian? (serbian? siberian?)
protectorate is close to
protector

of course there's your culture
a tradition of teachers and doctors
an elegant descent
from Phoenicians

but
immigration officials
and neighbors
employers
perplexed by exotics
non-anglo-saxon
non-westeuropean-nontoxic
attest
the best are
types here
longer

the immigration official
said to me,
syrian?
what's
that?

(and sallow
with a menacing
guttural tongue)

your teacher accused
arabic spoken
at home:
"you have an accent"
though fearing strangers
and the foreign school
I went
showed myself
clean   educated
stopped her

still she detested
your rivalling

the girl on her lap
whose braids she caressed
before the class

people don't mean
to be mean
nevertheless
better say
french

~

Charon drives his ambulance
over the bridge
an accomplice politely checks:
    all right?

on the stretcher
you are dozing
we are beside you
as the belly-swelling tumor
draws you to sleep

    decide, said the doctor
blood count's down
falling toward five
pills can comfort repose

or send her back
    to plasma
    pretense
    and chance

O father
we cruelly chose
with kindness

in the jaws of the screaming ambulance
I dream your life down
bottom of a hospital
swallows you again
transferred from
death accelerating
in bed at home
to death more slow-paced
laboring to mount the
plastic tubes
death seeping through injections
measuring
its pills

conventschool girlmother
your smile is that anointed place
unblaming

nurses appear
like nuns

the needles in you mommy
are not nice
they've stuck you all with pins
but why? having been
a good girl

your face is littler now
than mine
I'm all grown up

you're getting small
in that white bed

the nurses come
with pills and charts
they squeeze
the red bag hanging like a plum
with stem attached to you
slow drops come through

why can't they put
the juice in quickly?
make your checks
pretty again
your arms firmly giving
a hug

face become bird
triangular
over stertorian sleep
hard rattling

i.v. and plasma
worry your dying
you must die
to your own measure

in the room
of announcing departure
eyes are cool
for the journey

clattering like dice
anticipation

fall
to the grasses
of night
where death
accepts them
in silent weeds

within your death
engendering
my life,
ghostflower, lily
will not be detached
stem, umbilical
confers light
a pale ring
of petals
drawn outward

mother
at this distance in a dim light
your picture moves
the hands clasped under your chin
unclasp toward me
and I move close to see if it is real
that gesture
if you are living in my wall
if you are a glimpse of infinite youth
before I was born

I examine the frame
touch the glass that traps only paper

the sad smile printed there
lives in my mind

where you hold me

EUGENE P. NASSAR

Summer 1958

THE HOUSE was in deep shadow though it was noon. The wind had whipped up through the elm trees, the clouds were pushing fast and wild on the black sky and Mintaha could hardly hold herself up. As she wrestled with flapping sheets and clothespins in her apron pockets she hoped the rain would not come. The neighborhood was somber though it had been in bright sunshine two hours before.

But it was much the same to Mintaha as her life has been mainly within herself; she hardly knew the neighborhood, what was East or West. She knew other things; she knew moral beauty from moral ugliness, and courage from the lack of it; she knew a hardy plant, and she knew grief as the first cousin to joy. These she knew: some of the houses of Lebanese and a few others, a few stores, a few streets, and the people who came into her house. Her house was no longer a center; the father of the house had been dead one year and the house had half-died. Mintaha knew now the emptiness of a house without its father and husband and lost heart daily, but daily she struggled to gain heart, to not withdraw from what she knew was life; from duty and family and laughter. The thunder cracked and the wind blew furiously; the sheets snapped. Mintaha turned and at her side found Shafee'a.

"The Devil has a sick stomach today, Mintaha, soon his bowels will be moving."

"Ya, Shafee'a, I thought the Devil liked the ladies. Why then does he do this?"

"Mintaha, you don't know! The Devil comes to the ladies at night; in the day our Lord punishes the devils and ladies."

"My sweetheart, the Devil I'm sure came to me last night and brought me such a dream . . ."

"Stop with your dreams! You dream too much; I have heard enough of your dreams. Have you coffee?"

"If you want my coffee you must hear my dream."

"That is a heavy price to pay. Your cucumbers are not big yet. You have a few days left before your lady friends come to visit you. *Yellah*, here is your rain."

It began to sprinkle. They left the wash and the wind and entered the house. Shafee'a had seen that Mintaha was tired and dispirited and quickly made coffee and did around the kitchen what she saw had to be done, despite her friend's protest. She had been coming to Mintaha twice a week ever since Mike died and Mintaha looked forward to the visits since Shafee'a never cried. (Shafee'a damned up and down in Arabic and in the loudest tones of her loud voice the women who came to dump their load of misery in a house which had its share.)

"Speaking of Devils, Butros was in the house at seven-thirty this morning."

"But Butros, Shafee'a, is one of the biggest saints, isn't it so?"

"Saint! Butros, may his mother never rest, is a devil with six horns; he is Luciforus's own son. Every morning, every morning before I have even my coffee he runs across the street zipping up his pants as he goes and knocks on my screen door, 'Shafee'a, Shafee'a, may your sleep have brought you health.' I say to him, 'May this day see you in the river, Butros,' but he comes in and drinks my coffee and stirs up my blood with his malicious gossip and his drooping eyes. I tell him, 'Seventy-eight years old and still a fool, Butros? Is it not time at last to be a good man?' And he tells me, may the flames take his father's son, 'I bear your words lightly Shafee'a, because I know you love me.' Love him! If it were not Friday, I would cook him in the oven and eat him!"

They told Butros stories. One of Butros drunk rapping on Minnie's door long ago and asking for a tomato to be eaten in the right way, by plucking it off the vine. Then Butros prone on the ground between the tomato sticks plucking tomato after tomato off the vine, eating, and singing as loud as he could the praises of his home city and that of the good family of this garden.

Zahle, the decorated bride
Adorned by the feats of its men.

To which Mintaha, of Zahle, laughing, answered

Zahle, the distracted bride
Disgraced by the madness of its men.

Then Mike (may God be watching him) and Abdoo had returned from the Ah'we to find Butros sleeping among the tomatoes. They carried him home, up the stairs, and his son had opened the door. They were shocked to hear the son who had said "Take my father back to where you put him in this condition." And Mike had told him, "This is your father. If you do not respect your father, no matter what he does, you have nothing; you are less than he, you are nothing."

"Good for you, Mike," roared Shafee'a, "the father had some blood in him, the son is a worm."

When Mike came home, shaken, and told his wife of the incident, both he and she tried thereafter to be good to Butros (as good as cox-comb would let them be).

But one day during the war Minnie had gotten a telegram from her oldest son from Galveston, Texas ("Is *that* near Lebanon?" she had asked her youngest son). It read: "Have written great play. Wire starving artist—private $10. Kisses." Butros was at the table sipping coffee and eating olives with Mike when Minnie brought in the telegram and read it aloud.

"Well, Michael?"

"Well, Mintaha? Do you have it? If you have it, send it. What else?"

And Butros has whispered, "Ya Mike. You should control your wife. She is too much for her sons." And Mintaha had heard and turned fiercely, inflamed, "Butros, do you know what you are saying! Shame on you, old man. How can I respect your age when you speak so? I have brought the coals for your tobacco and put the sugar in your coffee. You are coming between a family, which does not befit your white hair. The money I send our son is all my husband's money. Please leave that chair where you have sat many times, and go through that door, and do not come back to this house." Yet six days later Minnie was preparing a smoke for Butros as he sat on the porch as he loved to do.

"Butros was born," said Shafee'a, "to test the endurance of us all, it is obvious. St. Peter will kiss the feet of Butros's wife. If he comes tomorrow morning I will serve him coffee with the turd of a dog and tell him it is honey of the old country. But what tornado of a dream did you have this time?"

"Shafee'a, I saw my father sitting at the table and he motioned to me to come to him, just like real, and he wanted me to bring him *leban* and bread. And I brought it and he wanted to kiss me, and I woke up. Does that mean he wants me, Shafee'a?"

"It means your father is not getting *leban* and Arabic bread in heaven. If it was true that heaven is run by the Jews they would have it, as the Jews I know love *leban*."

"No, Shafee'a, it was real. He was the same as the day he died forty-three years ago. Something is going to happen in the house of Kassouf."

"It would be more surprising if something did not."

They were all gone, her loved ones of the House of Kassouf in America, or were going. Her father first at forty-four of apoplexy upon working very hard on a hot day and coming into the house and asking his daughter Mintaha for ice water. Her Uncle John, that massive man she loved so dearly, who had loved her and raised her as one of his daughters in Pennsylvania, had gone quietly. Mintaha dreamed often of both of them. She dreamt of her husband and all the others, those long gone or of the near past, and they spoke to her in the simultaneity of the dreams.

Her Uncle John's wife, the sweet woman who taught Mintaha everything, had called for her from Utica when she was dying. She had heard that her Mintaha had gone partially deaf and had put her fingers on Mintaha's ears and prayed that she would hear. And Mary Kassouf had died and left a great hole in her companion Mintaha's heart. (She had asked Minnie to watch over her daughters but they had needed no watching.)

And without his wife Joe Kassouf had fallen into confusion and bewilderment, and had died. It was no life without her sitting silent at the center.

Mintaha and Mike had visited him one evening some six months after his wife had gone. Joe, heavy and tired, had taken Mintaha's hand and led her to the far room of the house. She did not know what to make of it as she sat down by him. She was afraid of what she might hear at Joe's lips.

"Ya, Mintaha, shall I tell you what I am thinking about?"

"Unless it is too sad, then keep it to yourself."

"My cousin, I have had the desire, which I cannot overcome, for kishik with onion, as Mary and you could make it and my daughters cannot. Mintaha, bless your eyes and as a Kassouf girl, make a kettle full of kishik for me and Mike."

"With all my heart, my cousin! I was afraid you might have wanted to marry again and had some unworthy devil in mind, to dishonor Mary and our House."

"Ya, Minnie, are you crazy? Even if I was such a fool, which thank Our Father I am not, what do you think? At my age the only bride is kishik with onion."

Mintaha smiled and Shafee'a was glad to see it.

"Ya Mintaha, I stopped before coming here to see Abdoo with some stuffed squash and he was on the porch. He can hardly see anymore and he said to me when he heard my voice, 'Shafee'a, my sister, my day is lightened. But do I not look like a ghoul with these teeth? To the Devil and his fires with this dentist, shoemaker, butcher, thief! Next time my son brings me I will take them out and bite him with them in a delicate place and leave them there.' 'You have charming morning thoughts, my brother Abdoo,' I said to him. 'Observe Shafee'a,' he said, 'my wife is gone, my job is gone, I cannot fish or drink or walk up and down the streets. Every day I ask God to take me! What the devil is the matter with him? He has plenty of room. There are only Lebanese up there and some Italian popes.'"

"Ah, Shafee'a, you remember they used to call Abdoo Mike's wife as they went everywhere together. One day the colored people at the mill invited Mike to their picnic and he brought Abdoo, who didn't know where Mike was taking him. When they got to the park, they were the only ones who were not black and Abdoo said, 'Ya, Mike my little brother, they will eat us.' But they were very good to them and so Abdoo sang an Arabic song for them and a Negro woman learned it on the spot and sang it with him."

"Confusion to your house, Abdoo, if you are not a rare thing! Do you recall how he would go fishing with Abdullah in the truck day and night and never come home with any fish? And his dear wife Nahail, said to him one day, 'Ya Abdoo, you are neglecting your family with this fishing that you love, but you catch nothing. Now, mighty hunter, I have a reasonable suggestion. Here is our washtub which I offer to fill with water and place in the middle of our kitchen. You can put your pole in it and sit all day till you are satisfied and your family will have you in its midst, and you will take no less fish for our table.'"

"Shafee'a, Shafee'a, do you remember Abdoo at Mike's funeral! How he came to the coffin after Abdullah had sung and he wished to sign a farewell to his friend and brother, and he had written the words on the paper in his hand. But he cried before he started and his sons had to take him home."

Mintaha had tears at her eyes.

"Stop, Mintaha! You will make me cry and I did not come to make a woman's concert. You must not cry when you have good sons! But wait, I have a story for you about a old lady in the old country who did not have good sons."

"Can this be a story to make one laugh?"

"We will see. The old lady was a widow and her children were married and neglected her so that she had little to eat and could hardly get out of bed."

"*Ya Botille*! She would have been better off bringing up swine."

"They were true swine but inedible. Her neighbor however was a good soul, but poor, and with many children. This honorable neighbor made up her mind to have the old woman fed by those damnable children in spite of themselves. So she visited next door and asked to borrow the old lady's best olive crock, which the old lady gave her with all the usual blessings. And the woman sat down in front of her place and painted the crock gold. Now the first lady that went by of course wanted to know what she was doing and was told in all secrecy that the crock was to be filled with the old lady's treasure and buried in the cellar. Meantime, every night for two weeks the woman took the crock of gold to the outhouse and relieved herself in it, and then she buried it and its treasure in the old lady's cellar."

"A swine's treasure indeed."

"And so the children were always in the mother's house and the daughter-in-laws cooked and cleaned and combed their mother's hair and dressed her in the highest style. And the boys, those *ackroots*, addressed their mother in high flown language, and she lived like a queen for six years, for which she thanked God and died."

Well, *yellah*, the priest and the lawyer scrambled over to the house after the funeral ahead of the villagers and discovered that the old lady had not expressed her wishes about the disposal of the crock of gold. Priest, lawyer, and children argued the whole day (assisted by the villagers) but finally it was decided that the priest would get his tenth and the children would get equal portions of the rest except that the lawyer for his past and future services also deserved a bit of it. The lawyer in his wisdom suggested that the crock of gold be placed on his head (he had a very flat head) and that it be broken with a stick, the treasure remaining on his head to be his. This was done with all haste, and lawyer, priest, and living children all got their rightful share of the treasure.

"This is a story that should be taught in all schools."

"You are right, Mintaha, except that it may cause a rash in places. Now, Mintaha, have you a story for me before I go?"

"You remind me, Shafee'a, with your priest, of the afternoon long ago when we were christening our youngest son and Abe Shalhoube and Father Lahoud, God bless them, were sitting on the couch in the living room and Abe told a story of a priest."

"The story, Mintaha. It may be good."

"There was a peasant in the old country who had a wife and eight children and one cow. From this cow they got milk and cheese and butter, enough to live from day to day. The peasant and his wife prayed incessantly that their lot be bettered. But the village priest had that typical frailty of man—covetousness—and could not bear that any cow be eating grass outside the fences of the church pasture. So on a Sunday at the pulpit, the priest turned directly to the peasant and spoke the words of the gospel that he who gives to God and His church of his house or his cow will have his gift returned to him three and four fold. The simple peasant saw the end to his misery and determined to give his cow to the church, whereupon his wife shrieked and his children wept. But he gave the cow to the priest (who accepted it with humility and grace) and went home in a blessed mood to await his fortune."

"His wife should have ready a crock of gold."

"Listen. The peasant's cow felt out of place among the clergy's cattle and too confined. Late at night it broke through the fence and for some reason the priest's cows followed. The peasant on his mattress on the floor of his place was awake and heard the pounding of hoofs. He looked out of the window on the moonlit night and saw his little yard full of cattle. He roused his wife and cried, 'It has happened my dear wife, it has happened. The Lord has given us twelve cows for one.'"

"This village Man of God was wild in the morning and rushed to the peasant's yard. 'It has happened, Father, as you promised,' said the peasant. Our father had to think."

"The swindler does not like to be swindled."

"You are too frank, Shafee'a. Say rather the shepherd found the perfect solution for the member of his flock. 'My uncle,' said the priest, 'God will tell us who deserves these cows. Whoever rises first in the morning and says "Good morning" first to the other shall keep them.' The sly priest was sure the peasant did not know that the morning began at midnight, and he was right. But the peasant had a plan of his own.

"Why waste words, Shafee'a? The peasant slept that night in the tree by the priest's house and placed an empty kettle at the door. Close to midnight the priest quietly arose, slipped out the door and knocked over the kettle. The peasant awoke and cried out 'Good Morning, Father, what the devil time is this to be out?'"

"Well done, Mintaha! And what said Father Lahoud to Abe's useful story?"

"'Ya Abe,' he said, 'I have no cows and you have only two beautiful daughters. We can do no business.'"

"Who can believe that both are dead, such men, such princes! Do you hear me, Lahoud and Shalhoube, it was not time to go! But for me it is time to go, I must begin supper. *Yallah*, Mintaha, into bed."

"Yes, I will go to bed. Run home quickly before the rain comes again. Kindest regards to Butros, if he comes to you this evening."

"A curse as I leave!"

"And my apologies to Abdoo. He will understand."

SHE LAY IN BED and she could not hear the thunder though she saw the lightening flash moment after moment. She wanted to think of her husband and her sons but only good thoughts. She needed to sleep and did not want to dream.

They were all they had had, Mike and her, and all that would have mattered in the old country. But America would take them, would swallow them up, would crush the family and obliterate the past. She would have to rely on their upbringing and their education but she had no idea where life would bring them.

She prayed that all would not be obliterated for that was twice death and what then was it all worth? But it *must* be worth; she could not bear the thought that it not be. And if it be, where was Mike to see it! It was too sad, and life was too risky, and yet one must keep going. And yet it was too hard.

Mike was gone and had not seen the blossoming of his sons. They had told him he was foolish to deny himself so much for his sons, the wicked people, and he would always say, "Ask my wife, she has the answers for you." And she would tell them, "Is not Wisdom both Goodness and Knowledge? We can hope to give them a good heart, but we cannot give them knowledge beyond what we have." And that would keep them quiet . . .

"Ya, Mike, what is to become of me, and of our sons! Take me Lord, before I am a burden, or before any disgrace!"

SHE AWOKE IN EXTREME DARKNESS for five o'clock. The storm had not come and yet kept hovering. She hardly knew the day or the year in this darkness. She had dreamt but could not remember, something of Mike speaking to her in the kitchen. But she must cook. She had only the one son home for supper tonight. The middle son was married and the eldest, the Harvard lawyer, was in Washington for something.

Lentils and rice she made, and her son all of a sudden was there beside her. She hadn't heard the door or his greeting.

"You scared me. Sit down. I fell asleep and had a dream."

"If it's bad, don't tell me."

"I don't know. Your father was sitting and saying something, but I can't remember."

"Maybe he was telling you that Tanous Kassouf has got a boil in a bad place. I just saw Selma and she said he went to the hospital today to have it fixed."

"Ah, I knew it, I told Shafee'a, and she said no. I told her we would hear bad news of the House of Kassouf."

"That's not bad news—that's nothing, a boil."

"My father wanted to tell me this morning; he looked just like real. Thank God it was not something worse. He will be sore but it will go."

"I studied pretty well. I took a walk and I had coffee in a place, and I saw some people in the library."

"You've got a good life, between school and the summer. Think of the men in the mill."

He had studied wretchedly. His whole body pounded and he had the cramps of wretchedness. He had had them all week as the time for him to leave again drew near. It was the nadir of his life this summer, with his father gone, his mother ill, and he, going overseas to study. He could not study, he could not think, he had roamed the streets as he had always loved to do, but saw only the sterility of his own mind. Having coffee had been better, human beings around him. He had wanted so badly to go home and lay on the bed, but he did not want his mother to see him miserable. He would walk tonight, go to a movie, anything to make the time pass.

"Good lentils, Ma. Did Shafee'a have any good stories?"

"Does she ever miss? We laughed and laughed."

And so did mother and son in their repetition.

"You ought to make a book."

"But stories alone don't make a book Ma."

"Don't print the book until I read it to see if there is anything in it which is not fit."

"Me, Ma! I'm your son."

"That's true, but the world is funny nowadays."

"Ma, tomorrow I won't go to the library. I'll go out and do some jobs in the yard."

"It's about time. Everything is falling down."

"Someday Ma, maybe next summer when I can come home, I'll paint the whole house inside and out."

"Someday water will come out of the water tap."

"Ma, if I go out for a while now and come home early will you be all right? I can stay home."

"No, I want you to enjoy yourself. Go out. I'll finish my jobs while you are gone."

Shortly her son kissed her and left. She did the dishes, wiped the table, turned the pages of the paper, then shut the light. She sat back in the heavy chair in the darkened house.

He is not happy now. Nor is his oldest brother happy. But they work. It cannot be that they will stay unhappy when they work, and they love each other. Lord, let them be happy.

Even the devils love something, and cry over something, even the dogs. Rose across the street, how she loved clean sheets and a clean sidewalk. And Frangesce when he came crying to me that morning! All because he took a rose from the bush. He never stole anything in his life, he said, but the rose in the night was beautiful, and he knew I hated to see them cut off the vine! Better to cut the vine from the bottom than to see that old man cry.

All of life is crying, crying, crying; cry for this one and cry for that one. What else is there to do but cry?

And Fate would come with a heavy axe in the next year, testing Mintaha's capacity for life even further. Shafee'a would die with her stories and laughter. Abdoo would die, even Butros would die. Shafee'a would fall on a street of a stroke, like a great elm felled. Then, later, mother and son would visit Abdoo as he sat under his grapevine almost blind and eating cantaloupe.

"Can we call this life, Mintaha. What is this nonsense? No longer the days of pleasure when your dear Mike and I would walk the streets as men. Get me God on the telephone! He has forgotten me and I demand to be gathered up! He is making a fool out of me."

And Butros would come to the house bent and with a cane, climb the stairs, sit in the porch chair, cry a bit, and call out for Mintaha.

"Ya, Mintaha, coffee, bless your hands, coffee and a sliced tomato from the yard. (Damn the doctors to the deepest devils.) Ya, Mintaha, Shafee'a is gone and Abdoo is gone! There is no house left but yours."

"And our house has its oppression also, Butros, but it does not give in."

She roused herself from the chair after an hour and walked out onto the porch where the sky had brightened up and people were walking back and forth. People nodded to her as she sat, and some stopped to talk and ask about her and her sons. She felt better, it was good on the porch. The neighbors respected Mintaha.

A little girl came by on a bicycle and asked for an apple.

"What is it, sweetheart, I can't hear you."

"Can I have an apple, lady?"

"I hate to cut roses off the vine and kill them, but a pretty girl like you, you can take one."

"No, I want an *apple*."

"An apple! Have three. And get me one too."

The little girl jumped and got apples. She came up and sat beside Mintaha and they ate green apples.

"Do you know any stories, lady?"

"Listen, and I will tell you a story you've never heard, about a lazy cat named Hassan."

"That's a funny name for a cat."

After the story the girl followed Mintaha back to the garden clothesline and put clothespins in the bag while the lady piled the white sheets on her arm. The evening had gotten quite nice, no wind and a mild blue sky. A sweet darkness was coming on. The girl and the lady looked at the garden getting shadowy and deep green. Then the girl ran to her bicycle and Minnie carried the sheets into the kitchen and onto the table.

Tomorrow she would iron. Tonight she hoped for no dreams, or good dreams, of the happy past, or the past or present made happy, of the dead alive and happy somehow, somewhere, or of the live laughing.

Laughter, tying the devil's tail. She undressed for bed and thought of her son who (like the girl) loved stories.

If I am still awake when he comes in the house, I will tell him the story of the wife who put the devil in a bottle.

Summer 1964

THE HOUSE was in the twilight calm of late August and late suppertime (the hour which Leonardo said was the best for seeing, when branches stood out clear against the sky). The shadows would climb the porch steps now. The grass which had borne all summer the burning sun at noon would in some days or weeks be nipped by frost in the dead hours of the morning. September would be the month of changes, of the dying of gardens, of the end of swimming and the beginning of schooling, of early darkness and old people moving back into the house. There was then for Mike's youngest son the touch of melancholy in all this quiet beauty as he stood with his brothers looking down on the neighborhood from the porch. Tonight he would walk.

Their father had died in September seven years ago. He had known his middle son's first child; he would have been equally delighted with the others. The brothers stood quiet for a moment looking out on the rooftops, yards, and wooden fences. Their father had loved to stand and look out here with his sons or to walk back to the yard with one or another.

"PA SHOULD BE HERE. It's ridiculous that he's not here."

"He could enjoy life now."

"He could have made the trip with Ma to the old country. That would have been the top of the world for him."

"He and your godfather, Abe, used to argue right here on the porch for hours whether a street in Zahle bent before or after so-and-so's house, and if the house had three or four arches, or if a stream was five or six feet wide as it passed his house or Abe's house."

"And yet they knew *this* town better than any of us."

THEIR MOTHER called them in for supper. They sat down at the table of their youth.

Mike's youngest son was day-dreaming of all the walking with his father; to the stores, to church, to the Ah'we, to relatives, to the mill, everywhere, up this street and down the other, back and forth, talking, watching, forming.

It was not possible to violate his father's trust (he told himself) as his father never thought of his sons as different from himself.

And he *was* his father (he hoped); otherwise he was only himself and that was not enough.

They had walked together into kitchens thousands of times and had enjoyed thousands of treats given from hand to hand.

"*YA TOUFIC, does a Khawajha [lord and gentleman] like you sit thus at the table in his long underwear?*"

"*Ya Khawajha Mike, it is the latest style. The Niswan [women] in this country show their underwear, and the men must follow their way.*"

"*Damn the Niswan, I'll keep my underwear to myself.*"

. . . HE KNOCKED ON TOUFIC'S DOOR. After a long while there was a fumbling on the other side. And then there was Toufic, with his few white hairs sticking up on his bald head. He was in the baggy pants and flannel shirt. When he saw Mike's son tears formed at the corner of his eyes and he embraced him. The house was empty, his wife had died, and his children lived elsewhere. Everything was seedy; the armchairs were soiled, the rugs were worn in places and spotted in places, the wall paper was of big flowers and full of oil marks. Ashes from Toufic's cigar were in most of the corners, the lights were all poor or defunct. A bedroom he caught sight of looked like a cell, nothing in it but a bed, a crucifix, a chair like those in the coffee house, and a dresser with nothing on top of it. It was like a ghost house. He could remember when it was full of noise, and people making spots on everything, and using with high spirits furniture of no aesthetic value.

Toufic's son that was a doctor lived now in Denver, Colorado for some reason and came to visit his father with his wife (not the children) every two years or so, and stayed at the hotel. His wife would not touch a thing when she came because she was on vacation. If Toufic tried to cook something or make a salad, she would protest that Lebanese food was too greasy, and bad for Toufic. They would pay a few duty calls hurriedly, drop in on a few of the better bars and restaurants, go up North to swim, and then fly back to Denver, leaving Toufic with pictures of the children. Toufic looked at the pictures all the time, and found his own face in all of his grandchildren.

Another son had had money in a downtown business, married a show girl and put up a seventy-five thousand dollar house. The business failed, the mortgage lapsed, and his wife absconded. She took with her her jewels, her silverware, a boy friend, and the two children that were the apples in their grandfather's eye. Toufic's wife died, maybe of shame, a year later. Father and son however still loved each other (no one could help liking Toufic's son), and he came fairly often to take his father to the races.

And he had a daughter that lived in New York City with her husband, an executive. They had no children after all these years, and she cried on her father's shoulder whenever she would come to see him (without her husband). She sent him letters every week and little packages often.

Toufic put a little gold pot of Turkish coffee on the stove. They sat down in the narrow kitchen, and Mike's son read him the letter from his daughter. As he read he remembered the girl who was older than he was, and how they had built up together fantasies of marriage, and pledged astounding feats of protectiveness and fidelity in this kitchen, and made every rung of every chair into a magical snare or deep, dark, entrance to an Arab tent.

Toufic took him by the hand and they went out the back door steps to the very small yard between all the houses. There the pear tree and the rose bush were that had come from the branches Mike had given to Toufic. They were both flourishing; Toufic was keeping the trust given to him by his friend who was gone now.

They went back into the kitchen and sat over their coffee. Khalil was gone, Joe was gone, Abdullah had died in the truck, and Aid was old, old, and could hardly take care of himself. The Ah'we was painted and full of young men, gamblers and drifters, and few of the old people went there any more. You had to go to someone's house to play cards now, and in each house there were too many memories, it was too sad. Across the street at the fruit stand there were no chairs anymore to sit down on. You tell a boy to go buy you a cigar, he says go to hell.

He got up to leave and Toufic came out with him, sat down on his porch steps and smoked.

. . . WARMTH. Living within traditional values, within its comedy. Laughter, real laughter.

When you have a home to go away from and come back to.

And loyalty, loyalty, loyalty . . .

Going away can be like falling in the ocean.

Or like a walk around the block, when you've never been away because nothing you've done has any meaning without your sense of home.

He turned onto his street.

. . . If you could walk rightly you see things you don't forget, and these take on meaning. And it gets important, not where you walk, but how you see.

How to describe the nights in which you walked, and what you felt. How to make language sing to you.

What to say about the light in the garage at ten o'clock at night, the big door open, the little old man wheeling a garbage can out of it, his granddaughter sitting in the driveway, pulling at the hair of her doll. Why was it so mysterious? Why, why does peace roll over you in waves, when you stub your foot on the cracked slate sidewalk, or when that woman sat on the porch step in the moonlight and peeled an orange?

But *that* love, strange beauty, is no good without a home . . .

. . . again the triangle . . .

. . . you'd be better off sleeping than thinking this stuff over and over . . .

He went up onto his porch.

He lay on the porch swing for a while with the breeze floating across. He got up and went into the house and put on the kitchen light. His mother turned over in bed and mumbled. He went into her room to see if she would wake up and talk to him. Suddenly in the dark room she twisted and called out, "Mike! Mike!" A burning and a freezing went through his body.

His mother woke up and he sat on the bed and listened to her dream. Then he shut the light off and went into the kitchen and sat down to eat something by himself. He looked around the kitchen and all the doors coming into it. He wished his father were alive.

He sat there in the dark room.

He got up from the kitchen table.

He went into the bathroom and washed, into the bedroom and undressed.

Abstractions about love are not the thing.

You say tell love stories, but is that enough?

If not, tell more, and then more.

He crawled into bed and looked at the pictures of his brothers on the wall.

Tell of . . . what? . . .

What else? . . .

Ma's love.

He worked it out in his head, the way he would write it.

SEVEN. *What do we live for but for our children. And they for their fathers and mothers?*

And the family. And those that love you.

When we are good it is that way.

When we are bad the devil is in us.

(I am going to kill the devil, Ma, if he ever comes in our house!)

And there are many that would like to break up families and make the worse the better path. It is because they are envious of a life of honor.

(Is it because they like our garden, Ma?)

Do not let them catch you, or ever be of their party.

Do not be too soft except to those who love you. And even then do not listen to women too much for women can tie the devil's tail.

(But ma, ain't you a woman?)

SEVENTEEN. *Be on the lookout for fakers. You have good eyes and I think you will be all right, but there are so many fakers.*

Your father does not know how to fake, nor your Godfather Abe (that's why we picked him), nor Joe, nor Shafee'a, nor their kind.

If Shafee'a ever asks you for anything, you run, and if she wants you to carry her on your back up the hill, you bend down, and if to feed her with a spoon, you ask, "Is there not something else I can do?"

She is honest, and will keep her promises to me. And she laughs, that is important.

Look out for the man who wears fancy clothes all the time, he will be a faker.

And the man who gossips about others, tell him to move over, and find someone else's ear.

And the silly girl who wants to talk about Love, and how much you love each other, she is a faker.

(nobody asked me yet, ma!)

Talk is cheap. You want a girl who is proud of herself and will throw the faker out the door even when her husband is a devil.

Find the strong, proud woman; it is the weak woman that will make your life a trouble.

But not the hard woman who wants what she wants.

(No! The soft woman, with long hair, ma.)

Do not be proud because you will have an education, which is lucky, but be proud if you have kept on the right road, and you have brought your children down the right road, and pray they keep on it.

TWENTY-SEVEN. *He can take me anytime He wants.*

I made a bargain with Him, first when I was sick, to leave me here till the boys grew up so that your father would not have to do it alone, and then to see you all finish schooling, and now it's done, and I'm ready.

(Don't talk like that, ma!)

We did, your father (pray for him) and I, something that was worth to be done, and I wish only that he had seen you.

But we live in you, and when people ask you who you are, say, I am Mike's son, of the House of Nasser, and a Kassouf on my mother's side.

(TELL ME AGAIN, *ma, for the hundredth time, of your courtship and marriage, today, tomorrow, and years from now.)*

MY UNCLE JOHN *remember was three hundred and sixty-five pounds, and tall and handsome. He took my father's place when he died after just bringing me to America, and he loved me so much, and nobody was like my Uncle John for me.*

We lived as one family in the big house, and there was Uncle's wife and my cousins, and Father Bschara. He loved me too, and he was round and comical, and when they ate, bless them, they ate for twelve. Wherever he went among the Lebanese all over the country, he would tell all the young men about Mintaha, the Kassouf girl in Pennsylvania, and it was all Mintaha, Mintaha.

And they came, all the rich ones, Maronite and Melchite, with rings and silks, and talked to my Uncle John. And he would ask me what I thought of this one and that one, and I would say, no, his nose is too long, and his eyes are too small, and he sees himself in his eyes, and they were all fakers. And the Maronites were all saying it was my Uncle, that he wanted only a Melchite, but it wasn't so, it was only that I was fussy.

Then Father Bschara was called to come to Utica to take care of the Melchite people there. And Joe Kassouf, God bless him, my cousin, was Melchite, and at his house Mike, your father, heard about me from Father Bschara. And they came all together, the three of them to Pennsylvania on the train and they stayed at my Uncle's house. And they came two more times and Father Bschara said to my Uncle that Mike was a very good man and did not gossip. And my Uncle John loved him from the first but he was so afraid for me because Mike had no money, and was unhappy without his family, and wanted to go back to the old country. And he came to me and asked me, "This one, Mintaha?" And I said "Yes." "And is not his nose too long, Mintaha?" he teased me. "His nose is fine," I said.

And the Maronites danced up and down. "See, see," they said, "John Kassouf did not want a Maronite. And now the Maronites have stepped on the neck of the Melchites!" And when my uncle heard they were talking like this, he called Mike to him and asked how they would get even. Mike said he would carry a sign on his back downtown that he had changed to Melchite for his wife's sake. "No," my uncle said, "just tell that to the House of Dahroogh when they come, and let us watch them jump."

(AND AS LONG AS FATHER BSCHARA *was alive we went to him, but when he died we went to the Maronite church.)*

AND SHMUNDAR OF THE HOUSE OF CHAMOUN *made a plan with Mike and all of the men in the house that had come from Utica to play a joke on me. And they were all watching and Mike came walking softly in the kitchen, and asked me for a kiss in the silly way. And I pushed him hard and he went back through the door and fell down the cellar steps. And all the dummies from Utica came out singing of the House of Kassouf, and Mike came up, and they said, "Now she deserves a kiss," but I still wouldn't give him one.*

(IT WOULD HAVE SPOILED THE WHOLE STORY, *ma, if you did!)*

AND WE HAD THE BIG WEDDING IN THE HOUSE, *and my Uncle John invited the whole world, and he cried and I cried all day. Abe came, and Abdullah sang, and Aid did the sword dance. And it was the long mass, and when Father Bschara had to say to your father, "And you must leave forever your mother and father, and stick to your wife," Abe, your Godfather, who was always comical, got up and said, "That is not a good thing for you to say, Father Bschara. I did not expect that from you." And everybody laughed, except my Uncle John.*

IT WAS PERHAPS six-thirty in the morning, breezy and fresh, the sun already up a while. He stood in the garden back behind the house. Mike's son had been brooding a little in bed, but here and now in the morning air he felt very happy.

Maybe he would catch the lady in black today. She had taken, in her old age, to stealing directly from gardens (some grape leaves, a cucumber, a tomato), and reserving the lamentations for later in the day.

He should fix the crack in his bedroom window.

The fence too he should fix, and pull up the weeds around the plants.

The sun shone on the squash that flopped and twisted along the fence and the tar-paper shack.

The plump deep-red tomatoes hung heavy on the stalks. The stalks were having a hard time keeping their backs up, even though the rags and sticks were lending their aid. The little bugs were swarming all over the garden, up the sticks, the stalks, through the spray and into the fruit, getting their share. The grape leaves waved lazily in the breeze, and the worm crawled over the snail. The water in the rain barrel shimmered and puckered. The bird on the clothes wire jerked his head in two directions and then flew down to the garden ground and jerked his head two more times. From the roots of the stump many little trees were pushing up all over the yard, and others were still under the ground. The cherry trees were elegant and conversed with each other alone. Over in another yard the gigantic elm lorded it over the blocks of the neighborhood. Streets radiated out and criss-crossed all over the city. Somewhere, all the time, adulterers were adulterating other men's wives, old men were talking together, and some people were leading deep moral lives; a man was swimming alone in the ocean, others were laying on beds, and one might be knocking sand off a chute in a plaster mill. He blessed the full world, the neighborhood bursting with all of life, the gardens everywhere the same and beautiful, and the feeling heart that rose and fell.

He picked a tomato off the vine, a pear off the tree, and went into the house and gave them to his mother.

NAOMI SHIHAB NYE

Yellow Glove

WHAT CAN A YELLOW GLOVE MEAN in a world of motorcars and governments?

I was small, like everyone. Life was a string of precautions: Don't kiss the squirrel before you bury him, don't suck candy, pop balloons, drop watermelons, watch TV. When the new gloves appeared one Christmas, tucked in soft tissue, I heard it trailing me: Don't lose the yellow gloves.

I was small, there was too much to remember. One day, waving at a stream—the ice had cracked, winter chipping down, soon we would sail boats and roll into ditches—I let a glove go. Into the stream, sucked under the street. Since when did streets have mouths? I walked home on a desperate road. Gloves cost money. We didn't have much. I would tell no one. I would wear the yellow glove that was left and keep the other hand in a pocket. I knew my mother's eyes had tears they had not cried yet—I didn't want to be the one to make them flow. It was the prayer I spoke secretly, folding socks, lining up donkeys in windowsills. I would be good, a promise made to the roaches who scouted my closet at night. If you don't get in my bed, I will be good. And they listened. I had a lot to fulfill.

The months rolled down like towels out of a machine. I sang and drew and fattened the cat. Don't scream, don't lie, don't cheat, don't fight—you could hear it anywhere. A pebble could show you how to be smooth, tell the truth. A field could show you how to sleep without walls. A stream could remember how to drift and change—the next June I was stirring the stream like a soup, telling my brother dinner would be ready if he'd only hurry up with the bread, when I saw it. The yellow glove draped on a twig. A muddy survivor. A quiet flag.

Where had it been in the three gone months? I could wash it, fold it in my winter drawer with its sister, no one in that world would ever know. There were miracles on Harvey Street. Children walked home in yellow light. Trees were reborn and gloves traveled far, but returned. A thousand miles later, what can a yellow glove mean in a world of bankbooks and stereos?

Part of the difference between floating and going down.

Arabic

The man with laughing eyes stopped smiling
to say, "Until you speak Arabic—
—you will not understand pain."

Something to do with the back of the head,
an Arab carries sorrow in the back of the head
that only language cracks, the thrum of stones

weeping, grating hinge on an old metal gate.
"Once you know," he whispered, "you can enter the room
whenever you need to. Music you heard from a distance,

the slapped drum of a stranger's wedding,
wells up inside your skin, inside rain, a thousand
pulsing tongues. You are changed."

Outside, the snow had finally stopped.
In a land where snow rarely falls,
we had felt our days grow white and still.

I thought pain had no tongue. Or every tongue
at once, supreme translator, sieve. I admit my
shame. To live on the brink of Arabic, tugging

its rich threads without understanding
how to weave the rug . . . I have no gift.
The sound, but not the sense.

I kept looking over his shoulder for someone else
to talk to, recalling my dying friend who only scrawled
I can't write. What good would any grammar have been

to her then? I touched his arm, held it hard,
which sometimes you don't do in the Middle East, and said,
I'll work on it, feeling sad

for his good strict heart, but later in the slick street
hailed a taxi by shouting *Pain*! and it stopped
in every language and opened its doors.

Jerusalem

"Let's be the same wound if we must bleed
Let's fight side by side, even if the enemy
Is ourselves: I am yours, you are mine."
—Tommy Olofsson, Sweden

I'm not interested in
who suffered the most.
I'm interested in
people getting over it.

Once when my father was a boy,
a stone hit him on the head.

Hair would never grow there.
Our fingers found the tender spot
and its riddle: the boy who has fallen
stands up. A bucket of pears
in his mother's doorway welcomes him home.
The pears are not crying.
Later his friend who threw the stone
says he was aiming at a bird.
And my father starts growing wings.

Each carries a tender spot:
something our lives forget to give us.
A man builds a house and says,
"I am native now."
A woman speaks to a tree in place
of her son. And olives come.
A child's poem says,
"I don't like wars,
they end up with monuments."
He's painting a bird with wings
wide enough to cover two roofs at once.

Why are we so monumentally slow?
Soldiers stalk a pharmacy:
big guns, little pills.
If you tilt your head just slightly
it's ridiculous.

There's a place in my brain
where hate won't grow.
I touch its riddle: wind, and seeds.
Something pokes us as we sleep.

It's late but everything comes next.

Holy Land

Over beds wearing thin homespun cotton
Sitti the Ageless floated
poking straight pins into sheets
to line our fevered forms,
"the magic," we called it,
her crumpling of syllables,
pitching them up and out,
petals parched by sun,
the names of grace, hope,
in her graveled grandmother tongue.
She stretched a single sound
till it became two—
perhaps she could have said
anything,
the word for peanuts,
or waterfalls,
and made a prayer.

After telling the doctors "Go home,"
she rubbed our legs,
pressing into my hand
someone's lost basketball medal,
"Look at this man reaching for God."
She who could not leave town
while her lemon tree held fruit,
nor while it dreamed of fruit.
In a land of priests,
patriarchs, muezzins,
a woman who couldn't read
drew lines between our pain
and earth,
stroked our skins

to make them cool,
    our limbs which had already
traveled far beyond her world,
    carrying the click of distances
in the smooth, untroubled soles
    of their shoes.

The Only Word a Tree Knows

Tonight the hens line up on a bamboo roost,
sides touching.
You can hold their evening in the palm of a hand,
wondering at restlessness,
the stranger people should never let in.
Pecans falling before we have cracked the ones from last year!
Squirrels building a nest under the roof!
There is nothing to do that isn't singular.
One meal, one letter, one memory roaring inside the head.

The trees promise to remember us.
Yes. It is the only word a tree knows.
Leaves dropping, it is the one thing left.

Tonight we will be branches loose in the wind of our bed,
a motion preceding and following everything we do.

The trees shrink on the wall of the sky.
Listen long enough, it sounds like
they're talking inside your head.
This bending, this rake—
a leaf lands, little boat, on a stair.
To be everywhere and know:
I was born to answer a tree.

Renovation

1.

It cheered me that the man and woman ripping our house apart were a married couple. Maybe this meant they would be more careful with things. Delia neatly packed all the belongings from the three rooms where mold was detected in large cardboard boxes marked KITCHEN ITEAMS and BATH—the mugs, spatulas, pots and pans, towels, bottles of shampoo. Chico draped large sheets of plastic from the 11-foot-high ceilings for "containment." Then they both donned plastic space suits and face masks and began smashing the hundred-year-old green-and-white tile of the kitchen counter and the blue Mexican bird tile in the bathroom to take it out. The mold was under wood and sheetrock. It likes to eat adhesive. A very subversive guest. Goodbye familiar cracks and rounded edges. Goodbye heavy wooden drawers and stained porcelain bathtub. Our neighbors felt scared when they saw the spacemen in the yard.

2.

We slept at a hotel three blocks from our own house for 32 days. We ate waffles and hard-boiled eggs for breakfast. The hotel served an unidentifiable form of mixed canned fruit in a big bowl. I heard people wondering about it at other tables, Is this papaya? A slimy peach? What the hell is this? We saw the traveling groups come and go, the deputy sheriffs of small-town Texas (very noisy group), the evangelical African American track stars of Houston, the glittery pre-teen Britney Spears fans of northern Mexico. The best thing about our hotel was the free happy hour from 5 to 7 every day, which I almost never missed. Carlos made a terrific Cuba Libre. He made two in a row, perfectly. I needed them, in order to be able to face our house during the rest of the day.

3.

Mold is not a very sexy topic but it could be growing inside anybody's walls at any moment, finding its own safe harbor of moist secrecy, spreading and thickening in green or black creepy glory. We had mostly green but a little black. It gave me asthma even before it started sneaking out of a hole in the ceiling over the bathtub. Thanks to a leak in the roof and two other unrelated leaks in two wall pipes, we had it. Our hundred-year-old cottage was sabotaged by a sneaky culprit. Truly, considering all the possibilities for leakage in this world, it amazes me that more things don't leak. It amazes me that poop goes into the poop pipe and relatively clean water comes out of the faucet. It all amazes me. I know some people who have had to bulldoze their houses and throw away all their belongings. Delia called me into the front yard to see the boards from our bathroom wrapped in plastic. She pointed. There, there it is. See those little black and green spots? It is going away now. We are hauling it to the DUMP. You won't have it any more.

4.

So we moved back into our house without any running water or toilets, it was like camping out at home. We ate peaches and icy cherry tomatoes from a big bowl. We drank coffee and made rum drinks in the afternoons, trying to replicate the happy hour at the hotel down the street, but it did not feel as delicious. We drove around in the summer heat through traffic to gaze at tile and bathroom fixtures in too many stores and talked to carpenters and lighting experts and tried to make decisions. There are some people in the world who are good at doing this. We are not among them. During all these minor movements of human beings, rain began falling in beautiful gray sheets and fell for 20 days and nights. Biblical fashion. I actually invited it to fall before it started, though harbor no delusion of my power. On June 28, when the annual south Texas summer water conservation measures were announced (you will only water between certain hours, on certain days, and only with a hose, not a sprinkler, blah blah blah), I said (this was Happy Hour talking), "Well I wish it would just start raining and rain for all of July." And then it almost did. Numerous Texans saw their houses float away downstream, in shocking TV newsreel footage played over and over. Such sights eclipsed our efforts at domestic improvement. Messages came in by e-mail, phone, "Are you okay?" Our inner-city neighborhood is protected by a multi-million dollar drainage system installed years ago. We made fun of it when downtown was all torn up, but have changed our tune. I had a panic attack at a granite yard among sheets and slabs of cut stone, then decided against granite, which seemed cold, hard and too chic for my humble leanings. How could you go from washing dishes in a red plastic pan in the yard to granite? Finally, after waking up with tile/grout nightmares, I decided on SILESTONE, a mysterious impenetrable reconstituted quartz substance supposedly popular in Europe for many years. Welcome to the United States. We selected elegant turquoise and green MISSION TILE from Mexico for the back-splash, a term that reminds me of elephants. Do you do much splashing in your kitchen?

And then we waited. For someone to come measure. For substances to arrive from different directions. For things not to be broken. For them to be re-ordered. For someone to be able to put them in. Renovation involves mostly waiting. For the electrician who knows you cannot deal with those wires yourself. For the evangelical electrician who says we will soon all be washing dishes in our yards. He does not like to go under the house if no one is home. For the carpenter who looks uncannily like my gynecologist. For the diverter switch to arrive at a plumbing warehouse. For windows. For the counter installers who wanted advice about their rosebushes at their house where they live together when they are not installing counters. How do you make a rose bush bloom more? What does it want and need? We start receiving mysterious catalogues like "Rest Room World."

5.

During all this, the Palestinians overseas were being confined to their homes, if they had homes, or to their shacks, rooms, tents, and hovels. They could not go out to buy fresh oranges. They could not go to school. More houses were being seized and demolished daily. The word "demolished" sounds softer than it is. But in the documentary movie *Gaza Strip* you can hear the terrifying crashing sounds of giant bulldozers as they knock down houses a hundred years old. One gets tired of saying or hearing the words but it keeps happening. The whole time we were putting our house back together, more Palestinians were losing their homes. Suicide bombers, those tragic people driven insane by oppression, do not come out of vacuums. They come out of demolished homes. They saw their fathers blindfolded, hauled off to prison in buses. They saw their friends gassed by poison, blown up, stomachs strewn in the dust. Their mothers wailing and bloody. Why is this almost never considered in the news? Where everything comes from? We pay our taxes to Israel for 53 years so they can brutalize and oppress an entire population then feel stunned when so many people start acting crazy blowing each other up. Sometimes where everything comes from is much more critical than where everything is going.

We washed dishes in a pan in the yard for two months and became related to all the people in the world washing dishes in the yard. If they had a yard. If they had dishes that weren't broken by someone with a tank and large guns who likes to break dishes, smash glass in picture frames, defecate on beds. Say this, American TV. Say what the Israeli soldiers do with the money we give them. Stop acting so pure.

6.

I hate this, said the teenager we live with, one rare night when I asked him to help me rinse. We had had company for dinner. It was fun to have company with no running water or bathroom. They were a little taken aback. I poured water over their hands from a pitcher. They tried not to look at all the boxes piled up in the dining room. The teenager scraping plates said, How long is this going to go on? Don't some people get their whole houses rebuilt in, like, a week? Why is it taking so long for this to be completed?

Just think, I said to him. This is never a good idea to say to someone, especially a teen person, but I said it anyway. Just consider someone coming and taking our house away, on top of it. While we're in the middle of fixing things. While everything is a mess. How would you feel? They would say your room is their room. Your computer is now their computer. Or they would blow up your room and say, Ah, too bad, we call it security, no one cares if you suffer.

What are you talking about? he said. I'd call the police!

What if you had no phone lines? What if the police had no power?

Stop talking like this. The mosquitoes are killing me. I hate washing dishes.

Amir & Anna

"It's unbelievable, this cycle of violence, and how neither party realizes they're both losing."
—Dr. Cairo Arafat, West Bank

Amir can't sleep.
He dives under his bed.
Anna is afraid of everything.
Parked cars, moving buses.
Anna is afraid of toast.
Their names begin with "A",
contain the same number of letters.

No one has given them
what they deserve.

Around both their houses,
all the Arab and Jewish houses,
red poppies sleep beneath
dirt and stones.
What do they know?
In March green spokes
with fluttering heads
rise and rise on every side.

Your Weight, at Birth

Watching the Palestinian men
emerge from the Church of the Nativity,
I considered birth: being born into light again
after so many cramped weeks inside,
born into air & space,
how we wish the best for one another when someone
is being born, born into deportation & exile,
born, & banished.

Across the street, their women were wailing.
They could not greet or hug them.
The men were shuffled onto buses
to be sent away.
On the white & dusty street of Bethlehem,
where so many travelers have stood
holding candles, wrapped in song,
the prisoner men, in their own town.

An American TV announcer's voice sounded excited
to be present at the births—
over & over again
he hailed the table of sandwiches & bottled water

provided by Israeli soldiers
who actually looked perplexed
whenever the camera came in close.

One is born to wear a helmet, carry large artillery.
One is born to be thin, to wear raggedy clothes
& be shot in the leg. And some are born
to wonder, wonder, wonder.

Supple Cord

My brother, in his small white bed,
held one end.
I tugged the other
to signal I was still awake.
We could have spoken,
could have sung
to one another,
we were in the same room
for five years,
but the soft cord
with its little frayed ends
connected us
in the dark,
gave comfort
even if we had been bickering
all day.
When he fell asleep first
and the cord dropped
to the floor,
I missed him terribly,
though I could hear his even breath
and we had such long and separate lives
ahead.

The Only Democracy in the Middle East

Please leave your house immediately.
Do not call it a home.
This is our home not yours.
And this is for security.
Always, always, for security. Our security.
Take nothing, ask nothing.
Stand over there, against the rubble, where
you belong. All young men, come with us.
A chance you will not see your families again.
You can't say goodbye or hug your son.
We have suffered too much thanks to you
and thanks to everyone
but you are the only ones we can touch.
Please don't give us any trouble.

Because of Poems

We were never alone.
Words had secret parties.

Verbs popped surprises
from their pockets.

Quietly stared out the window,
but someone—was it Befriend?—
wrapped a comforting arm around her.

Lost and Remember huddled
in the corner.

I was serving punch.

NAHID RACHLIN

The Calling

EVEN AFTER A WEEK Mohtaram could not believe that her sister, Maryam, was really with her in the living room of her house. But there she was, her polka dot chador wrapped around her, and sitting in a patch of sunlight on the rug to warm her legs, although it was late May and the temperature hovered around seventy-five. The house too had marks of Maryam's presence. The gifts she had brought—a cloth with paisley designs covered the kitchen table, a tapestry depicting a caravan hung on a wall. The smell of rose water that she dabbed on her clothes permeated the air.

It made Mohtaram feel more at home in her own house since her sister had come. She had not really anticipated what she was getting herself into when she sold all her belongings in Iran, after her husband died, and came to America to live near her son and daughter, how much she would be leaving behind, so much would be out of her reach. She had not even known that her son she had come to be near would not be that accessible to her. She saw Cyrus only a few moments every day when he stopped in before he went to the university in Athens to teach. His two children were at school and busy with their friends. Mildred, Cyrus's wife, had not learned Farsi and her own English was not all that good and they could not really talk to each other. Feri, her daughter, who had come to America shortly after Cyrus, was studying in Madison and was married to an Iranian engineer but they were busy with their own lives and Mohtaram rarely saw them. She had a few Iranian friends who lived in town but they were all younger than her with different concerns.

Ever since she came to America five years ago she had been asking Maryam to come for a visit. She wrote to her. "You will love Ohio. It's sparkling clean with no dust to settle on things. There are many trees and lakes and rivers . . ." Maryam had always refused, saying, "I have my prayer sessions starting next month," or "Bahman wants to get married and we're looking for a proper wife for him." What had prompted her to come now, Maryam had told her, was a dream she had. In the dream she was searching for Mohtaram and finally found her in a wide, well-lit but empty street, scratched and bleeding. The dream had so shaken her that she decided she must see her sister immediately.

Already, in one week, Mohtaram was falling into the old interdependency with her sister. Every day they woke at dawn, prayed, cooked and ate together, went out for walks. One day they went to the shopping center, within walking distance, to buy shoes for Maryam. She had been complaining that her feet hurt. Maryam put on her chador and Mohtaram a long-sleeved dress and a head scarf. Although Maryam complained about her feet and walked rather slowly, she gave the impression of being the stronger of the two with her sturdy arms and ample breasts. Mohtaram felt thin and frail by contrast and was aware that her fairer skin had wrinkled more. It was hard to tell, she was sure, which one of them was older, even though there was a five-year age difference between them. A few passers-by turned around and looked at Maryam in her long black chador and some smiled at her but just as often they acted as if they did not notice anything different. "See, they leave you alone here," Mohtaram said. "No one interferes in your affairs."

"But it's so lonely, it's like everyone has crawled into a shell," Maryam said.

It seemed to Mohtaram that it would be more natural to Maryam if people stared or even poked at her chador and asked her what it was.

One thing caught Maryam's attention which she liked, a pair of soft, flat shoes in the window of Payless store. "They look so comfortable. They'll be perfect for me," she said. "I keep changing shoes and never find any that fit."

They went in and Maryam tried on the shoes. They cost only ten dollars. She bought two pairs. She wore one pair on the way back. She said they felt as comfortable as they looked.

THEY RETURNED HOME to prepare for visitors. Today Feri and Sohrab were driving in from Madison to spend the weekend in Athens, planning to stay in Cyrus's house and visiting here during the day. They were all coming to the house for lunch today. Mohtaram had also invited the only Iranian couple she was friendly with. She had bought a side of mutton from the young man who slaughtered sheep in the *halal*, Muslim fashion, and sold it to other Iranians in town. Maryam helped her prepare—cutting eggplants, green beans, cucumbers, soaking the rice, raisins and lentils. On the mutton they used some of the spices Maryam had brought with her—turmeric, sumac, and dried ground lemon, a combination of coriander, cinnamon and pepper. The air was filled with scents Mohtaram associated with home. As they prepared Maryam filled in Mohtaram with more stories about the three brothers, nephews, nieces and aunts and uncles all living in houses near each other in a network of alleys off Ghanat Abad Avenue.

Mohtaram though thought with all the detailed account there was something imprecise and foggy about her sister's descriptions of people. She was filled with a longing to be with them in person.

Cyrus arrived first. He came into the living room and said, "Mildred had a cold and couldn't come but she sent this." He held out a large platter. "Apple pie, especially for you Aunt Maryam."

"You all have been so kind to me," Maryam said.

Cyrus walked into the kitchen and put the pie on the counter. He took out packs of beer from a bag he was holding also and put them in the refrigerator. He was only sixteen years younger than his mother, had alert brown eyes, curly hair and muscular arms from lifting weights every day. He came back into the living room and sat on the semi-circular sofa.

Maryam gathered her legs under her. "I ache all the time. I'm on the way to my grave."

"Don't say such things," Cyrus said. "People here get married at your age."

Mohtaram went into the kitchen to fry the potatoes she had sliced, but she kept her eyes half way on Maryam and Cyrus. She wanted to make sure no misunderstanding would develop between them—a few days ago when Cyrus dropped in, Maryam had told him bluntly that unless he had had a Muslim wedding ceremony his marriage to Mildred was not valid and Cyrus had flushed and had not answered. Mohtaram had explained for him, "I made sure to marry them with the Qu'ran myself. I said the words and they both went along with it. I converted her first into Islam and gave her the name Effat."

"Tell me all about Uncle Mohsen and Uncle Hoveida," Cyrus was saying to Maryam. "I haven't had any news from them for years."

"What's there to say about them?" But she went on to talk about her brothers at length. Uncle Mohsen had retired from his job as a clerk in the City Hall and spent his days going to the mosque or on pilgrimages with his wife. Uncle Hoveida had a gall bladder removed.

There were some sounds outside—a car pulling into the driveway, and then footsteps.

"It must be them, Feri and Sohrab," Mohtaram said from the kitchen and went to open the outside door. "Come in, come in." She kissed Feri and Sohrab and they all went in. Feri went over to her aunt and they embraced and kissed. Then she introduced her and Sohrab to each other.

"You're still as pretty as when you were a little girl," Maryam said to her.

"Thank you. I've been counting the days to see you," Feri said.

Then they all sat down. In a few moments Maryam took out from her purse two matching gold pendants with *Allah* inscribed on them in Arabic and gave one to Sohrab and the other to Feri. Feri and

Sohrab thanked her and put them on. Mohtaram thought the pendants looked a little strange on them with their short haircuts and jeans and wild looking T-shirts. Sohrab engaged Cyrus in conversation while Maryam and Feri talked between themselves.

"Have you thought of children yet?" Maryam asked Feri.

"I've been too busy to think about it," Feri said.

"You don't want to end up childless like me."

"Yes, Aunt Maryam, tell her that," Sohrab said, turning to them.

Feri laughed and leaned against his chest. He stroked her cheeks and then let go.

"Let's play some records," Cyrus aid. "Persian music for the occasion. Do you mind, Aunt Maryam?"

Maryam looked into space and nodded her head ambiguously.

He searched through the small stack of records next to the phonograph and put one on. A soft, nasal female voice began to sing, *Oh, my love, you're like a wild flower on the hills, out of my reach, out of my reach.*

A car pulled into the driveway. "Here they are, Abdul and Marzieh," Mohtaram said.

Momentarily Abdul and Marzieh came in. They glanced around the room, greeting everyone. Abdul was holding a basket with two chickens, their legs tied with strings. The chickens lay placidly in the basket.

"I brought these so that we can slaughter them in the *halal* way for Maryam *khanoom*."

"Thank you, please put them on the porch," Mohtaram said. "We already have a lot to eat."

"You can save the chicken for later."

"May God pay you back for all your troubles," Maryam said. "I can't thank you enough."

Abdul went out through the screen door and laid the chickens on the porch. The chickens began to cluck frantically as if they knew they had little time left to live.

Mohtaram and Maryam brought over the food and put it on the dining table—broiled mutton, two kinds of rice, a yogurt and cucumber salad, sharbat to drink, halva and the huge apple pie Cyrus had brought for dessert. "Let's sit down and eat," Mohtaram said.

After they finished eating the main food, Mohtaram served the pie. Maryam refused.

"It's just flour, sugar and apples," Mohtaram said, knowing what her sister was worried about. The first night she had arrived, Maryam had inspected everything in the house and asked her to read the ingredients in packaged items—crackers, cookies, bread—before she ate them. She had explained to Mohtaram that a young man in their neighborhood in Teheran had told her that they used pork fat in everything in America.

Maryam took a slice and began to eat it. "It's very good. May God give strength to your wife," she said to Cyrus.

Cyrus smiled. "I'm glad you like it."

After lunch the men sat in one corner and started to drink beer and talk while the women had tea. They talked rapidly and intensely, their voices occasionally rising above those of the men in the living room. Abdul was bragging about how much he won every time he went to the horse races, one hundred dollars last time. Sohrab talked about his engineering firm, how the salesmen always went after girls when they traveled, and, he added in a whisper, some call girls were arranged for them by the customers' companies. Then Abdul said to Cyrus, "You college teachers have all those young girls available to you. They want to be in your favor . . ."

Mohtaram was thinking how much closer she felt to her sister than to her children. Her children seemed aloof by contrast to Maryam. There was something offhand about them, even when they were trying to be nice. Their attitude toward the occasion, it seemed to her, was that of amusement. When children, they had been like all other Iranian children, dependent on her approval, thriving on her warmth, her cuddling and kissing them, but they had changed. They were cool and independent and egocentric. Maybe I have changed also, becoming a little like them. The knowledge hitting her for the first time really upset her. Then she thought maybe it is Maryam who makes me feel this way. I must be seeing things through her eyes, for this is how she must be viewing my Americanized children as she sits there looking on.

"There is this student in one of my classes," Cyrus was saying. She always sits in the first row, crossing her legs and . . ." He paused and then added something that Mohtaram, even though she strained, could not hear. Then the men began to giggle about something, a private joke maybe.

After a moment Abdul said, "They don't think of that as being loose morally. I used to think every time a girl smiled at me she meant something by it but that isn't necessarily the case."

The other two laughed again.

"American girls think nothing of such matters," Cyrus said. "And why should they?"

Mohtaram was aware of Maryam shifting tensely in her place. Just then Maryam broke her silence but with an unexpected remark. "Mohtaram, why did you do this to me, making me eat the *unhalal* food." Her face went white, her dark eyes rolled upward as if she were delirious.

"Oh, sister, what's wrong?" Mohtaram asked.

"I heard what they were saying in the kitchen."

She must be referring to Feri and Marzieh, who had gone into the kitchen to do the dishes.

"What did you hear?"

"The pie Cyrus brought over had been cooked in pig's fat."

"Who said that?"

"Feri said it."

"Feri, come over here," Mohtaram called urgently.

Feri came to the doorway.

"Did you say that the pie crust was cooked in pig's fat?"

"No."

"What did you say then?"

"I was talking about a pie I took to a picnic. I used bacon and ham in it. It was a quiche Lorraine, a French dish."

Marzieh came into the doorway also. "Yes, Maryam *khanoom*, that's what Feri was telling me."

"Apple pie in pig's fat?" Cyrus said.

"All the sinful talk in this room and the beer dripping on the rugs where we pray," Maryam said, in a near whisper, looking from face to face.

"We just finished the last beer so there won't be any more of it," Cyrus said.

"I'm spoiling the day for you. I should go back home soon," Maryam said.

"If you go back so soon we all will be heartbroken," Feri said.

Maryam lowered her face, in deep contemplation.

Everyone was quiet, enveloped in the tension hanging in the air. Then Cyrus got up and said, "I have to go home, I have a lot of work to get done. And Mildred is left alone." He said good-bye to everyone and left.

"We have to leave also," Abdul said. "I'll slaughter the chickens first. I brought along a good knife." He went out through the screen door to the porch. Then he came back and put the chickens, all cleaned up, on the counter. He washed his hands and he and Marzieh left. Then Feri and her husband also left to go to Cyrus's house.

"The light is fading. We'd better pray," Maryam said, now alone with Mohtaram.

"Let me put away the food first," Mohtaram said, going into the kitchen.

Maryam followed. "See how these chickens are lying there, dead and helpless? That's how we will be one day," she said, giving out a sigh. "And imagine if you get ill, who's here to take care of you? You know the dream I had that prompted me to come here. Maybe it meant something. You ought to go back with me. Put up this house for sale. We'll return together. Everyone will be happy to have you back. You could buy another house there or if you want the two of us will live together in my house."

Mohtaram began to cry, tears just trickling down her face as if a dam had broken. "My life has been empty without realizing it," she said. "If I had any sense I would go back with you."

Soon the two of them knelt together, chadors on their heads, facing the east, reclining and touching their heads on the *mohrs* they put on the floor.

Mohtaram had a hard time concentrating on her prayers. Her mind kept wandering to her childhood—she and Maryam sitting together in the hollowed-out trunk of a sycamore tree in their courtyard, going shopping in the bazaar running parallel to their alley, lying in a mosquito net on the flat roof of their house, talking and looking at the shapes the clouds made, the lit kites circling in the sky, the bright stars. As a child she had been the more gregarious. She recalled Maryam often withdrawing into a secluded corner of the courtyard and playing alone with her dolls, saying endearing things to them, picking them up and kissing or spanking them, but Mohtaram would intrude and insist on being included and Maryam would be open to her.

Maryam had been haughty and very pretty with greenish-hazel eyes and wavy brown hair, striking against her olive skin. Mohtaram was shorter with smaller bones and less striking features. When the time came Maryam married a jeweler and made the best of her marriage. She herself married a distant cousin, an accountant, she had always had a crush on, and they were happy together. He was hardworking and intelligent, the only educated person among a family of merchants. He was healthy and energetic, hard to believe he would die young, from a stroke. Mohtaram still could recall vividly that morning waking up and finding him staring with unmoving eyes into space. She touched him and he was ice cold and rubbery. She screamed and ran out to Maryam's house, a few doors down on the same alley. Maryam had kept her there for days, trying to comfort her . . .

THAT NIGHT Mohtaram lay in bed awake for a long time. Memories hit her again, more strongly and vividly in the dark. She saw Maryam and herself in their house, in the hollow of that tree. Now she recalled how the two of them used to sing together, a rhyme they had made up, *I belong to this tree, to this house, to this alley, and will never leave them as long as it is in my power to stay.*

She wished she could break out of the prison of this new self, and be reborn again into the old one. She fell asleep and each time she woke she thought the same thing: "Maryam is going to leave soon and the house will become impersonal, barren without her, one of the many houses on the street and yet quite isolated from them."

Near dawn, when she woke, she thought very clearly, I must return with Maryam. This is my chance.

ROGER SEDARAT

My Mother's 20 Persian Gold Bracelets

Marriage handcuffs say American wives.
One for every year Dad's family came,
Aunt Hishmet pushing rings on Mom's fingers.
At four years old, my hands the size of those boys' hands
that Persian dance through carpet-weaving looms,
I sit in her lap with my palm through her rings
to know why she's crying.

The sight of her scrubbing the kitchen floor,
stirring endless pots of stew each summer for Persians
who'd criticize her home then give her finely twisted
21-karat-gold jewelry. Her hand, like a dog trained to jump
through burning hoops, collecting rings for keeping secrets,
smiling when there's company and she picks up the phone
to hear an anonymous Texan tell her to leave the neighborhood.

The bracelets in a sour cream and onion dip container,
bits of grime floating in bleach, resin from planting onions
in the garden, gutting eggplants for *khoreshe bademjan*
after a full workday, so much digging for gold in her adopted
    country.
My Dad warns that one of her students might cut off her arm
for drug money. I watch her do dishes with a stump, a bloody
right hand palm up, finally at rest in her high school parking lot.

Coming home to my Father dead drunk in front of Ted Koppel
reporting on the fall of Iran,
she'd put him to bed only to lie beside nightmares,
have him punch and kick her out in his sleep,
music on her arm playing down the hall, dying on the couch.
Each ring a year, skin on her wrist indented patterns,
twenty lines of marriage in the morning deep enough to wonder
how blood moves through her fingers when she sleeps.

Like any son, growing up I take her for granted,
the jangle on her arm nothing more than a warning to stop
a dirty movie on the VCR, a tambourine announcing dinner,
deep metallic laughter bringing brownies from the oven.
Now that I am older and Dad's been gone, rings hanging in time
like petrified wood, she discusses the past, each bracelet
a medal for her American service to Iran.

San Antonio, 1979

Iranians never escape that year.
My Father said, *Tell people you're from France.*
For an eternity I'm forced to hear

This kid in third-grade science named Pierre
Asking, Ça va? I didn't have a chance.
(Iranians never escape). That year

They dragged me down the hallway by my hair
Blindfolded, screaming in Texas accents
For an eternity I'm forced to hear:

Hey Ayatollah you're not welcome here!
The U.S. is for us! As immigrants,
Iranians never escape that; year

To year we relive it whenever we're
in an airport and get looked at askance
For an eternity. I'm forced to hear

Customs detaining my father declare,
It's just routine. Voices that turn a man's
Ear on eons never escape that year.
For an eternity I'm forced to hear.

Khomeini's Beard

I.

In twilight the carpet weavers' threads change color;
soon the boys' fingers to reveal behind the red-blue forests
of lions and lambs, deep indentions, stone calluses,
as they wave east with their bodies in prayer,
corn husks flapping in the wind that comes singing
through the teeth of a pitchfork left stuck in the earth,
the farmer building a fire dropping his wood, the cupped
curl of his ear, pink as a newborn calf, hanging on each word
coming in the microphone static, coming like streaks of lightening
from Isfahan, white Arabic burning above a mosque's
gold belly, the echo of an Allah Akbar rolling like thunder,
like clouds of sand on the village trail beneath the feet of oxen,
stirring down from an olive tree, shooting an arrow into the stars,
each pair of wings flapping white and electric.

Outing Iranians

Andre Agassi.
He likes to stand close
to the line, pretending it's one long grain of rice

Christiane Amanpour.
How come she never really talked back
while interviewing Rafsanjani in a chador?

The Soup Nazi in New York.
A curiosity on Seinfeld, he's any one of
my uncles who take their cooking seriously.

Henry Kissinger.
(Just kidding).

Bijan.
Smell his cologne and you'll see a well-dressed
man with olive skin (he's gay, but don't tell my father
who refuses to believe Iranians can be homosexual).

Your daughter's homeroom teacher.
When you come to "Parent's Night,"
he insists that you eat the fruit he set out for you.

The boy your daughter decides to marry.
He's devilishly handsome and when he tells you
they'll honeymoon in Iran, won't say for how long.

The owner of the "Middle Eastern Restaurant" in your
    neighborhood.
If you ask him if he's Iranian and he wants your business,
he'll just smile and give you a free *doogh*.

CONTRIBUTORS

ELMAZ ABINADER is the author of a memoir, *Children of the Roojme: A Family's Journey from Lebanon*; a collection of poetry, *In the Country of My Dreams*; and several plays, including *Country of Origin*. She is cofounder of the Voices of our Nations Arts Foundation (VONA/Voices), and she teaches at Mills College in Oakland, California.

DIANA ABU-JABER'S new novel, *Birds Of Paradise*, is the winner of the Arab American National Book Award. Her novels *Origin*, *Crescent*, and *Arabian Jazz*, and her memoir *The Language of Baklava*, also won several awards, including the PEN Center Award, the American Book Award, and the Oregon Book Award. Abu-Jaber teaches at Portland State University.

SUSAN ATEFAT-PECKHAM (1970–2004) was an Iranian American writer who earned a PhD from the University of Nebraska–Lincoln. Her book of poems, *That Kind of Sleep*, was selected by the renowned writer Victor Hernando Cruz for a National Poetry Series Award in 2000. Her nonfiction book, *Black Eyed Bird*, was a finalist in the Associated Writing Programs Book Award series and a runner up for the *Beryl Markham Book Award in Creative Nonfiction*. Her work has appeared in many journals including *Borderlands*, *Texas Poetry Review*, and *The Literary Review*. Atefat-Peckham taught poetry, creative nonfiction, and fiction at the University of Nebraska–Lincoln and Hope College before joining the faculty of Georgia College and State University. She became the first poetry editor of *Arts and Letters*, a literary journal. On February 7, 2004, Atefat-Peckham and her son Cyrus were killed in an automobile accident while she was teaching on a Fulbright Fellowship in Amman, Jordan.

JOSEPH AWAD (1929–2009) completed graduate work at Georgetown University and was appointed Poet Laureate of Virginia in 1998. His poetry has appeared in numerous journals and his books include *Leaning to Hear the Music*, *The Neon Distances*, and *Construction Ahead*. He received the Edgar Allan Poe Prize of the Poetry Society of Virginia, *The Lyric* magazine's Nathan Haskell Dole Prize, and the Donn Goodwin Poetry Award.

BARBARA BEDWAY'S fiction and essays have appeared in *The Iowa Review*, *The New York Times*, *Flyway*, and *Mizna*. "Death and Lebanon," her first published short story, received a Pushcart Prize. She also writes on personal finance.

JOSEPH GEHA is the author of *Through and Through: Toledo Stories* and the novel *Lebanese Blonde*. His poems, plays, and short stories have appeared in numerous periodicals and anthologies. He was granted a fellowship from the National Endowment for the Arts. His fiction has been awarded the Pushcart Prize and chosen for inclusion in the Permanent Collection, Arab-American Archive, of the Smithsonian Institution. He is Professor Emeritus of the creative writing program at Iowa State University.

SAMUEL HAZO is director of the International Poetry Forum in Pittsburgh, Pennsylvania. He is McAnulty Distinguished Professor Emeritus of Duquesne University. His most recent books are *The Time Remaining* (novel), *Like a Man Gone Mad* and *The Song of the Horse* (poetry), and *The Stroke of a Pen* (essays). A book of poems entitled *And the Time Is: Poems, 1958–2013* is forthcoming in 2014.

JOE (FORMERLY JOANNA) KADI is a teacher, writer, and editor living in Calgary, Alberta, Canada. He teaches at Mount Royal University and University of Calgary. Kadi is the editor of *Food for Our Grandmothers: Writings by Arab-American and Arab-Canadian Feminists* and the author of *Thinking Class: Sketches from a Cultural Worker*.

PAULINE KALDAS is Associate Professor of English and Creative Writing at Hollins University. She is the author of *Egyptian Compass*, a collection of poetry; *Letters from Cairo*, a travel memoir; *The Time Between Places*, a collection of short stories; and the coeditor of *Dinarzad's*

Children: An Anthology of Contemporary Arab American Fiction. Kaldas was born in Egypt and immigrated with her parents to the United States at the age of eight in 1969.

LISA SUHAIR MAJAJ is a Palestinian American writer and a longtime scholar of Arab American literature. She is the author of *Geographies of Light* (poems) and coeditor of three essay collections: *Intersections: Gender, Nation, and Community in Arab Women's Novels*, *Etel Adnan: Critical Essays on the Arab-American Writer and Artist*, and *Going Global: The Transnational Reception of Third World Women Writers.* She is currently teaching at the University of Cyprus in Nicosia, Cyprus.

JACK MARSHALL, born in Brooklyn to Jewish parents who emigrated from Iraq and Syria, now lives in California. He is the author of the memoir *From Baghdad to Brooklyn* and several poetry collections that have received the PEN Center USA Award, two Northern California Book Awards, and a nomination from the National Book Critics Circle.

KHALED MATTAWA is the author of four books of poetry, most recently *Tocqueville* (2010), and the translator of nine volumes of contemporary Arabic poetry. He is the recipient of the 2010 Academy of American Poets Fellowship Prize and a Ford/United States Artist for 2011.

D. H. MELHEM (1926–2013) was the author of eight books of poetry and a trilogy of novels under the title *Patrimonies.* She has also authored over seventy essays, edited two anthologies, and written a musical drama entitled *Children of the House Afire.* Among national and international prizes for her poetry, she earned the CUNY Alumni Achievement Award, two Pushcart Prize nominations, and a New York Heart Association Media Award.

EUGENE PAUL NASSAR is Professor Emeritus of English at Utica College. A former Rhodes Scholar, Woodrow Wilson Fellow, and National Endowment for the Humanities Fellow, he is the author of several books of literary criticism and the editor of several others. His memoir of growing up Lebanese American in the Italian American neighborhood of East Utica, New York, is entitled *Wind of the Land.*

NAOMI SHIHAB NYE'S thirty-three books include *There Is No Long Distance Now: Very*, a collection of short stories; and *Transfer, Honeybee, and 19 Varieties of Gazelle*, poems of the Middle East, which was a finalist for the National Book Award. She lives in San Antonio, Texas.

NAHID RACHLIN attended Columbia University Writing Program on a Doubleday-Columbia Fellowship and then went on to the Stanford University MFA program on a Stegner Fellowship. Her publications include a memoir, *Persian Girls*; four novels, *Jumping over Fire*, *Foreigner*, *Married to a Stranger*, *The Heart's Desire*; and a collection of short stories, *Veils*. Her individual short stories have appeared in more than fifty magazines, including *The Virginia Quarterly Review*, *Prairie Schooner*, *Redbook*, and *Shenandoah*.

ROGER SEDARAT is the author of the chapbook *From Tehran to Texas* and two poetry collections: *Dear Regime: Letters to the Islamic Republic*, which won Ohio University Press 2007 Hollis Summers' Prize, and *Ghazal Games*. Current projects include a scholarly study of the influence of Persian verse on Emerson as well as a full-length translated collection of poetry by Hafez. He teaches poetry and literary translation in the MFA Program and Middle Eastern American literature in the Department of English at Queens College, City University of New York.